Be Careful What You Pray For

Be Careful What You Pray For

Nicole S. Rouse

URBAN
CHRISTIAN

www.urbanchristianonline.net

Urban Books, LLC
78 East Industry Court
Deer Park, NY 11729

ISBN 13: 978-1-60162-676-9
ISBN 10: 1-60162-676-2

First Mass Market Printing October 2014
First Trade Paperback Printing November 2010
Printed in the United States of America

10 9 8 7 6 5 4 3 2 1

Distributed by Kensington Corp.
Submit Wholesale Orders to:
Kensington Publishing Corp.
C/O Penguin Group (USA) Inc.
Attention: Order Processing
405 Murray Hill Parkway
East Rutherford, NJ 07073-2316
Phone: 1-800-526-0275
Fax: 1-800-227-9604

Be Careful What You Pray For

by

Nicole S. Rouse

This book is dedicated to:

Linda B. Rouse
My mother, my best friend, and my greatest
inspiration
and
Mary L. Booker.
My grandmother and my pillar of strength.

Acknowledgments

I would like to express my love and sincere thanks to:

God for being my strength and for making my writing career possible.

The Booker and Rouse families for their undying love and support. I am so proud of each and every one of you, and I feel blessed to have shared so many wonderful memories with you over the years.

My angels, Bernard J. Rouse Jr., Rev. Lula W. Rouse, and Rev. Bishop C. Rouse, for watching over me and giving me the inspiration and motivation to pursue and accomplish all of my dreams.

My father and webmaster, Bernard J. Rouse Sr., for creating and maintaining my beautiful Web site.

My agent, ShaShana Crichton, for understanding my needs as a writer and making sure I achieve my very best.

Acknowledgments

My incredible editor, Joylynn Jossel, for her endless patience, dedication, and commitment to the authors at Urban Christian.

My friends, Dannette Hargraves, Heather Morris-Gunter, and Marcia Tokich, for helping me fine-tune this story in the midnight hours.

My soul mate and best friend, Robert Bridges, for growing with me, believing in me, and loving me.

My beautiful sorors of Zeta Phi Beta Sorority, Inc., for their overwhelming encouragement and support. You are wonderful examples of true sisterhood.

I certainly cannot forget all of the bookstores who sell my books, the book clubs that read and discuss them, and the many readers who support each story. You all have made such a great difference in my life, and for that, I am forever grateful.

Isaiah 40:31
But those who trust in the Lord *will find new*
strength.
They will soar high on wings like eagles.
They will run and not grow weary.
They will walk and not faint.

Chapter 1

Kenneth's homemade chicken teriyaki greeted Maya as soon as she opened the door to the fifth floor apartment they shared near the art museum in Philadelphia. She closed the front door and placed her extra-large tote bag next to Kenneth's brown Salvatore Ferragamo shoes. No matter how many times she asked Kenneth to put them on the small area rug behind the door, he never listened. A few years ago, Maya would've complained, but after living together for six years, she had learned to let some things go. She'd rather maintain a happy home than bicker over a misplaced pair of shoes.

Maya leaned over and moved Kenneth's shoes onto the rug. Specks of dirt from the bottom of the shoes had settled into the light-beige carpet and she sighed. Before going to bed, she'd have to vacuum. Maya grabbed a stack of papers to grade from her bag and made her way to the living room. Although the windows were open, the tiny apartment felt stuffy. She set the papers on a small desk in the corner, and then walked to the window. Lifting the set of double windows as far as they could go, Maya pressed her forehead against the screen and peered down at the street. The Benjamin Franklin Parkway was bustling with activity. Across the street, the bright lights shimmering over the art museum made it difficult for her to see the new Cézanne billboard by the front entrance. Living near the museum had given her a deeper appreciation for the arts. On many weekends, she frequented the different exhibits and special events offered to the community and shared what she learned with her students.

Growing up in the heart of West Philadelphia, residing near the art museum was the last place Maya thought she'd live as an adult. She desired to live in the suburbs, away from the constant noise, but Kenneth wanted to be in the midst of all the city happenings. The rent for their one-bedroom apartment was steep, but over time, the location had proven to be ideal for both of them. The high rise was only blocks away from Center City—a hub for shopping, dining, entertainment, arts and culture.

Maya pressed her face against the screen, searching for a cool autumn breeze, but only hot air floated inside. The unreasonable weather mixed with the heat from the stove warmed the apartment more than she could stand. Pulling away from the window, Maya removed her light-weight sweater and draped it across the back of the chair next to her. If it were up to Maya, she'd keep the room temperature at a steady seventy degrees, but Kenneth didn't believe the air conditioner should run in the fall. He insisted the two fifteen-dollar window fans he purchased from WalMart would be sufficient until the weather changed.

When it came to money, Kenneth was a miser. The only thing he splurged on without complaining was clothes. His mentor was grooming him to become a future partner of the downtown firm where they worked, and as an up-and-coming attorney, Kenneth thought it important that he dress the part.

Kenneth wasn't like many men his age who adored fancy cars and expensive gadgets. He'd been driving the same car for ten years—a classic black BMW 323i, with leather seats, a sunroof and a five-disc CD changer. The car was old by many standards, and despite a few scratches on the rear bumper, it looked almost brand new. Maya didn't mind that Kenneth was so frugal. Since she'd moved in with him, he handled all of the bills and made sure they were paid on time.

Heading down the narrow hallway to the kitchen, Maya stopped briefly to look in the rectangular-shaped mirror along the wall. As she suspected, the humidity had caused her hair to swell. She'd have to wake up a half-hour earlier in the morning just to flat iron her short bob. Maya smoothed the few stray hairs sticking up on top of her head, and then wiped the perspiration from her forehead. Her stomach growled, and she rubbed it until the grumbling ceased. She couldn't wait to eat. Tuesdays had always been her night to cook, but she was exhausted. Being a third grade teacher, she barely had ten seconds of alone time during the day. And thanks to the shortage of teachers, Maya spent her free time covering the computer lab and babysitting students on lunch duty. Adding to her daily frustration, Patrick Gregorio, the new student in her class, was trying her patience. She would've pushed herself to make dinner tonight, but was relieved when Kenneth offered to cook. Thoughtfulness was one of the qualities she loved most about him.

Once inside the kitchen, Maya walked past the food on the stove and straight to Kenneth. As usual, he was facing the 15-inch flat-screen television on the wall, engrossed in a baseball game and didn't hear her come into the apartment.

This was an important game. If the Phillies won, they'd be in a great position to win the World Series, and Kenneth's law firm had promised him box seats for the next game.

With a light touch, Maya ran her fingers along his shoulder. "Oh, hey, babe," Kenneth said and kissed her hand before setting his eyes back on the television screen. "Did you ever get a hold of Patrick's mother?"

"No," she said. Maya had been trying to contact Patrick's parents, but believed he erased her messages from the answering machine before his parents could hear them. "I left a message at his father's job this time. Hopefully, he'll get back to me soon. I can't take much more of that boy." Maya could feel her pressure rising. Just the thought of Patrick angered her.

"I'm sure he will," Kenneth said, still focused on the game.

Everyone knew that Patrick Gregorio had been Maya's source of stress for the last month. New to the school, Patrick quickly adjusted to the environment by becoming the class clown. Maya had a low tolerance for misbehavior. Teaching at Samuel B. Huey in West Philadelphia for seven years, all of the students knew how strict she could be, and Maya was applauded by many of her peers for the way in which her students behaved. At four feet eleven, five feet two in heels, Maya was often mistaken for a mature looking eighth grader. For this reason, a few students would test her, but normally that only lasted a few days. But there was something different about Patrick Gregorio. No matter how many times Maya reprimanded him, he was determined to defy her.

Maya backtracked to the stove and lifted the lid to the simmering pan of chicken. She picked up the spoon, tasted the semi-sweet mixture, and smacked her lips in approval. Maya took two plates from the cabinet and scooped a mound of rice onto each one. Along with the chicken and rice, Kenneth had steamed fresh asparagus and doctored a package of instant garlic and butter mashed potatoes. She didn't understand why he cooked both rice and mashed potatoes, but didn't complain. Kenneth could be sensitive when it came to a critique of his cooking.

After grabbing a couple of forks from the dish rack, Maya tucked them between her fingers. Kenneth sensed her approaching and pushed the chair across from him out with his right foot. Maya placed the plates and utensils on the table and sat in her chair, then waited for a commercial break so that Kenneth could stop watching the baseball game long enough to bless the food. As Kenneth cheered for the home team, Maya paged through the latest Nordstrom catalog. Next week, she and Kenneth would be celebrating their thirteenth year as a couple. For their anniversary, Maya had decided to add a little variety to Kenneth's wardrobe. His idea of casual was a pair of comfortable khakis and a button-down shirt. Although he wasn't the kind of guy to change a tire or fix a leaky faucet, Maya felt he needed some jeans and sweats to lounge around in.

Before closing the catalog, Maya looked at the watch collection. Jewelry always made a nice gift. Browsing the his-and-her matching sets, Maya wondered what Kenneth had in mind for *her* this year. Although she desperately wanted to make their relationship official, she'd given up on a marriage proposal and knew better than to force the issue. "I'll propose when you least expect it," Kenneth said the last time she asked. That was six years ago. The best Kenneth had done since then was propose they move in together. "If we can survive this," he said the day they signed the lease, "then I know we're meant to be together forever."

Maya frowned. Living with Kenneth had been great, but over the past year, every time she stepped inside Monumental Baptist Church, she felt God was telling her it was time to make a change. Maya's mother had tried to change her mind up until the hour before she moved in with Kenneth, exclaiming, "God doesn't approve of shacking up!"

But Maya defended her decision. "We're living in different times. Besides, Kenneth and I aren't strangers. And we can save money to buy our dream home and have the big wedding every girl fantasizes about. Not to mention the horrendous school loans we need to pay off." Maya was thirty years old at the time and tried to convince her mother that it was a wise thing to do. "Many couples my age are doing the same thing," she reasoned.

Mrs. Richards had glared at Maya with a hint of a tear gathering in the corner of her eyes. In response to her daughter's remarks, she replied, "Just promise me you won't compromise too much for him."

At the time, Maya didn't understand her mother's words. But now, as she faced another year of an unfulfilled commitment, Maya realized that she'd broken her promise. Maya would never admit it to anyone, but she wasn't as confident as she was so many years ago that her journey with Kenneth was leading to marriage.

A commercial came on and Kenneth twirled around in his seat, his long, thin legs barely fitting underneath the table. "You blessing the food tonight?" he asked.

Maya placed the catalogue on an empty placemat. "Why don't you do it, baby. I need to rest my voice. I've been talking all day."

While Kenneth blessed the food, Maya stared at him, her stomach now grumbling nonstop. "Amen," she said when he was finished. She couldn't wait to dig in. "Patrick plucked rubber bands at three kids today when I wasn't looking," Maya said as she lifted a forkful of chicken to her mouth. "Shy, little Ciona almost cried. At lunch, the little bugger poked fun at Julian because he had a hole in his gym shoes. I told Patrick he had to stand on the wall while the other kids were playing at recess for the rest of the week." Maya dropped her fork while she chewed. "And then—"

"Baby, baby, relax! I can see steam coming from your head," Kenneth interrupted. "I thought we agreed not to bring work problems home. You'll be all tense tonight if you don't stop."

"I know," she said coyly. "You may need to give me a special massage."

Kenneth pulled his eyes away from the screen and flashed a crooked smiled. "I'll see what I can do."

Maya blew on an asparagus spear to cool it before putting it inside her mouth. Kenneth was right. Talking about Patrick did make her pressure rise. As she finished her meal, Maya substituted her thoughts of a troublesome student with thoughts of Kenneth's smooth hands caressing her back.

After dinner, Maya and Kenneth moved into the living room and settled into their regular routines—Maya grading papers on one end of their leather sofa and Kenneth typing on his laptop on the other end. Maya's favorite movie, *Love Jones,* was playing on BET. Films where true love ultimately wins touched a sensitive part of her heart. She watched attentively as Larenz Tate's character ran alongside an Amtrak train, desperate to get his love interest's attention before she left Chicago and his life for good. *How romantic,* Maya thought. She hoped Kenneth would go through such lengths for her if placed in the same position. Rarely did he express an intense emotion. Not even for a case he knew he was going to win. His passion and humble confidence made him an excellent child advocate, and it was his calm demeanor that caused the law firm to recognize his talent.

Kenneth hummed a Marvin Gaye tune softly as he typed. He was happy and content. And Maya should've been too, but tonight her heart ached. She didn't know whether it was the movie, being overwhelmed at work, or the fact that she'd been with a man who hadn't proposed to her after thirteen years, that caused her heart pain.

Kenneth sat his laptop on the round glass coffee table in front of him and stood up. "You want something to drink?"

Maya said no and watched him walk out of the living room. It was hard to say where all the years had gone. She just knew that too much time was already invested into Kenneth to let him go. And being single again at thirty-six was not an option she wanted to embrace.

While she waited for Kenneth to return, Maya recalled the day they met. That day was like a scene out of an old movie. They were both graduate students at Temple University, and during a break one afternoon, they were standing less than a foot away from one another in front of a lunch mobile on the corner of Broad Street and Montgomery Avenue. Kenneth had his head in a book, studying for an exam, and Maya hummed softly to an old Phyllis Hyman song that played through her earphones.

"Chicken cheese steak, mayo, no ketchup, no onions," shouted the cook, holding up a long brown paper bag, and both Maya and Kenneth reached for it. They had ordered the exact same thing. "I think the gentleman was here first," the cook replied and winked at Maya. "Your steak will be up in three minutes, pretty lady."

Although Kenneth ordered first, he let Maya have the sandwich, and every school day for the next two weeks, they met at that lunch mobile at the same time, their conversations a few minutes longer each day.

Kenneth reentered the room with a glass of carrot juice in his hand. Tall and statuesque with full lips and ears that seemed detached from his head, many people joked that he could be one of President Barack Obama's relatives. Much to her own surprise, Maya blurted, "Are you ever going to marry me?" before Kenneth could sit down.

Kenneth stood tall, wobbling a little and careful not to spill any juice on the carpet. "What just happened here?" he asked with a face full of confusion. "I've only been gone two minutes."

In a slightly timid voice, Maya repeated her question. "Are you ever going to marry me?"

"Where is this coming from?" Kenneth demanded. "Did Claudia say something to you?"

Claudia Marshall was Maya's best friend. Kenneth hadn't been fond of Claudia since Maya's birthday dinner blowup a few years ago. Tired of waiting for Kenneth to propose, Claudia drilled him in front of family and close friends about his intentions. Since then, every disagreement between Maya and Kenneth, whether big or small, was somehow Claudia's fault in his eyes.

"This has nothing to do with her," asserted Maya.

"Then what is it?" he probed.

Maya looked down at the floor. How could she explain what was going through her head when she barely understood it herself?

Kenneth put his glass next to his laptop on the coffee table. "Talk to me, Maya. What's going on?" Maya's lips started to tremble, and Kenneth rubbed her arm gently. "Is this about having a baby? I told you I was ready. I'm just waiting for you to stop taking the pill."

Maya couldn't believe her ears. She'd waited so long to hear those words, and yet the happiness she should've felt was replaced with sadness. In her mind, she'd rationalized living with Kenneth, but Maya knew she couldn't justify having a child before the promise of a ring. "That's not it," she said quickly and wiped her eyes before tears could fall. The strength and control she exuded at work was absent in her relationship with Kenneth. With him, she became one of her third grade students, shy and vulnerable. But tonight, she forced herself to be strong. Maya got up from the sofa and grabbed a coaster from under the coffee table. "I-I'm not really sure what it is," she said and put his glass on the coaster.

Kenneth was even more confused. "Then it must be your time of the month," he said. "You know how emotional you can be when—"

"It's not my period!" Maya snapped. "Do you realize that we've been together for *thirteen* years? Don't you think it's time for us to have this conversation?"

Kenneth's jaw dropped. He was about to speak, but then changed his mind. Instead, he headed out of the living room, and Maya quickly followed him.

"Don't walk away from me! We have to talk about this," she said, trying to remain calm. The phone rang and Maya rolled her eyes. "Whoever it is can leave a message," she said as Kenneth reached for the phone on the mantle.

"It's your mother," he said sarcastically, after looking at the caller ID. Kenneth took the phone off its base and handed it to Maya.

Maya rolled her eyes again. She wasn't in the mood to talk, but knew her mother would call all night if she didn't take the call. Quickly pulling herself together, she pressed the talk button. "Hey, Mom."

"Hey, Pumpkin," Mrs. Richards said joyfully. "Did you ask Ken if he could take Eddie to the airport tomorrow?"

Maya closed her eyes. She'd forgotten that her cousin was going to Texas for business in the morning. Although he had a number of "friends," Eddie preferred to have family drop him off at the airport. "No," she meekly replied. "I haven't had a chance to ask him yet."

"Ask him now." Mrs. Richards commanded. "I need to know now. It's going on ten o'clock."

"Okay," Maya answered with little expression.

"If he can't, I'll need to beg your father," added Mrs. Richards. "You know how much he hates driving to that airport."

Kenneth stood close to Maya, towering over her with the face of disapproval, and her heart beat faster. "I'm gonna have to call you back, Mom," she said, her voice shaky and weak.

"Why? What's wrong?" queried Mrs. Richards.

"Nothing. I just need to call you back."

There was a brief pause on the line. "Are you sure? I know when something's going on with my first born," Mrs. Richards noted.

Maya let out a puff of air. "Mom, I'm fine. Really, I am. I was in the middle of something that I want to finish. Okay?" Mrs. Richards didn't believe her daughter, but agreed to let her go without further interrogation.

"So that's what this is about?" Kenneth spoke as soon as Maya hung up. "Your mother got into your head? Did she tell you to ask me about getting married?"

"It's not what you think," responded Maya. "She wanted to know"

"Everybody can't have the perfect marriage like your parents," Kenneth remarked.

Maya slammed the cordless into its base. "Mom wanted to know if you could take Eddie to the airport tomorrow morning. And besides," she continued, "this isn't about my parents. I need to know if *our* relationship is going anywhere."

Kenneth's mood softened. "What kind of question is that? Of course it is, Maya. We're getting closer every year."

Maya stood firm, determined not to succumb to his soft eyes and sensitive touch. "Then why not marry me?" There was a long stretch of silence and tears surfaced. Maya didn't think the question was *that* difficult to answer.

"I don't want to end up like my parents and grandparents or brother and . . . need I go on?" Kenneth finally replied. "We've talked about this many times. You said you understood."

"That's a lame excuse, Ken." Maya sobbed. "We're not any of those people. Haven't we proven that already?" Maya swung her arms in the air and hit her elbow on the edge of the mantle. "I'm tired of catering to your needs. What about what I want?" Maya spewed and rubbed her elbow until the pain went away. "I want a house. I want children. And I want a dog," she cried. "I want to go on family vacations and—"

"We don't need to be married to do those things," Kenneth tried to argue.

"You don't get my point. I want to do all those things with *my husband*," she stressed.

"We're practically functioning like man and wife now," said Kenneth. "What more—"

"Then why not get me a ring to make it official?" Maya fired back.

"We don't need rings to prove that we're committed to one another," he declared.

Feeling the need to present a closing argument, Maya grabbed her cheeks in frustration. "Marriage is not about a ring. It's a public declaration of our love before people we care about," she explained, "and *especially* before God. It's a sign of our appreciation and gratitude to Him for bringing us together."

Kenneth was stumped. Deep inside he knew Maya was right, but stubbornness ruled his heart. "God knows how I feel," he said, and with his head held low, started to leave the room.

"I need you to make this clear to me," she urged and grabbed his arm, "'cause I feel like we should've been married at least eight years ago."

Kenneth's nonchalant demeanor was something Maya both loved and despised. It worked in the courtroom when he was fighting for children's rights; giving off power and confidence, but in a disagreement between them, it made her feel as if he didn't care.

"Don't push the issue, Maya. You're not going to win this one." Kenneth freed himself from her grip and stopped in front of the television on his way to the bedroom. "And you need to turn off that sappy movie. That's what probably got you all worked up in the first place."

"Fine," she mumbled and plopped back on the sofa. Rather than continue the argument, she complied as usual. Maya had learned not to challenge him. With his litigating skills, he'd win every time.

On television, *Love Jones* was nearing the end. The main characters were kissing in the rain, thrilled that they'd found one another again. Maya turned the movie off. Continuing to grade papers, Maya tried to keep from crying.

Kenneth poked his head out of the bedroom. "What time does Eddie need to be at the airport?"

"Seven-thirty," she sniffed.

Kenneth mumbled, "Okay," and then shut the door.

Maya wiped her face and used her pants leg as a towel to dry her hands. *God, what's wrong with me?* she whispered to herself. She hadn't cried this much since she was a hormonal and bratty, pimpled-face teen in junior high. Maya sighed and focused on the last paper she had to grade. As luck would have it, that paper belonged to Patrick Gregorio. Grading his paper, Maya was surprised that he had answered almost all of the problems correctly. Curious, she opened her grade book and looked at his test scores in other subject areas. Academically, Patrick was a good student. With the exception of a C in Language Arts and D in behavior, Patrick had a B average.

Maya needlessly dug into her tote bag to retrieve Patrick's home number, although she practically had it memorized. It was late, but she needed to solve at least one of her problems tonight. Since it was clear that Kenneth wasn't going to budge, Maya thought she might have more luck with Patrick's parents. She walked to the mantle and without hesitation picked up the cordless phone. She dialed the number on the card and was glad when an adult answered.

"Hello," a male voice said.

"Mr. Gregorio?" Maya replied, praying it was him.

"Yes, who's this?"

"Good evening. This is Ms. Richards, Patrick's teacher. I'm sorry for calling so late, but do you have a few minutes? I'd like to talk to you about your son."

Chapter 2

Maya sauntered down the hallway in her three-inch heels, confident that the students behind her were walking in a straight line. Occasionally, she'd hear a few snickers and have to turn around. Each time she did, she'd catch Patrick jumping back in the line with a feigned innocence on his face. *If he were my child, I would take him in the bathroom and* . . . Any other day, Maya would've had a word with Patrick, but this Friday afternoon, she let the incident pass without comment. She'd received word from the main office that Mr. Gregorio had arrived for his scheduled conference. Tight-lipped, Maya walked down the hallway, praying that Mr. Gregorio was standing by the main window where he could witness his son's behavior firsthand as the class marched by.

As instructed, the students stopped by the stairs leading to the gymnasium while they waited for the double doors to open. Maya walked alongside her students, stopping near the middle, when she heard noises from behind. Reminiscent of the human beat box pioneer, Biz Markie, she turned to find Patrick making music with his mouth and hands. Before reacting, Maya wondered where he'd learned the art. Patrick was too young to even know what beat boxing was. A few children laughed nervously behind covered mouths, and Maya had to say something or she'd risk losing control of the class.

"There go your father," announced the child behind Patrick before Maya reached him.

Advancing toward the end of the line, an older version of Patrick dressed in a navy uniform was approaching them. Maya guessed that he was a mechanic or truck driver. "There *goes* his father," Maya corrected her student, and silently thanked God.

Patrick faced forward, now silent and attentive, pretending he'd been a model student all along. Trying to conceal the smirk on her face, Maya greeted Patrick's father. "Mr. Gregorio?"

"Yes," he said, extending his right hand. Although Mr. Gregorio had strong African American features, Maya detected a mild Hispanic accent.

Standing eye to eye with him, Maya placed the composition book she was holding under her

arm and shook his hand. "I'm Ms. Richards. I'll
be with you in a few minutes. You can wait here
or in the office."

"I'll be in the office," he responded in a friendly
manner, and before walking away, gave his son a
stern glare. Maya wished she had a camera to
capture the nervous look on Patrick's face.

The doors of the gym opened at exactly 1:15,
and Lloyd Bradford, the gym teacher, appeared.
"Good afternoon, Ms. Richards," he said, then
gave the students a special signal to get changed.
Anxiously, they charged to the locker rooms and
Maya quickly waved good-bye.

"Did they find a replacement for the computer
lab yet?" Lloyd asked before Maya could escape.

Maya paused by the stairs. "A new teacher is
supposed to start on Monday."

"I know you're happy about that," he said.
"Did she say anything about lunch duty? It
would be nice if teachers could eat lunch with
adults again."

It was clear that Lloyd wanted to talk, but
Maya couldn't today. Mr. Gregorio was waiting
for her in the office. "I know how you feel," she
agreed. "I need peace and quiet while I'm eating
too."

For a man that looked about ten years Maya's
senior, Lloyd was in great shape and looked as

good as any thirty-year-old man on the street. He wasn't quite Kenneth's height, but had well-defined muscles, probably from his long-term interest in playing several sports.

"I should come to your room one day. I never get any quiet in the gym," said Lloyd.

The children started to trickle out of the locker rooms in their blue and white uniforms and Maya was relieved. Lloyd's invitation caught her off guard. They'd been friendly colleagues for several years, and he seemed down-to-earth, but Maya wanted to be careful that she didn't send the wrong signal. Although she was upset with Kenneth, Maya only had eyes for him. "I better go," she replied. "I have a conference with Patrick's father."

"Really? He's a hard man to track down," Lloyd said.

"So you understand why I'm in a hurry," Maya joked, then whispered for Lloyd to turn around. Patrick leisurely walked out of the locker room with a dismal look on his face, and without exchanging words, both teachers knew what the other was thinking.

When Maya stepped inside the main office, the secretaries were giggling like schoolgirls.

"What's so funny?" she asked them, casually scanning the room for Mr. Gregorio.

Ms. Covington, the younger of the two, stared at Maya in awe; her Baby Phat glasses slipping to the tip of her long and narrow nose. "Do you need to borrow these?" she asked, pointing to her fancy frames. "Did you *see* Mr. Gregorio?"

"If I were ten years younger and hadn't been married for almost twenty years, I'd slip him my number," Mrs. Harris, the other secretary, chimed in.

"Obviously I haven't studied him as closely as you two have," Maya said in a hushed tone, "but you do remember who his son is, don't you? Are you ready to be *his* stepmother?" The two women looked at one another and shook their heads. "Now," continued Maya, "would you happen to know where I could find Mr. Gregorio?"

"He's in the counselor's office," Mrs. Harris replied.

Maya should've thought to look there. Claudia, the school's guidance counselor and her good friend, had offered her office for the meeting because she wanted to speak to Patrick's father as well. But as Maya approached the office, she heard Claudia talking about something completely unrelated to Patrick or education. Through the slightly open door, she saw her friend sitting on the edge of her IKEA "therapy" sofa, engaged in an upbeat conversation about traveling. Seated at the small table in the corner of the room, Mr. Gregorio was just as friendly, responding to Claudia like they'd been friends for years. Maya was confused. Only two hours earlier, Claudia mentioned that she couldn't wait to give Mr. Gregorio an earful about his son.

Maya tapped lightly on the door and Claudia pulled it wide open. "Ms. Richards, please come in," Claudia said excitedly and stood to her feet. "Did you know Mr. Gregorio is from Guatemala?"

"Born and raised," Mr. Gregorio added. "I've only been here for eleven years."

"And you still have that accent," Claudia said, running her manicured fingers through her naturally blonde hair.

"My family still speaks Spanish, so it's hard to lose," he informed her.

Claudia moved closer to Mr. Gregorio and her recent trip to the tanning salon was more evident. "He was telling me about all the cool Guatemalan dishes I can make," she stated.

How they'd gotten on that subject was a mystery, but Maya didn't have time to shoot the breeze. She only had twenty minutes to talk. There was a teacher's aide covering for her in the computer lab. "I'm glad you two had a chance to meet, but I don't have much time to talk," she stated, and sat in the empty chair across from Mr. Gregorio. "Do you mind if I interrupt?"

"He's all yours," Claudia said, slowly closing the door as she eased out of the office. When she was certain Mr. Gregorio couldn't see her, Claudia winked at Maya, and before the door closed all the way, Maya gave her friend "the eye."

Directing her attention back to Mr. Gregorio, Maya placed the composition book she purchased specifically to document Patrick's behavior on the table and opened it. It was October, and she'd already recorded seven pages of notes. After Maya explained the purpose of the book, Mr. Gregorio laughed aloud. Not amused, Maya looked up and the smile on Mr. Gregorio's face immediately disappeared.

Mr. Gregorio wasn't a bad looking man. He had what many called the "it" factor, similar to the R&B singer, Maxwell, or rocker, Lenny Kravitz. Much like those famous men, Mr. Gregorio exuded sex appeal and charm, but no matter how attractive, Maya refused to succumb to his charismatic nature as her co-workers had done.

"He has a B in almost all of his subjects, and he seems to like math the most," she continued in a serious tone. "He can multiply three-digit numbers easily. That's pretty impressive for a third grader."

Mr. Gregorio leaned back in his chair and sighed with relief. "At least he's using his brain."

Maya fought the urge to roll her eyes. She began to see where Patrick learned his behavior. "Yes, he is a good student academically, but he has to learn how to behave as well. Your son enjoys being a class clown."

"I have to admit, Ms. Richards, Patrick gets that honestly," he replied.

Detecting a hint of pride in his remark, Maya slid the composition book to Mr. Gregorio. "Being a comedian isn't always appropriate," she retorted. "Please take a few minutes to read my notes. You'll see how often he disrupts the class. I've been told that he acts the same way in other classes too, like music and especially art."

Mr. Gregorio lost his smile again and leaned forward. He turned each page, shaking his head continuously, and by the fifth page, he closed the book and sighed deeply. "Please accept my apologies."

From experience, Maya knew a story was forthcoming, and as Mr. Gregorio leaned back in his chair, she prepared for a lengthy explanation.

"This is all new to me," he began. "I'm ashamed to admit this, but I haven't exactly been a good father to Patrick. He's been giving his mother a hard time for the last year, and I decided it was time for me to step in. Maybe I can make a difference, but being a full-time parent is hard." Mr. Gregorio looked down so that Maya couldn't see his watery eyes. "He's been with me since July, and his mother hasn't come around much. I think Patrick is lashing out because of that."

Maya had to check her emotions. There was something about Mr. Gregorio's deep brown eyes that softened her heart. She could tell he was hurting and realized that his comedic responses were covering up pain. His words seemed sincere, unlike some of the other parents who came to meetings crying and looking for sympathy. Maya imagined the difficulty he was facing and felt for him, but also knew she couldn't make an exception for one student.

Despite what she felt, Maya kept her voice steady and firm. "While I applaud what you're doing, Patrick needs to learn how to control his emotions and redirect his anger into something more positive. Does he have any hobbies?"

"He does," Mr. Gregorio answered, "and I promise you I'm trying to work with him. It's just so hard with my hectic schedule. When he gets home from school, I'm there long enough to make sure he eats. When I get home from work, he's on his way out the door for school. That's the insane life of a truck driver," he explained.

"You drive at night?" Maya inquired, noticing the small Wendy's emblem embroidered on his uniform.

"Yes, I'm working on changing my hours, but that's hard to do when you're not at the top of the seniority chain," he said. "My sister helps me out, but . . . a man just isn't meant to be a single parent."

Something inside Maya snapped, and before she knew it, "And women are?" came out of her mouth.

A sly grin crossed Mr. Gregorio's face. "That isn't what I meant. I should've said that it's not meant for one parent to raise children alone." Mr. Gregorio paused briefly before continuing. "Do you have children, Ms. Richards?"

Maya didn't like sharing personal information, but felt compelled to answer. "None of my own," she replied. "Just the thirty-one in my classroom."

Mr. Gregorio laughed, and involuntarily so did Maya. In that moment, she understood why Claudia felt so at ease with him. He seemed more like a childhood friend than a parent. It would've been easy to get off topic and discuss something more pleasant, but Maya pulled herself together. "Well, Mr. Gregorio," she said, "I'd like to come up with a plan of action to correct Patrick's behavior. It's going to take a lot of effort from all of us, but I think it can work."

"You seem like a teacher who genuinely cares about her students. If you think this will help my son, I'll do all I can to make it work," he assured her.

After mapping out a behavior plan for Patrick, Maya escorted Mr. Gregorio through the main office. Claudia was sitting next to Mrs. Harris, discussing the ingredients she used in an Asian cuisine she cooked for her husband the previous night. "Enjoy the rest of the day," Claudia said as Maya and Mr. Gregorio passed by. Mr. Gregorio waved and flashed a winning smile that made all the women in the office blush.

"Well, Mr. Gregorio," Maya said and shook his hand, "thanks again for coming. I'll be in touch."

Mr. Gregorio let go of Maya's hand. "I apologize for what happened in the hallway earlier. I'll work on Patrick's long-term behavior, but I can guarantee he'll be fine for the rest of the afternoon."

"I don't mind taking baby steps," Maya told him and smiled.

"Do you think I can have a word with him before I leave?"

"I don't think Mr. Bradford would mind," Maya said and directed him toward the gym.

When Mr. Gregorio was out of the office, Maya backed up and directly into Claudia, who was standing behind her. "Were you able to get anything accomplished?" Claudia asked and stepped back to add space between them.

"You ought to be ashamed of yourself. Your husband would be crushed," Maya answered, and then faced the secretaries. "*And* the man is my height in heels. That's way too short for any of you."

"Who cares?" Ms. Covington charged back as she sorted the day's mail.

A first grade student walked into the office, tears running down his cheeks and on the verge of hyperventilation. A regular to the office, everyone knew he was sent by one of the teachers to see Claudia. "What's the problem, Adam?" Claudia asked the crying child. "You've been good all week."

"It's not my fault, Mrs. Marshall," Adam sobbed, as a small stream of drool dripped from the side of his mouth. "Paint fell on the floor and Mrs. Garrett blamed me, and I tried to tell her it wasn't me, but she wouldn't listen," he explained between gasps for air. "She just told me to get out 'cause I was yelling at her, but I wasn't."

Adam used his sleeve to wipe his wet face. "I really wasn't," he pleaded. "I was only explaining."

It was no surprise that the art teacher had sent him downstairs. She was responsible for half the students sitting on the bench waiting to see Claudia on any given day. This wasn't a common practice for most teachers, nor was it normally tolerated by Mrs. Bridges, the school principal, but Mrs. Garrett was retiring in June. She'd been at Samuel B. Huey over forty years, longer than any other teacher there and longer than most of them had been alive. Her patience was limited, and she'd never been one to follow rules.

"C'mon, Adam," she said and gently grabbed his pudgy left ear. There were still fifteen minutes until the period ended. "Chill out on my sofa for a while."

"I better get up to the computer lab," Maya said and left the office. "I'll catch up with you ladies later." On her way to the elevator, Maya saw Patrick tearfully leaning against the wall by the gym with his lips poked out as his father gave him a lecture. She shouldn't have been happy, but she was. Maybe now classroom instruction would have fewer interruptions.

Chapter 3

For the first time in years, Maya arrived at Monumental Baptist before her parents. In need of some alone time with God, she asked Kenneth to drop her off at the front door while he searched for a parking space. Available spaces were hard to come by on a Sunday morning. The church had its own lot, but it often took such a long time to exit after service, that Kenneth preferred finding a spot on the street.

Walking down the aisle, Maya quickly greeted the few members scattered in the sanctuary before claiming her place in the middle section, five rows from the pulpit. Right away, she placed six church bulletins along the pew to secure seats for her family. As she placed the last bulletin, an usher Maya didn't recognize approached her. Believing the usher was coming to introduce herself, Maya prepared to say hello.

"Good morning, sister. Are *all* of these seats for you?" the usher asked, pointing a white gloved finger at each bulletin as she spoke.

Although Maya was taken aback, she kept the smile on her face and simply replied, "Yes."

"You need the *whole* row?" the usher queried. The inflection of her voice was indication that she didn't approve of Maya hoarding so many seats.

Maya didn't understand what the problem was. Everyone at Monumental knew the fifth row belonged to Mrs. Richards's family. It had been that way since her mother retired from the usher ministry two years ago. Before she could respond, Sister Hawkins, a veteran usher came to the rescue. "It's okay," she said and winked at Maya. "Her family will be here in a few minutes. I just saw them in the lobby."

The novice usher wanted to challenge the statement, but refrained. "Enjoy the service," she said snidely and marched to the back of the church.

"This is her first week at second service," the elder usher whispered. "She'll get used to things."

"Thank you, Sister Hawkins," Maya said and sat in her seat, third space in from the end of the row. *The usher ministry must be desperate.* Ushers were supposed to be warm and inviting people.

Maya closed her eyes and relaxed enough so that she could pray about her relationship. The argument she had with Kenneth about marriage made her nervous about their future.

"Maya?" a woman's voice called, interrupting her prayer. "Maya Richards?"

Maya looked to her left and barely recognized her old college roommate, Kafi Davis. The last time Maya saw her, Kafi was moving to North Carolina. That was five years ago, and Kafi was twenty pounds heavier, with a reddish-brown, natural haircut and was dressed in a black leotard and ankle length Bohemian skirt. The woman in front of her had a honey-brown weave down the middle of her back and carried a super-sized Makowsky handbag to compliment her haute couture tailored suit. Maya stood up and hugged her long lost friend. "Kafi Davis. What a pleasant surprise!"

"It's Kafi Booker now," she corrected and flashed a huge diamond wedding ring.

Speechless, Maya stared at the emerald-cut ring. It was too flashy for her taste, but was apparently Kafi's new style. Gaudy or not, at least she had a ring. "Congrats," Maya pushed herself to say.

"Thanks," Kafi replied. "Alvin and I have been together a year in December."

For as long as Maya had known her ex-roommate, she'd never had a serious relationship—plenty of acquaintances, but nothing substantial, and that's the way Kafi had liked things. "A woman in her twenties and thirties is supposed to explore different people, places and things without the pressure of commitment," Kafi would shout as she twirled about their dorm room in one of her filmy gypsy skirts. Kafi never understood Maya's relationship with Kenneth, but respected her choice to be bound to a man.

Once Kafi settled in North Carolina, she tried to persuade Maya to join her. The cost of living was cheaper, and Kafi was convinced Maya would enjoy southern living. There was also the hope that she'd meet a southern man and leave Kenneth for good, but Maya couldn't bring herself to leave Philadelphia. Philadelphia was home. Her family was there, her friends were there, and more importantly, Kenneth was there.

Over time, Maya grew tired of defending her relationship, and after several frustrating conversations she purposely ignored Kafi's calls. Eventually, the phone calls stopped coming and the two friends lost touch.

Kafi must've detected Maya staring at her ring with envy, and covered her finger with her bag. "So what's going on with you?"

"I'm still teaching third grade at Huey," Maya nonchalantly replied.

"And . . . are you still with Kenneth?"

"Yes, he's still the love of my life," Maya affirmed without hesitation. Although Maya meant her words, at the moment she said them more to save face and make herself feel better. The truth was, she was embarrassed. Maya couldn't believe Kafi had gotten married before she had.

Before Kafi could ask, Maya volunteered what she knew was running through her friend's mind. "We're not married yet. We're waiting for him to become a partner at the firm," she fibbed, and instantly begged for repentance.

"When you do, be sure to invite me," Kafi said, as she pulled out the latest BlackBerry from her purse. "Listen, give me your information, so we can touch base from time to time."

Maya didn't really want to keep in touch, but entered her information into the BlackBerry anyway.

"Is Ken still in West Oak Lane?" Kafi asked.

For a quick minute, Maya felt as if she were being judged. "*We* live near the art museum," she snapped.

"I was thinking he and my husband should meet. Maybe they can play ball or something while we're in town," Kafi said, and Maya felt like a fool for overreacting.

An awkward silence passed between them, and Kafi put her BlackBerry back inside her bag. "Well, I see some other people I know. Let me go mingle before service starts. It was great seeing you." Kafi gave Maya a weak hug and kissed her on the cheek. "Don't be a stranger."

Upset and in disbelief, Maya sat down. Kafi was the last person she expected to see married. Before she had time to sulk, a familiar, robust laugh caught Maya's attention, and she turned around. As expected, her parents were strutting down the aisle in their Sunday best. Always unpredictable, her mother's latest brown and copper snakeskin hat and her father's matching tie and copper shoes were the center of attention.

Following her parents, Kenneth strolled down the aisle, shaking hands with various people, reminding Maya of a politician on a campaign trail. When they reached the fifth row, Maya stood up and greeted her parents. "You look sharp, Daddy," she said and winked once everyone was seated. Mr. Richards let out a docile chuckle and smiled at his daughter.

"You are going to take that off during service, right?" Maya asked her mother, referring to her colorful and large hat.

"I might," Mrs. Richards said playfully and stared hard at her daughter. "Are you wearing makeup?"

"Yes, Mom," Maya huffed.

"You should try a little more color. Maybe something with a hint of red in it," Mrs. Richards said and rummaged through the five compartments of her purse for a sample. "So you have another anniversary coming up. Any special plans for this one, Ken?" she called down the row.

"Mom," Maya whined and looked to her father for help, but Mr. Richards pretended to read the church bulletin. Maya was afraid her mother would begin her infamous speech about making an honest woman out of her daughter.

"We're planning a quiet dinner at home," Kenneth responded.

"Umm," Mrs. Richards sounded, making it clear that his response wasn't the answer she wanted to hear. She studied Maya's dark gray Donna Karan outfit. "Nice suit by the way. You're keeping your body toned, Pumpkin. Still working out?"

"Yes," Maya answered, eager for service to start so that her mother would stop talking.

"I need to come with you one day. My can is getting too big," Mrs. Richards continued. Mr. Richards laughed aloud, and Mrs. Richards nudged his side. "Don't pay attention to your father. He could stand to lose a few pounds himself."

"I have no complaints," he teased. "I like a round-bottomed woman."

Mrs. Richards ignored her husband and resumed the search for the lipstick. "Here it is," she announced and handed the tube to Maya. "Try a little of this."

Maya did as she was told, smoothing the new shade onto her lips without using her compact mirror to check for accuracy. At the moment she didn't care if she looked like a clown. Her only priority was to appease her mother.

"Perfect," Mrs. Richards said and handed Maya the tube of lipstick. "You can keep it. That color brightens your lovely round face. Brings out your doe eyes, doesn't it, Ken?"

Kenneth gazed into Maya's eyes and sincerely replied, "She's beautiful with or without makeup."

Maya's father leaned forward. "Good answer, son."

Mrs. Richards responded to her husband's remark, but her voice was drowned out when the praise and worship team started service with an upbeat musical selection. Ready to sing along, Mrs. Richards removed her hat and fluffed her thinning curls with her fingers. "Thank you," Maya said and moved down a little to make room for the massive bonnet.

Disregarding her daughter's comment, Mrs. Richards stood to her feet and let the music lift her spirits. Soon, the choir added their divine voices to the instrumental melody and shouts and praises filled the sanctuary as the congregation worshipped God. Feeling God's presence, Mrs. Richards added her own special hand clap. Maya knew it wouldn't be long before her mother danced her way to the pulpit.

In the midst of worship, the usher from earlier stopped by Maya's row again, this time with a couple standing behind her in search of a seat. "Are you *still* holding these seats?" she asked Maya directly.

"Yes, sweetie," Mrs. Richards intervened. "My sisters are in the ladies' room."

Frustrated, the usher turned away and Mrs. Richards leaned into Maya's ear. "Where's Gwen?"

Maya shrugged. She hadn't spoken to her younger sister in two days. She prayed Gwen hadn't forgotten to set her alarm.

Five minutes into worship, Maya's only two aunts came down the right aisle—Mary, the eldest, clinging tightly to Bess because of a recent hip replacement. Weak from her surgery, Mary depended heavily on her baby sister. She recently moved into the house Bess once shared with her ex-husband and only son, Eddie. Both sisters had been without men in their lives for many years. Widowed in her late twenties, Mary dedicated her life to educating the youth and serving the Lord. Bess had been divorced for five years, and at forty-nine was still energetic and sassy. Every time Maya looked at her aunts, she saw an older version of herself and Gwen, and prayed they wouldn't spend their latter years the same way.

As the middle child, Mrs. Richards was close to both sisters. They lived in the same neighborhood and talked to one another at least twice a day. Maya didn't know how her father survived being married to her mother. An only child from a small town in southern Georgia, he moved to Philadelphia on a work assignment. That assignment turned into something permanent when he met Mrs. Richards at an outdoor Sister Sledge concert. Her father told her once that the best way to handle her mother and aunts was to be silent, nod occasionally, and keep busy.

Maya watched Kenneth patiently position Aunt Mary in her seat. Once she was settled, the women blew kisses at one another and jumped into the flow of worship.

During the church announcements, Gwen pranced down the aisle in a pair of brown slacks and an off-white sweater that revealed more than Mrs. Richards thought was acceptable for church. Unlike Maya, her sister had no problem displaying a little cleavage. Although both sisters resembled their mother—petite, hazel skin, and thick, wiry hair, they differed in personality. Maya was more reserved like their father, speaking only when necessary. Gwen was full of energy, outspoken and demanded constant attention.

Mrs. Richards gave Gwen a stern glare—the glare that many mothers give their children when they've done something wrong. "Good morning," Gwen mouthed as she folded her coat in her lap. Working for an independent magazine, Maya knew Gwen was out late following low-key celebrities throughout the city in search of a newsworthy story.

Mrs. Richards made a disapproving face. "Why so late?" she asked Gwen.

"Traffic," Gwen whispered and shoved her coat under the pew in front of her.

"At least you made it before the Word," Maya said softly when their mother wasn't watching.

The sanctuary was lively and more energized than Maya had seen in months. People shouted and caught the Holy Ghost all through the offering. Mrs. Richards danced so hard, she wiggled out of her suit jacket and shoes. When there seemed to be a lull, a worshiper would jump up and start a chain reaction of praise again. If the worship leader hadn't moved the service forward, they wouldn't have heard the message until dinnertime.

Wearing a thick white robe with purple trim, the first lady of the church stood before the spirit-filled congregation. Radiant and classy, the light from the ceiling reflected off the small diamond studs in her ears, giving her an angelic glow. Maya respected First Lady Williams. Many people did. She only preached a few times each year, but worked tirelessly behind the scenes for many of the church ministries. Her preaching style was different from her husband's. Pastor Williams was a dynamic and powerful preacher, inciting people to their feet ten minutes into his sermon. Whenever the first lady brought forth the Word, the message started off slow like boiling water, but by the end of her message, everyone who could stand was up on their feet.

"The atmosphere is set. God is preparing a way for change. The shift that's coming isn't going to destroy you, but will make you better," First Lady Williams announced in a serene and comforting tone. "Jeremiah 29:11 says, I know the plans I have for you. Plans to prosper you and to give you hope."

"Thank you, Jesus! Thank you!" a lady behind Maya shouted, repeating the phrase until she buckled into tears. Other cries rang throughout the sanctuary; some of joy, some of pain.

"For some, the change about to occur will bring about great pain," the first lady said above the cries of the congregation, "but hold on in those dark hours. Remember the pain has not come to destroy you."

In the midst of the sounds surrounding her, Maya heard an unfamiliar voice whisper crisp and clearly in her ear. *It's time to move on.* The words couldn't have come from Gwen, so Maya turned around. The woman behind her was standing with her eyes closed and hands stretched above her head. Doubting the words had come from her, Maya stared straight ahead. *Trust me,* she heard again in the same voice, but different ear. Confused, Maya dropped her head in her lap. Having never experienced the Holy Ghost, Maya wondered if God was speaking to her, though she couldn't understand why He would. She didn't have a strong relationship with God. Her prayer life was random and mostly limited to quick moments in the shower and even shorter moments in her car. If it weren't for her mother's persistence, Maya wouldn't have attended church on a regular basis.

Trust me, the voice repeated and Maya started to cry. Was God telling her to break up with the man she loved? Why couldn't God just help Kenneth with his insecurities about marriage? He was a good man, *and* he was saved. He wasn't a womanizer, or a criminal, and he wasn't bipolar like so many of the men she'd heard other women complain about. Couldn't God make their relationship work? *I'm overreacting again,* Maya told herself. *Is a ring really all that important?*

Move on, the voice called and Maya reached for Gwen's hand and held it tightly. Although the message was clear, Maya couldn't bring herself to submit to God's call. She wanted to be absolutely sure He was speaking to her before she walked away from thirteen years.

Maya felt a light tap on her shoulder and lifted her head. Kenneth was standing over her. "You okay, babe? I've never seen you react this way before."

Maya wrapped her arms around Kenneth's slender frame, frightened that their days as a couple were numbered. And as she cried, Maya made a promise to God. "If he doesn't propose on Tuesday, then it's clear what I have to do."

Chapter 4

Early Tuesday morning, Maya smoothed on the Plum Berry lipstick her mother had given her in church. Today was her anniversary, and she was nervous. If Kenneth didn't propose by midnight, Maya intended to keep the promise she made to God, no matter how hard it was going to be.

Maya stared in the mirror and posed at various angles. Last night she washed her hair and set it in medium-sized rods, making her straight bob curly. She wanted to look nice for Kenneth.

Kenneth's alarm clock buzzed and Maya finished getting ready for work. There was barely enough space for two people to fit in the bathroom without feeling cramped, so she had to hurry. In their early years, getting dressed at the same time was fun and endearing. They'd shower together, and when one was brushing their teeth, the other would floss and rinse. While Kenneth shaved, Maya would curl her hair. But over the years, they'd grown to appreciate personal space.

Lacking a full eight hours of sleep, Kenneth yawned as he entered the bathroom. His eyes partially closed, he slid behind Maya and gently kissed the back of her neck. "Happy anniversary, sweetheart," he said, his breath stale and tart. "Cute hair."

Ignoring his morning breath, Maya faced him. "Thanks, babe. Same to you. Will you be home at your normal time?"

"I'm meeting a new client at three, but I should be home before five," he replied and gave her a quick kiss on the lips.

Kenneth stretched his long arm and turned the knob in the shower. Once the warm water kicked in, he dropped his pajama bottoms and took off his undershirt. Maya stared at his flat, smooth stomach as he stood by the bathtub half-asleep. The defined six-pack he had when they met was gone. Since his caseload at work had increased, they stopped going to the gym together. And despite his lack of effort, Kenneth maintained an ideal weight. Maya was jealous. She had to work out four times a week just to stay in size six jeans.

Before the water from the shower fogged the mirror, Maya applied a natural shade of eye shadow above her eyelids, and then rushed out of the bathroom before the steam caused her hair to frizz. She put her makeup case away and wiped the few loose hairs from the counter, then walked down the hall to the bedroom.

As she did every morning before leaving the house, Maya made the bed and opened the Venetian blinds. The weather was finally changing. Tree leaves had turned into beautiful fall colors, and it was time for lined, leather coats. The sky was bright blue and clear, and the fluffy clouds looked as soft as cotton balls. It was days like this that her grandmother would say, "God is happy." Maya couldn't help but wonder if God was pleased enough to change His mind about her and Kenneth. Since Sunday, things between them had been close to perfect. Maya knew God's Word was final, but there was no harm in praying He would have a change of heart.

Maya tiptoed to her shoe closet, careful not to tear a hole in her ultra-sheer stockings. She pulled a pair of black ankle boots from the top shelf, then sat on the side of the bed. Once her boots were zipped, she grabbed her Tiffany necklace and fastened it around her neck as she walked out of the bedroom and down the hall. When she reached the bathroom she opened the door to let the steam rush out before poking her head inside. "I'm heading out, babe. Love you!" she yelled.

"Love you too!" Kenneth hollered back over the running water.

Maya left the door cracked and headed to the living room, praying the day would end as great as it had started.

Three o'clock had crept up on Maya before she had a chance to appreciate the flowers on her desk. While she waited for the dismissal bell to chime, she stared at the radiant arrangement of pink and red roses, carnations and lilies Kenneth had delivered to her job. Coats on and bags packed, Maya's students wrote in their journals while they waited for the day to end. If they were talking or clowning around, Maya hadn't noticed. In her mind, she imagined the different scenarios in which Kenneth might propose. There was no guarantee that he'd propose, but just in case, she wanted to be ready.

Maya removed the card from her floral surprise and read it again.

The future is where you and I dream; coexist . . .

Her cheeks flushed from the sentiment of Kenneth's words, giving her hope that today was the day she'd been waiting for. She was *finally* going to be Mrs. Kenneth Green.

"Ms. Richards," Patrick said, jolting Maya back into reality. "You didn't give me a behavior grade today."

Maya looked at Patrick and smiled, the first time she'd done that since he showed up in her classroom. She put the card back in the envelope and picked up the pen next to her hand. Per the conference with his father, Patrick had to have Maya and the specialty teachers sign his notebook daily. Mr. Gregorio would also have to sign it. This was their means of constant communication. At the end of each week, if Patrick behaved well, Maya and Mr. Gregorio would come up with a special reward.

Patrick slid the notebook across the desk and Maya flipped to the latest comment from the art teacher. Below his C grade, Mrs. Garrett scribbled: *Patrick continues to talk back when asked to be quiet.* Mrs. Garrett had about the same level of patience as a newborn. Although Maya didn't always agree with her ways, she respected the veteran teacher.

Separating Mrs. Garrett's remark from Patrick's performance in her classroom, Maya wrote, *You're doing a great job!* next to a B+ grade and drew a smiley face behind her signature. She thought Patrick would be thrilled, but his sour expression said otherwise. "What's wrong, Patrick?"

"When am I gonna get an A? I thought I was good today. My dad is gonna buy me a football if I get one A. All I need is *one*." Patrick pouted even more, hitting his leg with his fist as he waited for Maya to respond.

Even if she wanted to, Maya couldn't change his grade. She didn't want him to think he could use his puppy dog eyes and high-pitched whine to get what he wanted. "I want to see all A's. You're very capable of getting an A everyday."

Patrick looked as if he were about to cry. Since her heart was in a good place today, Maya looked in her drawer and took out one of the glittery pencils she gave away for outstanding improvement. "But tell you what. If you continue to do well for the rest of the week, I'll give you that A. And in the meantime," Maya handed Patrick the pencil, "here's a little something for your effort."

Patrick put the pencil inside the spiral of his notebook. "Thank you," he mumbled and frowned as he walked back to his seat.

The dismissal bell rang and the students quickly put their journals inside their desks. Maya walked to the door and called the children, table by table, to line up. Once all of the chairs were on top of the desks and every child in line, Maya escorted her class to the stairwell. She'd normally walk them all the way outside, but she was in a hurry to leave the building. She walked them halfway down the stairs and waited for the last child to exit before running back to her classroom.

"Are you ready for tonight?" Claudia asked from the doorway, as Maya packed her bags.

"I'm trying not to seem anxious, but I can't wait to get home." She was beaming and threw a few colored markers in her bag.

"I've been praying for you all week," Claudia replied. "I don't even want you to talk to me tomorrow morning. All I want to see is a diamond flashing in my face." Maya stuffed a stack of construction paper inside her bag and Claudia stopped her. "You're not gonna have time for this tonight. What's wrong with you?"

"You know Mrs. Bridges. She'll have my head if this board isn't done by the first," Maya retorted.

Claudia took the construction paper from her friend. "That's a week away, Maya."

"You're right," Maya replied. "I'm so used to working every night."

"Well, not tonight," commanded Claudia.

Maya grabbed her coat from the back of her chair and put it on. "Guess I better get going then."

"I hear you received some beautiful flowers today," Lloyd said as he glided into the room, startling the women. "Special occasion?"

"Just another anniversary," Maya gloated as she zipped her coat.

Lloyd looked at the floral arrangement on Maya's desk. "Wow! No wonder you've been glowing all day."

"She deserves every flower in that bunch," Claudia stated.

Maya knew better than to comment. Claudia would've given Lloyd a list of reasons why. She reached into her purse and turned on the ringer of her cell phone. The message icon flashed and Maya navigated through the buttons to read the text message. Hope ur ready 4 a nite of romance. Hurry home! I'm waitn 4 u. Maya stared at the screen lovingly.

"Aww, I remember when Bishop used to make me blush like that," Claudia reminisced. C'mon, Mr. Bradford, we'd better let Ms. Richards get home to her boo."

"He's one lucky man," Lloyd said. "I hope he's good to you."

Maya's smile grew wider as she returned Kenneth's text: I'm on my way! "He's very good to me," she replied, and prayed tomorrow she'd have proof of that on her ring finger.

Heaven must be operating in my favor, Maya thought when she entered her apartment twenty minutes earlier than normal.

Hearing the door close, Kenneth walked out of the kitchen. "I wasn't expecting you this soon," he said and helped Maya take off her coat. "Dinner is ready if you want to eat now."

"I'm starving," she replied and followed Kenneth into the kitchen. Even though she wasn't hungry, Maya was eager to get the evening underway.

As part of Maya's anniversary gift, Kenneth tried to replicate the first meal they shared at Olive Garden. Not quite the same as the famous Italian restaurant, Kenneth's presentation was a surprisingly close second. The mushrooms were sliced thin, the mussels tender, the shrimp plump, and the scallops grilled to perfection.

As tasty as the meal was, for the last hour Maya struggled to eat it all. Twirling the last of the linguine in her seafood Portofino around her fork, Maya soaked the thick noodles in the garlic-butter wine sauce.

"How was dinner?" Kenneth asked.

Maya removed her last mussel from its shell. "Absolutely delicious," she responded, and although she really enjoyed the food, she'd been on edge all evening, waiting for Kenneth to pop the question. When he handed her a glass of wine for a toast, Maya's eyes zoomed to the bottom of the glass in search of a ring. Every time she slurped up a noodle or opened a mussel shell, she hoped to come across a shiny diamond. She tried to relax, but this night was too important. By midnight, she'd either prepare for a fabulous wedding or end an important relationship.

"Shall we open our gifts?" Kenneth asked.

Maya clapped her hands together like a four-year-old on her birthday and jumped up from the table. She went to the hallway closet for the Nordstrom's bag full of the clothes she'd purchased for Kenneth. When she returned, Kenneth had already put the dirty dishes in the sink and was standing next to a Tiffany bag on the table. Maya practically leaped in the air. The shiny turquoise bag was a little too large for an engagement ring, but that didn't matter. She was confident the moment she'd been praying for had finally arrived.

"Ladies first," Kenneth said, grinning at Maya's excitement.

Slightly embarrassed, Maya calmed down. "No, baby, you go first."

"Are you sure?"

"Positive," she replied. Maya wanted to save the best gift for last.

One by one, Kenneth lifted each article of clothing from the large gift bag. "Guess you don't like my style," he joked, commenting on the casual items inside. "You calling me a prude?"

"Not at all," Maya confessed. "I just want to see my man in some jeans once in awhile."

Kenneth leaned down and kissed her forehead. "I think I can handle that for my special lady," he said and put his clothes across the back of the kitchen chair. "Thanks, babe. Now it's your turn."

Excited, Maya pulled the Tiffany bag close to her side, wondering when Kenneth was going to drop down on one knee. She reached inside the bag and felt several items. First, she pulled out a brochure on Australia, and when she opened it an airline ticket fell to the floor.

"This is the only country you talk about visiting," Kenneth said, then picked up the ticket and gave it to Maya. "I made plans to go during your spring break."

Tickled, Maya put the ticket back inside the brochure. "So you do pay attention to me," she said, then took out a glittery envelope from the bag. Inside were a few gift certificates for service at an expensive downtown salon.

"For those stressful days," Kenneth informed her.

"Think I'll need more than three free massages," Maya said and set the envelope on the table. The last gift inside the bag was a long, velvety jewelry box. She thought it strange that a ring could be housed in such a large container, but figured Kenneth was trying to throw her off. Slowly, she lifted the lid of the box and her eyes beamed with anticipation. But when she saw the link bracelet inside, her heart sank.

"It matches the necklace I bought you last Christmas," Kenneth said proudly. Careful not to frown, Maya closed the lid and put the box on the table next to her other gifts. Kenneth looked puzzled. "Everything okay?"

"Everything's beautiful, Ken," she said, teary-eyed.

Kenneth pulled Maya close to him and delicately kissed her lips. "I love you," he said.

Maya found strength to look him in the eyes without crying and replied, "Ditto."

"I've got another surprise for you," Kenneth said, but give me five minutes to get it ready."

Kenneth ran out of the kitchen like a schoolboy and Maya stood by the table and stared at the Tiffany bag. Maya never thought a piece of Tiffany jewelry could make her sad, and before she realized what she was doing, Maya picked the bag up and turned it upside down, shaking it frantically. Nothing but crumpled tissue paper came out. Disheartened, Maya set the bag down and tossed her presents back inside.

The sensuous vocals of Maxwell's debut CD flowed through the speakers in the bedroom, and instinctively Maya rolled her eyes. Taking her time, she strolled down the hall and stopped when she reached the bathroom. Kenneth was sprinkling red and pink rose petals into the bathtub. "What are you doing?" Maya asked, although Kenneth's romantic gestures were clear.

"I saw this in one of your love movies. I thought you'd like it. I hope I'm not wrong," he answered. "The water's nice and warm. Want to get in?"

Kenneth helped Maya undress, and once she was submerged in the water, he took off his clothes and joined her. Maya's heart was overwhelmed, and she temporarily forgot about the proposal. As they slowly bathed one another, Maya and Kenneth talked and laughed together, just as they had during the beginning years of their relationship.

Shivering as they exited the water, Kenneth rushed to get Maya's towel. He gently dried her delicate body, and then wrapped the towel around her before drying himself. "I've got one more surprise for you," he announced cheerfully, reminding Maya of her earlier disappointment.

Kenneth briefly left the bathroom and returned with matching exotic, tiger-print pajamas—a skimpy bra and panty set for her, and long bottoms for him. Maya tried not to frown. She didn't feel like wearing the outfit, and she wasn't ready for a night of passion.

"What's wrong?" Kenneth asked, concerned about Maya's lack of expression.

"I'm fine," she lied, forcing herself to look happy. "I guess it's getting near my bedtime." Maya reached for the lingerie and put it on. At this point, all Maya wanted to do was get the night over with.

"You look like a *Jet* centerfold," Kenneth complimented. Admiring her beauty, he lifted Maya into his arms and carried her to bed. Gently, he lay her down, kissing her body softly until he noticed his affection wasn't being returned. "You sure you're okay?" he asked, clueless to Maya's inner turmoil.

"I'm okay, babe," she tried to assure him. "Just enjoying the moment."

Maya tried to relax so that she could focus. She put everything she felt aside—the sermon last Sunday, the small voice that spoke to her, and the promise she made to God—and made love to Kenneth with great passion, possibly for the last time.

An hour later, Kenneth held Maya tight. "Thank you for thirteen beautiful years. I look forward to sharing the next thirteen with you."

Chapter 5

A sudden chill awakened Maya and she sat up in bed. With the weather changing, she'd have to buy some caulk from Home Depot to eliminate the draft coming through the bedroom window. As usual, Kenneth had pulled all of the covers to his side of the bed. Maya tugged at the comforter wrapped around his body until it loosened and grabbed enough to cover the bottom half of her legs and feet. There wasn't much time before she had to get up and begin her day, so she curled her body into a fetal position and thought of warm places, hoping that would be enough to psych her body, so she could fall back to sleep. But just as she closed her eyes, music from her alarm clock sounded. Maya rarely used the snooze button, but this morning she needed an extra ten minutes.

In nothing but a T-shirt, Maya tilted her body and faced Kenneth, who was sleeping as soundly as a baby. He'd tired himself out last night, waking up three times to make love. Watching him, Maya wanted to believe he'd one day marry her, but last night was Kenneth's last chance. She couldn't risk living another year without being his wife, or break the promise she made with God.

Maya rubbed her feet together under the comforter and started to drift, and as soon as her body went numb, the alarm sounded again. Though tempted to hit the snooze button a second time, Maya turned it off and got out of bed. If she didn't get up now, she'd mess up Kenneth's strict morning ritual, and both of them would be late for work.

Dragging her tired body across the room, Maya stepped on the fancy bra Kenneth had given her and broke the clasp. Reluctantly, she picked it up and examined the damage. Kenneth hated the thought of wasting money and would be upset if a gift she'd worn for less than five minutes couldn't be repaired. Figuring there was nothing she could do, Maya tossed the bra into the dirty clothes hamper and prayed he wouldn't notice.

Sluggishly, she walked into the bathroom and turned on the shower. Before getting in, Maya cleaned up the few stray hairs Kenneth left in the sink after shaving the day before. Rose petals from the bath he prepared last night were still scattered on the floor, and when she touched a petal with her foot, she instantly started to cry. Though her anniversary was near perfect, Kenneth's expressions of love couldn't take the place of an engagement ring this time.

Crying softly, Maya took off her T-shirt and stepped into the shower. As the water beat on her skin, a wave of emotion rushed through her. It was clear that the relationship was over. Kenneth was never going to propose, and she had to leave.

Pressing one hand against the wall, Maya leaned forward and silently cried out to God. How was she going to leave Kenneth? And when? Writing a letter seemed too impersonal, and breaking up over dinner would be torture. Should she wait until their lease ended next June?

The stress of the decision she had to make caused her stomach to cramp. She massaged the troubled area with her fingers, but the deeper she pressed into her stomach, the more intense the cramping became. "Why is this happening to me?" she sobbed. "God, where am I going to go?" Maya's cries grew louder and she covered her mouth with her hands, praying her voice hadn't carried into the next room. Through her moans of sorrow, Maya heard that same voice whisper, *Trust me*. As tears rolled steadily down her cheeks, Maya finished showering.

Ten minutes later, and feeling a small amount of relief, Maya stood lifelessly in front of the bathroom mirror, wrapped in a beach-sized towel. It was hard to get motivated. When Kenneth's alarm buzzed, she snapped out of her daze and snatched her face rag from the rack. Quickly, she wet the rag and covered her face before he walked in. Maya didn't want him to know she'd been crying. It was bad enough she was running behind schedule. By now, her teeth should've been brushed, her hair done, and her skin covered in lotion.

On schedule, Kenneth walked into the bathroom. "That was a great night, baby," he beamed.

"Umm," Maya moaned and slowly lowered the rag, praying the tear streaks had been wiped away.

Kenneth stood behind Maya, making her nervous. She was afraid her eyes revealed her sorrow. "Running late?" he asked.

Relieved, Maya squeezed toothpaste onto her toothbrush. "Yes, I needed a few extra minutes of sleep. *Someone* kept me up all night," she replied and brushed her teeth.

Kenneth laughed and turned on the shower. "I slept like a baby."

Maya couldn't smile. Her night hadn't been as easy. She spit the toothpaste into the sink and rinsed with citrus-flavored Listerine. Swiftly, she cleaned the counter and sink, and then glanced in the mirror. Her hair was a mess. The curls she worked so hard to style were ruined. Maya reached for a fashionable scarf in a side drawer, then combed her hair back and twisted it into a short ponytail. She wrapped the scarf around her hair until she had a small bun, and hoped she looked presentable.

Out of habit, Maya reached for her makeup case under the sink. It was amazing what the slightest touch of foundation and color could do. Rifling through her case, Maya searched for lipstick, but was unsuccessful in her hunt, and instead of wasting more time, she closed the case and shoved it back under the sink.

Pressed for time, Maya rushed to the bedroom and slid into a wrinkle-free, multicolored rayon dress that Aunt Bess had given her last year. Maya put on an old pair of stockings and slid into her thick-heeled shoes, then stared in the full-length mirror on the wall and shook her head. She looked like a preschooler had dressed her. The gold friendship ring Kenneth had given her several years ago twinkled in the reflection of the mirror and she yanked it off of her finger. People at work were expecting it to be replaced with an engagement ring. What was she going to tell them? And how was she going to face Claudia?

The shower stopped, and Maya pulled herself away from the mirror. Backing away, she wiped the few tears that had formed and threw the ring in the top dresser drawer as she walked out of the room. Although her footsteps were drowned out by the sound of Kenneth's electric razor, he expected Maya to announce her departure.

Maya touched the bathroom door, and right before she pushed it opened, dropped her hands. She couldn't say good-bye to him without falling apart. Maya continued down the hall to the coat closet by the front door. After putting on her coat, she took a deep breath and placed her hand on the doorknob. If Maya was going to leave Kenneth, as she'd promised God, she'd have to do it today.

Sitting in her car at a nearby gas station for the last twenty minutes, Maya had decided not to go into work. She called the school, hoping it was early enough for the answering machine to pick up, but was disappointed when Ms. Covington answered. "You must have a ring," she said, after Maya mentioned she wasn't coming into work.

Maya didn't want to admit the truth. Before the morning bell rang, Ms. Covington would have told the entire staff. "No, that's not it," she said in a mellow tone. "My emergency sub plans are in the thick, blue binder on my desk."

"How are you gonna make us wait to hear about your anniversary? I want to hear all the details," Ms. Covington insisted.

"It wasn't anything big," said Maya, ready to get off the phone, but Ms. Covington continued to press for information. Unable to handle her questions, Maya burst into tears.

Seconds passed before Ms. Covington spoke again. The sobs heard through the line spoke volumes. "Things didn't go as planned?" she asked. Identifying with her pain, Ms. Covington suggested Maya take a couple days off. "As a matter of fact," she said, "take off the rest of the week."

Without argument, Maya agreed. She had plenty of sick days to use. She hung up with Ms. Covington and before she had a change of heart, called her sister.

"This better be good," Gwen said in her morning voice.

Knowing Gwen, she'd been asleep for a few hours, and only answered the phone because she was expecting to hear details of Maya's engagement. "I'm leaving him," Maya stated.

Still a bit groggy, Gwen replied, "It's too early for jokes, Maya."

"I'm not going to work so I can . . ." Maya began, and had to stop because she started to cry.

Realizing that her sister wasn't playing around, Gwen became more serious. "Maya, you've got to calm down and tell me what happened."

"I want to move out today," Maya uttered between sobs.

"Are you serious?" questioned Gwen, although from Maya's cries she already knew the answer. "I take it Ken didn't propose," she said, full of attitude. Gwen wasn't shocked that he hadn't. What surprised her was the fact that Maya finally had the guts to end the relationship. "Did you guys have an argument?"

Maya reached into the glove compartment and pulled out a package of tissues. She pulled one from the pack and blew her nose. "No, he doesn't know I'm moving out."

"Where are you now?"

Maya sniffed softly. "At a gas station. Can you help me?"

"Of course I can," replied Gwen.

Maya's other line beeped, and Kenneth's number flashed across the screen. He was probably calling to check on her. Rather than answer and give him an excuse, Maya let the call go to voice mail. "I just don't understand, Gwen. What's wrong with me?"

"There's nothing wrong with you. Ken's just a wimp," Gwen said with an attitude. "Do you want me to tell Mom?"

Maya sighed. "I guess I'll have to move back home. Do you think Mom will mind?"

"I have a sleeper couch. That has to be better than living with Mom again." Gwen tried to make Maya laugh, but she didn't get a response, not even a faint chuckle. Moving back home wasn't something Maya was looking forward to.

"I guess you should call Mom and let her know I'm coming home," Maya responded. She would've called, but she didn't feel like answering a bunch of her mother's questions.

"I'll do it now," Gwen said and made plans to meet at Maya's apartment in an hour.

The time on Maya's dashboard read 7:13 when she hung up. Before pulling out of the gas station's parking lot, she checked the message Kenneth left. "Hey, babe. You left without saying good-bye." There was a hint of hesitation in his voice. He must've detected that something was wrong. "I guess you were running late and forgot. Well, call me during your prep. I love you."

Maya hit the END button and tossed her cell phone into her purse on the passenger's seat, then drove a few blocks back to her apartment. As she turned onto her street, she spotted Kenneth driving out of the garage. Immediately, she hit the brakes. The car behind her honked its horn and Maya didn't know what to do. If she kept driving, she'd ride right past Kenneth, and he would recognize the sorority bumper sticker on the back of her metallic gray Maxima. The car behind Maya honked again, and she heard an angry shout through the window. Maya looked in her rearview mirror, as the man behind her raised his hands in the air and mouthed what Maya was certain were obscenities. It was rush hour, and Philadelphia was full of impatient drivers; not the best time for Maya to pull such an act.

Slowly, Maya proceeded forward before the annoyed driver attracted more attention. Her heart was beating fast and her left leg jumped up and down, reminding her of someone in a restless leg syndrome commercial. The traffic light ahead turned red, and the car two spots ahead of her motioned for Kenneth to cut in. Maya was relieved. Although she was out of the woods, Maya ducked just enough in her seat to avoid being seen. When the light turned green,

Maya pressed her foot on the pedal, giving more gas than needed, and sped into the garage.

Driving up the ramp, Maya tried to calm her nerves. Her adrenaline hadn't been that high since her college days. Exiting on the third level, Maya parked in her assigned space near the elevator and sat in her car until she was sure Kenneth wasn't going to pull into the space next to hers.

When she thought it was clear, Maya got out of the car and walked to the elevator. The door opened as soon as she hit the button. She stepped inside and as she rode to the twelfth floor, reflected on all the things that would have to change. She and Kenneth had acted as one in so many ways—the joint lease, shared bank account and vacation savings plan. How would she determine the fair amount of money to withdraw from the accounts? She wasn't worried that Kenneth wouldn't be able to afford the apartment once she was gone. He'd handled most of the bills for the last six years.

The elevator door opened, and Maya walked a few steps across the hall to her apartment. Key already in hand, Maya's body shuddered as she turned the lock. Closing the door behind her, Maya sighed at the thought of packing. Most of the items would be hard to separate. Though

Kenneth had paid for most of the furniture, nothing was ever considered *his* or *hers*.

Maya stood in the center of the living room and looked around. "God, where do I begin?" she said aloud. There was six years of living to move out, and she didn't have boxes, packing tape or a truck to transport her things. Overwhelmed, Maya walked to the window. As hectic as the neighborhood could be, she was going to miss the high energy and entertainment, not to mention the walks along the parkway and multicultural festivals. *So many memories,* Maya thought, recalling all of the fun times she'd spent with Kenneth, and suddenly the fear of being alone engulfed her. It was hard to believe that she'd wake up tomorrow morning and he wouldn't be by her side.

A sharp pain shot through Maya's temple and she closed her eyes. Either she was hungry or the many tears she'd shed earlier had spawned a headache. Maya rubbed her temples, and then placed her hand over her forehead until the pain was less excruciating. Lightheaded, she eased down on the sofa and laid her head against the padded arm. There was no use in trying to get anything done until Gwen showed up.

Maya jolted awake when the intercom buzzed. She didn't know how long she'd been asleep, but she could've used more time to nap. Easing off the sofa, Maya buzzed Gwen inside the building and waited for her by the elevator across the hall. Expecting to only see her sister, Maya was surprised to also see her parents and her cousin, Eddie, when the elevator door opened. Maya was glad Eddie was there. At twenty-four, it was usually hard to get a hold of him. He worked unusual hours and enjoyed an active bachelor lifestyle. God was clearly on Maya's side today. Eddie's Chevy Trailblazer and additional man-power would be a relief to her sixty-five year-old, retired father.

Mrs. Richards wasted no time getting to her daughter, and without saying a word, Maya fell into her mother's arms. She hadn't realized how much she needed her mother's tender touch. Mrs. Richards put one arm around Maya, and used the other to direct everyone inside the apartment. "Oh, Pumpkin. I know you're hurt right now, but trust me. Everything's going to be okay. Momma's here now."

Once everyone was inside, Mrs. Richards had Maya walk through the apartment and tag the items she wanted to take with sticky notes—mostly clothes, music, movies, candles, toiletries, and other knick knacks—giving her family plenty to do while she and Mrs. Richards went into the kitchen.

Mrs. Richards made breakfast—cinnamon oatmeal, beef bacon, and toast. Maya didn't want to eat, but her mother insisted the food would ease her headache. Nibbling on a cold piece of toast, Maya watched her mother clean the dishes and put them away in silence. This was the first time Mrs. Richards had ever been so quiet. "Why is this happening to me, Mom?" Maya asked.

"I know it doesn't feel like it now, but you're doing the right thing," Mrs. Richards said as she turned to face her daughter. "And you're not staying with Gwen on some sleeper. You're coming home with me."

Maya shoved the last piece of toast inside her mouth. "You sure you want your thirty-six-year-old child back at home?"

Mrs. Richards let out the dishwater and cleaned the suds from the sink. "No matter how old you are, you and your sister can *always* come home."

Staring at her uneaten oatmeal, Maya ran her finger along the top of the bowl. "Why would Ken do all those nice things? Our anniversary was perfect, Mom. We hadn't celebrated like that in years."

Mrs. Richards folded the dishrag and towel and lay them across the faucet. "Ken knew you were getting antsy. He needed to do something to get you over this hump; something good enough to make you hold on. But," she said and sat in a chair by the table, "everything is going to be all right. God has a reason for everything."

"I thought God had given me Kenneth," Maya replied glumly.

Mrs. Richards wiped a few breadcrumbs from the table into the palm of her hand and put them in a napkin. "You'll meet someone nice. But take this time to focus on yourself while God heals your broken heart."

"Do you think God's mad at me? I mean . . . I haven't been saved all my life, and until a year ago, I didn't go to church all the time." Maya played with her fingers and started to cry. "I don't pray all the time like you, and . . ."

Mrs. Richards placed her hands on top of Maya and held back her own tears. "Don't ever think that God doesn't love you. Sometimes, He teaches us tough lessons to get our attention. But no matter how bad you're hurting, now is not the time to give up on Him."

"Why couldn't my relationship work? Claudia had a baby when she was sixteen. Then she met Bishop and married him only six months after their first date," whined Maya. "And I saw Kafi at church. She never wanted a man, and now she has a husband."

"Don't covet your neighbor's house," Mrs. Richards replied, reciting an all too familiar scripture from the book of Exodus. She often shouted those words when Maya and Gwen were kids complaining of unfair treatment or crying about the things their friends had that they couldn't get. "What God chooses to teach you isn't necessarily the same lesson for someone else. Don't compare your situation to anyone else's. You don't know what God plans to do with them. Just know that He's doing what He knows is best for *you*." Mrs. Richards removed Maya's plate and the empty juice cup from the table and put them in the dishwasher. "It's going to be hard, Pumpkin, but you've got to hold on to your faith."

Listening carefully as her mother preached, Maya could feel her faith slowly slipping away. The house phone rang and Maya checked the caller ID on the cordless next to her hand. "I better get this, Mom. It's Claudia," she said, and with little enthusiasm, Maya hit the talk button. "Hello."

"Are you okay?" Claudia asked right away. "Ms. Covington told me Kenneth didn't propose last night."

"I guess everyone knows, huh?"

"Don't worry about the people at school. *We* care about you." Claudia's attitude was evident. "I knew that buster wasn't going to do it! I tried to convince myself that he was going to change, but I should've known better. How are you feeling?"

"I'm moving out," Maya stated blandly.

"You're moving out?" Claudia repeated, surprised. "You'll be better off without him. This is his loss, Maya. I hope you know that."

With her mother staring at her, Maya tried not to cry. Though she knew Claudia was right, Maya wasn't ready to accept her words of comfort. "My family's here," Maya said, letting Claudia know that she couldn't talk in great detail. Claudia understood and Maya promised to call once she was settled in her mother's house.

"It's getting late," Mrs. Richards said when Maya hung up the phone. "I better go see how things are going."

Mrs. Richards got up from the table, and as she left the kitchen, Maya lay her head on the table and tried to relax.

Twenty minutes later, Maya stood in the bedroom alone. There was little trace that she'd once shared the room with Kenneth. An old picture from one of his office galas was all that was left behind as a reminder of the life they once shared.

"He'll regret not making you his wife," Mr. Richards said as he walked into the bedroom. "And when he does, it'll be too late."

Maya poked out her lips and sighed. "Thank you, Daddy. I just wish we could've worked it out."

Mr. Richards hugged his daughter. "If it helps, I never liked him."

Maya laughed aloud and looked up into her father's eyes. This was the first time she noticed the new wrinkles near his eyes and across his forehead. She couldn't remember when he had aged. His stomach was a lot fuller, and he took twice as long to complete his chores, but Mr. Richards was still the strong man she adored growing up, the man who always made sure his girls were well taken care of. "Thanks again, Daddy," she said and held his hand, "but I know you don't mean that. You're gonna miss the male bonding."

"I don't mean to interrupt your daddy-daughter moment," Eddie said from the door. "But we're finished moving everything."

Wow, Maya thought. It took less than two hours to remove six years of living. "Then we better get moving," she said and followed her father out of the room.

When Maya walked into the living room, Gwen was sitting on the sofa, reading an old *Urban Influence* magazine with her feet crossed on the coffee table. "Is that your anniversary gift on the table?" she asked.

"Yes, and I should probably leave that stuff here. I hope he can get his money back," Maya said.

"You're crazy," Gwen replied and got up from the sofa. She went to the table, and without permission, went through the bag. "You better take this stuff."

"I can't do that," Maya stated firmly.

"He's keeping *his* gifts, isn't he?" questioned Gwen, and Maya didn't answer.

"Well, I'll take the spa certificates. I've always wanted to try that place." Gwen thrust the bag into her sister's hands. "You should take the bracelet. You deserve *at least* that."

"It doesn't seem right," Maya said and put the bag down.

"It doesn't seem right that he would lead you on for *thirteen* years. But I won't go there today," Gwen snapped and put the jewelry box into Maya's purse.

Maya didn't have the energy to argue with her sister. "I should leave him a note," she said and took a pen out of her purse.

"If you must leave something," Gwen replied, "leave a picture of a wedding ring next to the apartment keys."

Eddie burst out laughing. "I like that, cuz."

"Now, now, don't be mean. I raised you girls better than that," Mrs. Richards interjected as she made her way into the room.

Gwen rolled her eyes and leaned close to Maya. "Keep the gifts," she whispered. "Now can we get out of here?"

One by one, everyone exited the apartment. The last to leave, Maya slowed down and stopped by the picture of her and Kenneth on a seven-day cruise, last spring, hanging on the wall. Life with Kenneth was officially over, and once she walked out the door, there was no turning back.

Mrs. Richards pulled lightly on her daughter's arm, but Maya needed a few minutes alone in the place that had been home for so many years. "Go ahead, Mom," she said. "I'll catch up."

"Don't stay too long, Pumpkin," Mrs. Richards replied and continued to the elevator.

When all was clear, Maya backtracked to the table. Reluctantly, she removed the apartment keys from her key ring and placed them next to the Tiffany bag. She lightly rubbed the keys and bowed her head. *God, how am I going to live without him? If I have to move on, I'm gonna need your help.* Maya lifted her head and put the straps of her tote bag on her shoulder, then slowly backed away, pausing at the same picture on the wall one last time. She put her lips on the glass of the frame and kissed Kenneth's image. "Good-bye, my love," she whispered, and walked out the door.

Chapter 6

Of all the rooms in the house, the kitchen was the place Mrs. Richards kept practically spotless. When Maya heard her mother walk through the front door, Maya knew she was going to be disappointed. Maya didn't know how the kitchen got so cluttered or how time had slipped away, but it was too late to clean up now.

Mrs. Richards stood at the entrance to the kitchen and dropped her keys on the glass table. The last thing Mrs. Richards wanted to see when she walked in the house was a sink full of dishes. Slouched in a chair, Maya pretended not to notice the strained look on her mother's face as she walked by.

Still in her fall coat, Mrs. Richards walked to the cabinet under the sink and pulled out a plastic trash bag. Immediately, she began cleaning off the counter. She tossed a crumpled Quaker oatmeal packet and a greasy butter wrapper into the bag, then leaned across Maya and grabbed two ginger ale cans from the table. An open jar of grape jelly sat dangerously close to the edge of the table, and Mrs. Richards searched through paper towels and granola bar wrappers to find its lid. Unsuccessful in her attempt, she gathered all of the mess on the table and threw it into the trash bag.

In silence, Maya focused on an old episode of *Judge Mathis* on TV and nursed a warm glass of soda. When her mother was in this mood, it was best to remain quiet and stay out of her way.

Mrs. Richards surveyed the kitchen and spotted the jelly lid on her new granite countertop. She grabbed the lid and twisted it on the jar before putting it back inside the refrigerator. Frustrated, Mrs. Richards looked at her electric stove. Grease stains from the bacon Maya cooked for breakfast were everywhere. She dropped the trash bag, grabbed a dishrag from the counter, and mumbling to herself, attacked the stains. She scrubbed the oily spots so hard Maya thought her mother was going to remove the finish on the stove. As Maya listened to her mother's grumbles, she considered leaving, but was afraid to move.

Mrs. Richards threw the rag in her hand aside and faced her daughter. "I hope you're planning to wash these," she said, pointing to the full sink.

Maya looked at the pile of dishes and couldn't believe she'd eaten so much. "It's only two o'clock. I'll have them done before dinner."

Mrs. Richards took off her nursing shoes and smock, and as she walked out of the kitchen snapped, "You need to do them now."

Feeling like a teenager again, Maya started to get up, but Mrs. Richards had returned, holding a leather coat in her hand. "You left this on the banister. You do know we have a place for this," she said sternly. "It's called a closet." Mrs. Richards dropped the coat in Maya's lap and stormed off.

To ease her mother's nerves, Maya hung her coat up, and then ran dishwater. As she waited for the sink to fill, Maya listened to Judge Mathis deliver his verdict for a burglary case. This was Maya's favorite part of the show, especially on days when the plaintiff and/or defendant had gotten on his nerves. Maya stopped the running water and suddenly, the television turned off. Unsure of what happened, Maya faced the television to find her mother staring back at her.

"I'm not going to let you become addicted to these reality shows," Mrs. Richards said and put the remote on the table. "Have you been out of the house today?"

"I went to Genardi's," she replied and started washing dishes. Today was the first day Maya had gone out of the house since she moved in with her parents. That was four days ago.

"You went to the grocery store like that?" Mrs. Richards remarked, referring to Maya's discolored and wrinkled jeans and bleach-stained sweatshirt.

"No one noticed me," she said faintly. She wasn't ready to sort through her numerous bags of clothes.

Mrs. Richards pulled a green and white silk scarf off Maya's head and placed it in her pocket. "I bet they noticed the rag tied around your head. You've been wearing that thing for the last two days."

Maya ran her fingers through her hair until her bob lay straight. "I was only in there long enough to get a gallon of milk. I'm sure no one recognized me."

Mrs. Richards gave her daughter a disapproving glare. "Well, just don't do it again," she said and left to go change her clothes.

When she was gone, Maya dropped the dishrag in the warm water and closed her eyes. She wasn't sure how much of her mother she could take.

"Why is this towel on the toilet seat?" Mrs. Richards shouted from the upstairs bathroom. "The toothpaste belongs *under* the counter."

The bathroom cabinet slammed and Maya jumped. In that moment, she regretted her decision to move back home. *God, you've got to have something better in mind for me,* she prayed, fighting the temptation to call Kenneth.

Maya was normally as anal as her mother, but lately she didn't have the energy to worry over her environment or personal appearance. And it was now obvious that if she and her mother were going to live under the same roof, Maya would have to get her act together.

Mrs. Richards walked into the kitchen and started scolding Maya again. "I'm not going to let you sit here day after day and feel sorry for yourself. It's been how many days?" Mrs. Richards took a can of Diet Coke from the refrigerator and sat down. "Ken is just one man. There are plenty of men in this city. And believe it or not, there is one that will marry you. God has someone special for you. So stop sulking!"

"I'm not so sure you're right about that," Maya said in return.

"Death and life is in the power of the tongue, Pumpkin," Mrs. Richards reminded her daughter.

"Then I'm hoping Kenneth and I will get back together," Maya said, "or that I at least find someone who'll *really* love me."

"So you spent too many years in the relationship. Nothing happens by accident, Pumpkin. Everything in life is a lesson. Look for the lesson God was trying to teach you." Mrs. Richards opened the soda can and took a sip. "You're still young . . . and cute when you fix yourself up. You'll find another love in time. For now, enjoy being alone. Do what *you* want for a change. I love your father, but Lord knows I miss my single days."

While Maya finished the dishes, Mrs. Richards silently reminisced on the early days of her life with her husband. When she met him, she was twenty-four and fresh out of college. Between working at a hospital, going on mission trips, and traveling with friends, she had little time to be bored. "The only way to keep me still was to marry me," she said with a fresh twinkle in her eyes.

For a brief moment, Maya envied her mother. "What you and Daddy have is rare. Not too many people stay together for thirty-eight years."

"God will send your mate. But don't wait around for him," Mrs. Richards replied, grinning like a schoolgirl. "By the way, I told First Lady you'd be a great Sunday School teacher."

"That's a big commitment, Mom. I'm not sure I'm ready for that, but I'll give it some thought," she said to appease her mother.

"Good," Mrs. Richards responded and drank more soda. "In the meantime, your sister and Claudia are coming over for dinner tonight."

Maya hadn't seen Claudia since she moved out, and she wasn't ready to deal with her sharp tongue. "Maybe they should come next week. I won't be good company today."

"Don't be that way, Pumpkin. You should be grateful God blessed you with people who care about you." Mrs. Richards sat her soda on the table and got up to open the refrigerator. She took out a frozen chicken for tomorrow's dinner and put it on the counter. "Put the chicken in the sink when you're done with the dishes. I need to take a nap before your father comes home. Between you and my patients, I'm worn out."

Maya finished the dishes, and then went upstairs to her bedroom. She needed to mentally prepare for her sister and best friend's arrival.

For over an hour, Maya sat on her bed, next to Gwen, listening to stories about the celebrities she'd recently interviewed. Claudia sat Indian-style on the carpeted floor, eating her third slice of vegetable pizza, begging Gwen to reveal any gossip she'd heard in her travels. Maya pretended to be interested, forcing a shallow grin every time either of them glanced her way.

"Are you gonna be quiet all night? When should we talk about what happened?" Claudia asked, tired of Maya's nonchalance.

"I don't want the evening to turn into a therapy session," Maya said solemnly.

To many people, Claudia and Maya were unlikely friends. Maya grew up in the heart of West Philadelphia, amidst a revived African-American community and attended private schools. Caucasian, and raised in Smyrna, Delaware, a small rural town two hours south of Philadelphia, Claudia attended public schools. Maya wasn't a true introvert, but was careful with the way she crafted her words and dealt with people. Claudia, on the other hand, was very direct, and for those who didn't know her, a bit curt. As a teen, she was given the name, *Schick,* because her tongue was as sharp as a razor.

The two women had worked together nearly two years before they became friends, speaking only in passing. It wasn't until they were teamed together at a teacher's retreat one summer that they had a chance to talk more in depth, and much to their surprise, they had a lot in common. Friends since then, they'd become each other's strength. Maya tactfully expressed what Claudia felt in sensitive situations, and Claudia sternly stressed what Maya felt in situations that required a more direct approach.

Gwen lightly pushed her sister. "I know you're going through something, but what's up with your clothes? Mom said you left the house like that." Gwen sniffed the air playfully. "Did you even shower today?"

"Those jeans are from the eighties." Claudia chuckled. "All you need is a neon ribbon for your hair."

Gwen jumped up and sang a few verses of *Material Girl* by Madonna, reminiscent of their preteen era, and the women laughed. Imitating dance moves from that time, Gwen was so excited that she accidentally kicked a soda can with her foot. The room suddenly grew silent, and on cue, Mrs. Richards appeared at the door. "Well, don't just sit there staring at each other, go get some paper towels."

Gwen ran out the room, giggling softly, while Maya and Claudia snickered behind Mrs. Richards's back. "You might need the vacuum too," Mrs. Richards said loudly as she guarded the stain. "There are pizza crumbs all over the rug."

"You just can't help yourself, can you?" Claudia asked. "Why don't you go downstairs and enjoy the rest of the night. We'll clean up."

Mrs. Richards looked at the garbage bags around Maya's room and decided to take Claudia's advice. "While you're at it, why don't you help her tidy up."

Gwen ran back to the room with a roll of paper towels and unraveled enough to clean the damp area. She was glad Sprite was her drink of choice this evening and not her favorite, Dr. Pepper.

Mrs. Richards reached for the paper towels, and Claudia held her arm. "We'll take care of this."

"All right, I'll leave you young ladies be," Mrs. Richards said and slowly backed away.

"Girl, I don't know how you can do it," Claudia whispered when Mrs. Richards was gone. She picked up the two pizza boxes and stacked them on the edge of the dresser. "My kids know they're out of my house after graduation. Now that my oldest is in college, she better not *think* about coming back. I don't even want her home during the breaks," Claudia joked.

"Now you know Debbie can come home whenever she wants. I bet she'll be the one to live at home until she's married," Gwen replied.

"Don't believe it!" asserted Claudia. "Listen, when I married Bishop, we struggled for several months. I worked a second job, and we lived in a dump, but I refused to live with either of our parents. If Maya's smart, she's saving money to buy a place of her own."

Maya ignored Claudia's last comment. She'd never lived alone, and the thought of buying her own place never crossed her mind. After college, she and Gwen shared an apartment, and Maya lived there until she moved in with Kenneth. Her dream had always been to get married and stay home to raise children. Being the PTA president and soccer mom was exciting to her. A house without a family wouldn't be a home to Maya. It would just be an empty and quiet place to dwell. "I want the first home I own to be with my husband," Maya said and immediately sensed Claudia's disapproval.

"Get with the times, Maya. This isn't the forties and fifties anymore. Women have evolved," Claudia said. "You don't need a husband to own a house."

Gwen put the pizza boxes in a garbage bag along with the rest of the trash and made a knot at the top to keep it closed. "That's easy for you to say. You're married," she replied. "Who knows? Maybe Kenneth will take this as a wake-up call and come by with a ring tomorrow. Men don't realize they had a good woman until she's gone."

"I wouldn't say yes if he did. A woman shouldn't have to jump through so many hoops for a man to be her husband."

"Now you know men don't think like we do when it comes to marriage," Gwen retorted. "Women already have their wedding planned before they even have a man in mind. If it were up to a man, he'd never bring up marriage."

"Well, I think," Claudia voiced, "Maya needs to look out for herself. Life doesn't revolve around a man. God forbid, if Bishop were to leave me today, I'd be crushed. But the reality is I would've done all I could do. Nothing's going to change his leaving. He'd be living his new life, and I would find the strength to do the same."

"Not every woman wants to be so independent," Gwen barked and set the garbage bag by the door. "There's nothing wrong with wanting to be a housewife and mother. That's part of the problem with kids these days. If more mothers stayed home, kids would be happier."

Claudia rolled her eyes. She and Gwen could challenge one another all night, if time permitted. Digging into people's lives through questioning was what they both did for a living. "So you're saying when you have kids, you'd give up your writing career to play mommy twenty-four/seven?"

"It depends on the situation. I won't know what I'd do until it happens. But this isn't about me," Gwen said and lay across the bottom of the bed. "I just want to point out that women have choices, and people, *especially women,* shouldn't make them feel bad about it."

Claudia wasn't used to biting her tongue, but realized Gwen was right. Tonight was about encouraging Maya, so she changed the subject. "Has he called you?"

Maya shook her head.

"Maybe you should call him," Gwen suggested. "There's nothing that says you can't make the first move."

"Are you serious, Gwen? *He* messed up. *He* should be the one to call," Claudia charged.

"Why, Claudia?" Gwen snapped and sat up. "She obviously needs to get closure. We're not in high school anymore, and they didn't have a short-term affair. They were together *forever.* That's what's wrong with so many women today," Gwen dictated. "We play too many games, and in the end wind up hurt. We need to be real with these men and *honest* about *our* feelings."

"This isn't one of your articles," Claudia snapped. "Men get away with too much because

we pacify them all the time. But more importantly, God says let *the man* do the chasing. That
cuts out who should call first or make the first
move."

"She's not chasing him," Gwen huffed and
looked at her sister. "If it'll give you some peace
of mind, call him."

Maya had learned not to interfere when Claudia and Gwen debated over a topic. The few
times she did, Gwen and Claudia would be silent
for two minutes, then pick back up where they'd
left off. "Do you think God is punishing me for
moving in with Ken?" she asked, hoping Gwen
and Claudia would switch their focus.

Claudia leaned against the dresser and crossed
her arms. "God understands that we make mistakes," she said, her tone more sensitive and
caring.

"Who says this was a mistake?" asked Gwen
with a raised brow.

"You can't be serious right now, Gwen," Claudia remarked.

"I don't think—" Claudia began, but she was
immediately cut off.

"It's not what you think that's important,"
Gwen blurted. "Everyone's not in the same place
spiritually. So the best thing would be to pray
that God speaks to Maya. It shouldn't matter
what *you* or *I* may think or feel."

Clearly annoyed, Claudia remained silent.

"Don't get me wrong. I do have strong opinions about moving in with a man before marriage, and God is a large part of that. But those are *my* opinions," Gwen preached. "Church folks need to stop criticizing one another when someone does something they believe is wrong. If God thinks it's wrong, *He* should be the ultimate and really *only* judge. Let God be the one to tell a person they're wrong and how to change."

Claudia uncrossed her arms. "I've never judged Maya for living with Kenneth. I don't agree with it, but it doesn't mean I love her any less or question her relationship with God."

"Humph," Gwen moaned.

"Just because I happen to believe that living with a man before marriage isn't the best thing to do, and for the record," Claudia stressed. "God makes it pretty clear *why* He doesn't want us to . . ." Claudia continued, and then stopped talking when she realized Maya was crying. "See what you did?" Claudia directed to Gwen and rolled her eyes as if it were her fault.

Maya sat up and leaned against the headboard as she held her pillow tight. She sobbed, "Now do you see why I didn't want to talk about Ken?"

Gwen scooted close to her sister and rubbed her arm. "Claudia and I don't agree on many things, but we do love you," she said. "It doesn't matter who calls whom first. Just be prepared when you do speak to him. At this point, you're either going to respect his views on marriage, or you're going to bite the bullet and let this one ride."

Not wanting to say too much more, Claudia added, "We're here to support you, no matter what you decide to do."

"I'm here too, Pumpkin," Mrs. Richards announced as she stepped inside the bedroom.

"How long were you outside the door?" Maya asked and smiled.

"I was on my way downstairs, but then I heard all the commotion," Mrs. Richards replied. "For a minute there, I thought Gwen and Claudia were going to need a referee."

Maya wiped the last trace of tears from her eyes and looked at the three women around her. "I know I haven't been myself the last few days. But I'll get it together and pray on what to do."

"Now that's the best advice I've heard from this room all night," said Mrs. Richards. "If it's your desire to be married, Pumpkin, pray for God to bring the man *He* designed especially for you."

"I know that's right," Claudia concurred.

"Well, it's been a long day and I think I've had my fill of women's night," Maya teased and rolled off the bed.

"Is that your way of telling us to leave?" Gwen joked.

"You know I love each of you. But if I'm going to get my life together, I have a lot of thinking and praying to do," Maya replied and looked around her room. "And I should probably start by unpacking these garbage bags."

"Amen to that!" Mrs. Richards cheered and danced to the door.

"And on that note," Claudia added as she put on her shoes, "we should probably leave."

When everyone left the room, Maya closed her door for more privacy. She walked back to her bed and used the remote by her pillow to turn on the television. It was almost midnight, and although she needed to organize her bedroom, it was too late to start such a tedious task.

There wasn't much on television at eleven o'clock, so Maya settled for watching a rerun of her favorite drama series, *Law and Order*. When a commercial came on, she connected her cell phone to its charger. *Why hasn't he called me yet? Doesn't he miss me?* she questioned silently, and raised the ringer volume to ten. She couldn't believe that Kenneth let so many days pass without attempting to reach out to her. Maya stared at the phone and realized that Gwen was right about one thing. She did need closure.

Without thinking, Maya hit speed dial, and before the call connected, she pressed the end call button. As bad as she wanted to speak to Kenneth, God had asked her to trust Him, and that was what she was going to try to do. Maya lay her phone flat on the nightstand and was suddenly moved to kneel by the side of her bed. It'd been so many years since she prayed on her knees that Maya hoped God wasn't angry with her for abandoning Him. Maya didn't know how to begin, but as she positioned her hands, the words seemed to flow from her lips like running water. *Lord, I'm sorry I've been a stranger, but I am going to do better. My heart is heavy today, God. I feel like I have so much love to offer, and no one to share it with. If I can't share this love with Kenneth, please send someone I can share love with . . .*

Chapter 7

In hopes of avoiding other teachers, Maya entered the building from a side door. Today was Maya's first day back to work since her anniversary, and thanks to Ms. Covington, everyone knew why she'd taken three days off. Maya hurried up the back stairs and down the second floor hallway. As she passed the elevator, the doors opened.

"Ms. Richards," Mrs. Garrett called and held the door open with her free hand. "I must've hit the wrong floor," she said and stepped out of the elevator. "It must've been meant for me to see you. There are no accidents, you know."

Lucky me, Maya thought.

Mrs. Garrett walked toward Maya with a look of sympathy. "How are you holding up?"

Out of respect, Maya answered, "I'm good."

"I don't know why some men are afraid of marriage. Men like that either end up alone for the rest of their lives, or marry when they're too old. Be glad it's over. Your fella was selfish. How could he lead you on all these years?"

Maya shrugged her shoulders. Though she was tired of everyone's opinions concerning her relationship, she was taught to mind her elders. "I wish I had the answer to that, Mrs. Garrett."

Mrs. Garrett pressed the up elevator button and the doors opened. "Relationships can be complicated. But hold on, you'll find someone else," she said and stepped into the elevator.

Maya smiled politely until the elevator doors closed and continued down the hall to her classroom. "You'll find someone else," she muttered under her breath. If she had a dollar for every time someone said those words, she'd be rich. Maya didn't want someone new. She wanted Kenneth to come to his senses. In church yesterday, Maya saved a seat for him, hoping he'd show up. But he never did. After service, Maya overheard one of the choir members say that Kenneth was at the 8:00 service, and she rushed to her car and cried. Going to an earlier service meant that he was purposefully avoiding her. But why?

Maya heard a set of keys coming from the main stairwell and sighed inwardly. She prayed it wasn't someone that wanted to talk, but as Lloyd advanced down the hall, his old school and smooth stride more apparent, Maya was disappointed that her prayer wasn't answered.

"Good morning," Lloyd said.

Maya waved, and then stopped cold in front of her classroom. After missing three days, the classroom looked like a tornado had swept through. Chairs were scattered around the room when they should've been on top of each desk so the cleaning team could mop the floor. Thinking of the time she'd need to straighten up, Maya sighed and walked inside, careful not to step on the balled up papers, candy wrappers, crayons, and pencils spread across the floor. As she glided across the room, she noticed an instructional math poster ripped in one corner and partially hanging from the wall, and the chalkboards covered in kid-writing.

"Welcome back," Lloyd said from behind her. "This must've happened on Friday. Mrs. Bridges was in a meeting at the school board all day."

Maya placed her bag on the chair behind her desk. "Good morning," she replied glumly, and then glanced at the handmade cards lined across the desk. Off to the side, there was an envelope addressed to her. Maya removed the three-page letter and read the substitute teacher's detailed notes on her students' behavior. When Maya reached the end of the letter, her eyes froze on one sentence. *I had to move his desk next to yours.* Maya dropped the letter and looked to the side. Sure enough, Patrick's desk was attached to hers. She considered moving it, but thought it might be a good idea to have him away from the other children for a while.

"Ms. Covington mentioned that you and your man broke up," Lloyd said as he moved the desks back to their original state. "Sorry things didn't go the way you wanted them to. I've only seen your guy once. I thought he looked like a fool then, but now I know it for sure."

"Yes, it's over," Maya said and put the letter away.

"He's missing out on a good woman."

"I'll be fine," Maya said coldly and examined the damage to the room again. "You know, you don't have to help straighten up."

"I don't mind," Lloyd said coolly and his lip twitched. "I just want to see that pretty smile of yours."

Maya turned away. Lloyd's compliment almost made her blush. "I'll erase the boards," she said and headed to the back of the classroom. The students had used the colored chalk Maya kept hidden in the closet to write on the board. They knew Maya only liked white chalk. Any other color was difficult to erase without leaving a faint residue.

For almost an hour, Lloyd helped Maya arrange the classroom. And although she initially thought his presence would annoy her, Maya welcomed his assistance and small conversation.

Lloyd picked up a gum wrapper and looked at the clock on the wall. "The bell is about to ring."

"Where did all the time go?" Maya responded and headed to the door.

"You stay here," Lloyd told her. "I'll go get them."

"You've done enough already, Lloyd. I can—"

"Really, it's no trouble," Lloyd said, and left the room before Maya could object.

Maya walked back to her desk and reviewed her lesson plans until she heard the patter of feet coming down the hall. Slowly, the children walked into the room as if they were on a death march and lined themselves in front of the chalkboard.

Still seated, Maya looked up from her desk. "After you put away your belongings, write in your journals until the morning announcements."

The children didn't move when Maya stopped talking. Instead, they turned to Lloyd for further instructions. And like a drill sergeant, Lloyd stared into their worried eyes, and then faced Maya. "They shouldn't give you any problems today. But if they do, call me." Lloyd gave the children another stern glare, and then motioned for them to take their seats.

"Thank you," Maya mouthed and Lloyd nodded before he walked out of the classroom.

"Do you need any help, Ms. Richards?" Patrick asked before sitting at his new desk.

Guilt makes you tilt, Maya thought, recalling a phrase her mother often used when a person knew they'd done something wrong. Such must've been the case for Patrick. He'd never offered to help Maya before. "I read a long letter from the substitute this morning. Your name was mentioned too many times to count. I guess that explains why she moved your desk."

"I'm sorry," Patrick said and frowned.

As she watched the children move around the room, afraid to speak, Maya prayed God would give her the strength to make it through the day.

Maya turned into the Westover Crossing community where her parents lived in Norristown and parked in their driveway. She was thankful that the day had gone by quickly. From the small porch, she smelled the aroma of her mother's homemade spaghetti and instantly missed preparing dinner for Kenneth.

"Hey, Pumpkin. How was your first day back?" Mrs. Richards yelled from the kitchen when Maya opened the front door.

Maya hung her coat in the closet then joined her mother. "Everyone treated me like a porcelain doll."

"You know that'll wear off soon," Mrs. Richards said as she chopped a small garlic clove into pieces. "I made your favorite tonight. I even put jumbo shrimp in the sauce, instead of meatballs."

"Sounds good," Maya responded and looked at the thick, chunky sauce simmering in a pot on the stove. "Where's Daddy?"

Mrs. Richards sprinkled the freshly cut garlic over several broccoli florets. "He was at a deacon's meeting all afternoon, but he called a couple hours ago from Gwen's house."

Maya watched her mother pour a few drops of olive oil over the broccoli before putting the tray in the oven. A few years ago, Mr. Richards suffered a heart attack, and as a result, Mrs. Richards stopped frying foods and cooked healthier meals. Surprisingly, Maya thought she'd miss her mother's southern-style fried chicken and catfish, but had learned to enjoy her baked substitutes.

"Everything smells wonderful," Maya said, missing the smells of her own cooking.

"Go change, Pumpkin," Mrs. Richards replied. "We'll eat as soon as your father gets here."

Maya dropped her bag in a dining room chair and headed upstairs. While she waited for dinner, she'd catch up on her lesson plans and ungraded papers. Inside her room, Maya took her cell phone from her purse and made sure the ringer was still on. No one had called all day, not even a telemarketer. She poked out her lips and connected the phone to its charger before setting it on her nightstand. Staring at the phone, Maya wondered when or if Kenneth was going to call. It'd been almost a week since she'd left. Maya kicked off her shoes, and before she dwelled too much on the past, changed into yesterday's lounge gear and went back downstairs.

Before sitting down, Maya took her students' writing assignments from her bag and spread them across the dining room table. From her seat, Maya had a clear view of her mother cooking. "I don't know if I can wait for Daddy," Maya said.

"It shouldn't be too much longer," Mrs. Richards called back as she stirred sugar into a fresh-brewed pitcher of iced tea. You know, as much as I love to cook, it would be nice if you helped me out sometimes."

"When I lived with Kenneth, I used to cook three times a week. Weekends were a free-for-all," Maya reminisced.

"You have a different life now, Pumpkin," Mrs. Richards reminded her firstborn. "One night a week would be fine. But I like the weekend free-for-all."

"How's Monday?" queried Maya, then quickly recanted. Monday had been Kenneth's night to make dinner. "Well, maybe Thursday."

Mrs. Richards smiled and squeezed half a lemon into the pitcher. "How convenient. This Thursday just happens to be Thanksgiving. Why don't you start next week?"

"Deal," Maya replied.

"Great," Mrs. Richards said, and then verbally mapped out an entire meal for the holidays while Maya tried to concentrate on her work. Maya hoped that her mother would get the hint when her occasional "Yeah" and "Uh-huh" mumbles had ceased, but Mrs. Richards continued to talk, clueless to the fact that she'd lost her audience.

The dryer in the basement buzzed loudly and Maya's body jerked.

"Can you get the clothes from the basement while I finish the tea? My hands are covered in lemon juice," Mrs. Richards shouted from the kitchen.

Slightly annoyed, Maya dropped her pen. "Sure, Mom."

Maya couldn't take the constant distractions, but realized it was something she'd have to get used to. In less than three minutes, Maya went to the basement, put the warm linens in a laundry basket, and then carried them back upstairs so that she could finish her work. *Please don't let her disturb me again until dinner,* Maya silently pleaded with God, but her prayer request was short-lived. Ten quiet minutes later, Mrs. Richards came from the kitchen and stood next to her. "What do you think about having a white-potato pie this year? Mary used to make them all the time when I was in high school."

"Only one, Mom." Mrs. Richards and her sisters were the only family members who enjoyed the special pie. The recipe had been passed down from three generations, and Maya was glad it stopped there. Neither she nor Gwen were fans of the semi-sweet dessert.

"You're right," Mrs. Richards said and dragged the laundry basket to the steps. "My sisters and I will probably be the only ones eating it anyway. Did you hear about Eddie's new job?"

Maya shook her head, and for the next ten minutes listened to her mother give her an update on her cousin's life as she folded the linens in the basket.

"Uh-oh! I forgot to pick up butter for the rolls. Pumpkin, can you run over to Genuardis? We can't eat the rolls without butter."

Maya put the papers she was grading inside her tote bag. There was no way she would get any work done before dinner. "No problem. I just need to get my sneakers," she told her mother and went up to her room.

Frustrated, Maya changed into her workout shoes and reached for her phone. Still, no one had called. As she combed her hair, Maya heard the front door open, and shortly after, she heard Gwen and her mother complaining about a tree. Maya threw on a sweater and walked back downstairs, surprised to see her father and Justin tugging a live Christmas tree through the front door as Mrs. Richards followed closely behind them with a broom.

Maya was saddened. Picking a Christmas tree was a tradition her father had done with Kenneth the last ten years, during the first weekend in December. "Old age getting to you, Daddy?" Maya asked in jest. "It's not even Thanksgiving yet."

With Justin's help, Mr. Richards carefully set the tree by the balcony door, and then sat down. "We're celebrating early this year, Pumpkin," he replied, breathing loud and heavy.

A puzzled looked crossed Maya's face. "Why? Is there some special occasion I'm not aware of?"

"We're going to Arizona for Christmas and New Year's," Mrs. Richards said as she swept the loose bristles into a dustpan.

"What?" Gwen exclaimed, and emerged from the kitchen holding a venti-sized cup of Starbucks coffee. Sophisticated and sassy, she looked like the national spokeswoman for a Starbucks advertisement.

"What nothing," Mrs. Richards snapped and emptied the contents of the dust pan in the trash. "Your father and I are grown. We don't have to tell you girls *everything*."

"You could at least consult us before deciding to bail out on Christmas. Gheesh!" Gwen replied and took a sip of her coffee.

"Did you buy the tickets yet?" Maya asked. For a moment, she considered going with them.

"I told her to tell you girls," Mr. Richards added.

"I'm telling you now," Mrs. Richards said and sat on the step to finish folding the items in the laundry basket.

Justin laughed aloud and everyone looked at him.

"This isn't funny, babe," Gwen told him and rubbed his balding head.

"Guess we'll have to finish this convo later. I need to get to the store, so we can eat." Maya went to the closet and took out her jacket.

"Wait a minute, Maya," Gwen said. "Justin and I need to leave, but since we're sharing things . . ." Gwen held Justin's hand. "This seems like the perfect time to make an announcement."

Mrs. Richards dropped the pillowcase in her hand and grinned ear to ear. In contrast, Maya's heart sank in anticipation of hearing news of an engagement.

"Justin and I—" Gwen began, and looked into her man's eyes. "We're moving to California."

Mrs. Richards's expression quickly changed. She looked at her husband, and then back at Gwen. "Why would you want to go to *California?*"

"I accepted a job at NBC Universal." Gwen waited for a response, but everyone was in shock. She would be the first member of the family to live so far from home. "Justin's got a job too. He'll start in February, but I start right after the holidays."

Unable to look at her daughter, Mrs. Richards stared at Justin. Sensing that he was going to be the blame for the move, Justin spoke up. "This is a great opportunity for Gwen. She has to go, and because I'd miss her too much, I decided to look for a job too."

"It's a small writer's gig, but there's a lot of potential," Gwen said, hoping her mother would understand her reasons for wanting to move so far away.

Mrs. Richards resumed folding the laundry. This was bittersweet news. "You have anything to say, honey?" she said to her husband.

"I'm very proud of you, Doodle," Mr. Richards told his daughter proudly. Doodle was the name he'd given her as a toddler. Gwen had been given a time-out many times for writing on the walls of their house.

Maya's childhood name was derived for a different reason. Until the third grade, she'd held on to her "baby fat." "You're as round as a pumpkin," Mrs. Richards had said many times, and eventually, the name stuck.

"Thanks, Daddy," Gwen replied, and then looked at her mother.

"Naming you after that Chicago poet seems to be paying off, huh, Doodle?" Mr. Richards said.

"Well, I hope Maya doesn't get any ideas," Mrs. Richards remarked forcefully. For the first time, she seemed to regret naming her daughters after her favorite literary icons, Maya Angelou and Gwendolyn Brooks.

"I'm not going anywhere," assured Maya as she put on her coat. It would be hard to see her sister leave, but Maya was glad Gwen's news didn't involve getting married; although she had a feeling marriage wasn't too far off. Justin had only been around for six months, but Maya knew her sister. Gwen was in love. By this stage in Gwen's relationships, either the men would become frustrated with her work ethic and independence, or Gwen would become bored and call it quits.

Justin was unlike any other man Gwen had dated. He dressed in clothes that never seemed to go together and wore odd pieces of jewelry. Many women would've given up on Justin based on looks alone, but Gwen was drawn to his artsy nature. Maya remembered the night Gwen rushed home from a photo shoot, talking nonstop about an eccentric photographer she'd just met. Maya knew then that Justin would be around for a while.

"I'm going to look for an apartment after Christmas," Gwen said. "Justin's going to look for one too."

"I wouldn't normally encourage a couple to live together, but in this case," Mrs. Richards said solemnly, "I think it'd be best for your safety, and less worry on me."

"Don't worry, Mrs. Richards," Justin replied. "I'll keep a close watch on her."

Tired of all the talk about moving, Maya interceded. "Well, this certainly is a lot to take in all at once," she said then faced the happy couple. "Congratulations."

Gwen gave Maya a hug and kissed her cheek. "I'll need someone to watch my cat while I'm in Cali, looking for a place. Think you'll be up for it?"

"Of course," Maya said and left Gwen alone to deal with their parents.

When she got into her car, it suddenly dawned on Maya that she'd be alone for the holidays. Maya backed down the driveway in a hurry, but before she could make it out of the development she had to hit the brakes. Maya was overwhelmed by the changes taking place all around her, and could no longer hold in the pain buried deep inside. "Lord, what have I done to deserve this?" she moaned. "Why can't I be happy like everyone else? Why do I have to be alone?" Unable to control her tears, Maya parked on the side of the road then dropped her head on the steering wheel, where she stayed until the tears stopped flowing.

Chapter 8

New Year's Eve . . .

Stretched across the sofa in the living room, Maya stared at the white blinking lights on the Christmas tree while Anita Baker's holiday CD played softly in the background. Next to her, Gwen's cat, Langston, lay flat on his back with his paws in the air, as Maya gently rubbed his plump belly. Long-haired and frisky, Langston should've been a Hollywood cat. He loved attention and automatically posed every time someone pulled out a camera. Mrs. Richards would've complained if she saw him on the sofa. His mixture of black, white, and brown hair stuck to the suede material.

A cramp formed in Maya's left leg and she wiggled it rapidly until the sensation went away. Langston flipped over on his stomach and waited patiently for Maya to get comfortable, then placed his head on her thigh. It was New Year's

Eve and Maya was alone. She'd been by herself since Gwen left for California, on Christmas Eve, and during that time, Maya and Langston had become close.

Maya picked up her cup of eggnog from the table and took a sip. Besides Langston's company, the creamy beverage was the only part of the holiday she enjoyed this year. Maya gulped the rest of her drink then set the mug on the coffee table. It was almost six o'clock. If she didn't get ready for church, she'd find herself asleep on the sofa when the New Year arrived. Maya didn't want to go to church, but her aunts insisted she be there.

"If you're asleep at midnight, you'll sleep your way through the whole new year," Aunt Mary had told Maya an hour ago. And although Aunt Mary's words made sense, at the moment, sleeping through the year didn't sound like a bad plan.

Unmotivated, Maya leaned back and dropped her head on the arm of the sofa. At least she didn't have to pick up her aunts. Aunt Bess mentioned that they were going early to meet up with friends. She hoped those same friends would take them home. Maya also promised Claudia that she'd attend her annual holiday soiree.

Langston jumped on her lap and Maya rubbed his furry tail. Since there was no getting out of her evening plans, she closed her eyes and prayed that God would lift her spirits. "God, please fix my attitude so that I can enjoy the evening," she prayed aloud. "And I know I shouldn't be selfish, but can you *please* send me someone special? This is the last holiday I want to spend by myself."

Wearing a winter-white pant suit, Maya walked two blocks to church. By the time she reached the front doors, her cheeks were red, her nose frostbitten, and the tips of her toes numb, but she waltzed into the sanctuary in her pointy-toed boots with a smile on her face.

When Maya reached the fifth row, she almost turned around. There was an unfamiliar man sitting in the seat where Kenneth used to be. Although Kenneth had been going to the early services, she hadn't expected to see someone sitting in his place. "Excuse me," Maya said politely.

The gentleman stood up and Aunt Bess did too. "Maya, this is my friend . . . Michael." The way Aunt Bess said *my friend,* told Maya that Michael was something more. She wondered how long he'd been around, and where her aunt had met him.

"Nice to meet you," Maya greeted and shook his hand. It was almost uncanny how closely he resembled Aunt Bess's ex-husband. They both looked like an African Santa Claus, with salt and pepper hair and beards.

Maya slid down the row and stopped in-between her two aunts. After taking off her coat, she folded it under the seat in front of her and sat down. "Something you want to tell me?" she whispered in Aunt Bess's ear. "Could he be the reason why you've been so busy lately?"

Aunt Bess blushed and tapped Maya's knee. "Hush up, child."

Despite her feelings of loneliness, Maya was happy for her aunt. Aunt Bess had been divorced for five years, and to her knowledge, she hadn't been on a date since then. Maya subtly browsed the sanctuary for people she knew, especially Kenneth. New Year's Eve was the one service he looked forward to each year, so he had to be there. But by the time praise and worship ended, and Pastor Williams had positioned himself behind the podium, Maya hadn't spotted him amongst the crowd. So instead of worrying about Kenneth, Maya sat back and tried to enjoy the pastor's sermon.

***

After service, light refreshments were served in the multi-purpose room. Maya wanted to leave immediately after the benediction, but Aunt Bess wanted to mingle, more than likely to show off her new beau. Standing in line for an orange-flavored punch, Maya reflected the pastor's sermon. "Come out of the cave!" he shouted at midnight. At the sound of those words, Maya felt a jolt in her soul and prayed she was about to experience life in a new way.

When she was close enough, Maya grabbed two small cups of juice from the table and navigated through the mounds of people back to where her aunts were waiting. Along her path, she spotted Kenneth talking to one of the youth ministers and felt butterflies in her stomach. She moved forward at a medium pace, careful to keep her hands stable so she wouldn't spill the drinks. As she grew closer, their eyes locked and Kenneth smiled. This was the first time Maya had seen him since the day she moved out. Being so close to Kenneth reminded Maya of the love they once shared and made her nervous. Just as they were close enough to speak, someone touched Maya's arm and pulled her attention away from him.

"Happy New Year," First Lady Williams said in the even-natured manner that Maya adored.

"Same to you," responded Maya half-heartedly and slowly she took her eyes off of Kenneth.

"Your mother tells me you're interested in teaching Sunday School."

At a loss for words, Maya made a mental note to speak to her mother about the matter later. She hadn't considered joining the ministry, but didn't want to speak out against her mother. "Maybe I should visit a class before making a final decision," Maya suggested.

The first lady smiled softly. "Why don't you come next week? I'm teaching the ten-to-twelve age group."

From the corner of her eye, Maya watched Kenneth walk away and tried to hide her disappointment. "Sure," she told the first lady.

Puzzled by Maya's expression, the first lady asked, "Did you enjoy the service?"

"Very much," Maya admitted with a little more fervor, but was still preoccupied with Kenneth's whereabouts. "It made me realize that it's time to make some changes in my life. Like pastor said, I've got to stop hiding behind my pain."

Maya glanced off to the side and saw Kenneth talking to her aunts. First Lady Williams touched her chin. "That's right, sweetheart," she said, and turned Maya's head to face her. "God didn't create you to hide behind anything, or anybody. I'll be looking for you next week, okay?"

As Maya watched the first lady walk across the room, she wondered how much information her mother shared about the breakup with Kenneth. Mrs. Richards meant well, but sometimes she offered more information than what was needed to her church friends.

Maya walked toward Kenneth and her aunts and noticed that he was wearing a pair of jeans she'd bought for their anniversary. And either he'd gotten more attractive since she'd moved out, or Maya had forgotten how handsome he really was.

"I was wondering when you were gonna make it over here. I'm parched," Aunt Mary said when Maya reached her. "I was about to get it myself."

Maya laughed as she handed a cup to each of her aunts.

"I see Aunt Bess has a friend," Kenneth teased, as he watched Aunt Bess walk to the end of the table to talk to Michael. Maya was tickled that he still referred to Bess as his aunt.

"I'm glad she's getting out more," stated Aunt Mary, already finished with her juice. "She's not home to boss me around all the time."

Kenneth rubbed Aunt Mary's shoulder. "You're still a comic," he said, and then studied Maya's suit. "You look nice."

Feeling like they were meeting for the first time, Maya blushed. She wanted to tell him how handsome he looked in his jeans, but decided to hold off. "I was looking for you in the sanctuary at midnight. I thought you'd gone to a different church this year."

"You knew I wasn't going to miss my pastor. Things haven't changed *that* much. I was in the balcony with my sister's family. It wasn't hard to locate you though."

"I don't think we'll ever change our seats."

Kenneth grinned. "The fifth row has the Richards name on it," he joked. "But that's not what I meant. I always loved the way that suit looked on you." Lost for words, Maya looked down at her boots. "Do you have plans for tonight?" he asked coolly, as if nothing had changed between them.

And though Kenneth despised conflict outside the courtroom, Maya had expected their first encounter since the breakup to be awkward. "I'm going to Claudia's soiree," she replied in a child-like tone.

"That's right. She and Bishop do that every year."

"What about you?" Maya asked.

"I got stuck watching my nephew," Kenneth answered. "We're going to play video games all night."

Maya wanted to be with Kenneth, but was too afraid to ask. She wanted to talk about what went wrong in their relationship, and ask if there was a chance they could work it out. But if Maya didn't go to her best friend's party, Claudia would have a fit. "Make sure you give everyone a kiss for me," Maya said.

"I'll do that," he said and leaned down to kiss Maya's cheek.

As he walked away, flashes of holidays past came to mind, and Maya drifted into a subtle trance. "He misses you," affirmed Aunt Mary. "And I think you miss him too."

"I'm just happy to see him," Maya said unconvincingly.

"You're not fooling anyone, my dear niece," Aunt Mary replied, then looked at her watch. "We should probably be heading home. It's getting late. You should tell Michael to go and get the car."

Maya chuckled to herself. Though her aunt would say otherwise, Maya knew that she was having a difficult time getting used to Aunt Bess's new beau. The two sisters clung to each other for nearly ten years. "Sure," Maya said, and eased down to the end of the table to relay Aunt Mary's message.

It took ten minutes to get to the lobby, but Maya didn't mind. Aunt Mary refused to use a wheelchair or a walker to get around unless it was absolutely necessary. "I'm not in a rush to get anywhere," she'd tell her family every time someone suggested she take it easy and use one of the walking aides.

The three women slowly maneuvered to the main door of the church and Maya couldn't help but think about Kenneth. Seeing him again, she really hoped God had changed His mind about them being together.

"Maya?" a male voice called, and Maya looked to the right.

"Mr. Gregorio?" Maya said and blinked a few times to be sure her eyes weren't deceiving her. This was the first time she had seen him out of uniform. *Not bad*. Either she really missed Kenneth or Mr. Gregorio was as handsome as the secretaries at school had said.

"This is a nice surprise. Happy New Year," he said and gave Maya a hug.

Taken off guard, she barely hugged him back. "Same to you," she replied, and quickly pulled back. "You attend Monumental?"

"My baby sister and I are thinking about joining," he said, and grabbed the hand of an attractive woman standing behind him. Her urban Mohawk was flawless, and her skin even toned. "Sydni, this is Ms. Richards, Patrick's teacher."

"Hello," Sydni said. Her thick accent and doe eyes complimented her pleasant personality.

"Well, I know I'm biased, but this is a great church. I think you'll enjoy being a member. I've been here since I was ten. It's my family church," Maya answered.

"Seems like a good place for Patrick too. He would've come tonight, but he's been with his mother for the last three days," Mr. Gregorio shared. "I hope he hasn't been too much trouble lately."

"He's improving," Maya replied, and noticed a small, oval birthmark at the base of his arm. "He told me you promised to get him a signed McNabb football, so he's making an effort to be good," Maya said.

Mr. Gregorio laughed aloud. "Well, if you give him an A, I'll know he *really* deserved it."

Maya could've talked longer, but Aunt Mary pulled lightly on her arm. Though Aunt Bess's new companion was capable of helping her to the car, Aunt Mary insisted Maya assist her. "Well, I need to walk my aunts outside. Have a great evening," she said and waved good-bye.

Mr. Gregorio and his sister waved back, and then joined a small group of people by the stairs.

"That's a nice looking man," Aunt Bess commented. "And charming."

"Yes, he is," Maya replied on the way to the door, now understanding what Claudia and the secretaries saw in him.

Chapter 9

Standing in the middle of a guestroom in Claudia's Wynnefield home, Maya stared at the outfit on the bed. She really wanted to get under the covers and watch Dick Clark's New Year's special, but she'd promised Claudia that she'd stop by after church. The party had already started by the time Maya got there, and she could've mingled with the guests in her winter-white suit, but was afraid someone would accidentally spill something on her.

Maya wasn't in a hurry to join the jolly group downstairs. This was the first soiree she'd attend without Kenneth or Gwen. But it was already a quarter to one, and if she didn't hurry, Claudia would come looking for her. Maya took off her suit and placed it neatly in her garment bag, then changed into a cranberry off-the-shoulder sweater Gwen gave her for Christmas and a pair of jeans.

Once she was satisfied with her appearance, Maya walked downstairs and straight into the living room. As she headed to the food table, Maya sensed a few men ogling her in an uncomfortable manner. Immediately, she regretted the revealing sweater and turned her back to them. After piling a few mini-spinach quiches and cocktail shrimp onto a small plate, Maya headed to the family room.

"There's my friend! I thought I was gonna have to come get you," Claudia announced. Wearing a reindeer sweater and elf hat, she stood by the fireplace, holding a tray of stuffed mushrooms. "You look great!" she complimented, and then informed Maya that their colleagues were in the basement. "I'll be down in a minute," Claudia said, and swatted at someone trying to take a mushroom from her tray. "These are for my husband," she chided and bent down close to Bishop, who was trying to light the logs in the fireplace.

Maya watched Claudia pamper Bishop for a few minutes. After several years of marriage, they still behaved like newlyweds. Claudia often shared the story of God's perfect timing. Both Claudia and Bishop agreed that had they met before maturing, their union wouldn't have lasted longer than a week.

As a teenage parent, Claudia's attitude was fierce. She'd chase away many potential suitors because of her uncontrollable tongue. Bishop was a high school drop-out and lacked positive direction. Because of his unstable lifestyle, he wasn't serious about committing to a woman. They'd both given up on finding real love when their lives finally connected one summer at Claudia's grandmother's house in Chester, Pennsylvania. Claudia and her twelve-year-old daughter, Debbie, were living there at the time and had hired an old family friend to build a patio in the backyard. When the family friend became ill, he sent Bishop and his brother as replacements. Six months later, Claudia and Bishop were married. Maya looked away and wondered how God chose to grant some people the gift of love. Rather than sulk over the love she no longer had, Maya headed to the basement.

The lights grew dim as she made her way downstairs, reminding her of the basement parties Gwen used to drag her to as a teenager. Only in this situation, dozens of warm bodies weren't smashed together on a tiny dance floor. The heat generated from this crowd was caused by holiday drinks and repeated games of bowling on the computerized Wii gaming system.

"Come on, Maya," a fourth-grade teacher yelled over the jazzy holiday music playing in the background. "You can be on my team."

Maya hadn't bowled in years, nor had she ever played a Wii game, but she was ready to have fun. She set her food on a table and joined the mixture of friends. And twenty minutes into the game, Maya was at ease and had bonded with the other players.

Patiently waiting for her turn, Maya sat on the edge of an armchair and felt someone press into her side and she looked up. "Happy New Year, beautiful," Lloyd said, wearing a huge grin on his face.

Maya leaned back to add some space between them. "Same to you."

"I was hoping you'd be here," Lloyd confessed and blocked Maya's view of the television screen. "Now I know my year will start off right."

"So I'm your good luck charm?" Maya asked playfully and repositioned herself in her seat.

"If not, I'm sure hoping you'll be," Lloyd replied smoothly.

Since the breakup with Kenneth, Lloyd had been talking to her more often. During a lunch break one week, he told Maya that there was a good man for her, waiting in the wings. Each time they talked, Maya wondered if Lloyd believed that "good man" was him.

"It's your turn," an excited colleague shouted and tossed Maya the Wii baton.

Having trouble coming up with a response to Lloyd's re-mark, Maya was relieved the teacher rescued her. "I'll be right back," Maya told Lloyd, and then walked to the front of the television screen. Holding the baton as if it were an actual bowling ball, Maya moved side-to- side until she found a comfortable position.

"You can do it!" Lloyd shouted from behind and her knees slightly buckled. In order to focus, Maya tuned out the cheers, then swung her right hand backward and forward quickly as she released the baton button.

Almost immediately, the ball on the screen flew into the gutter. That was the first time she'd made a bad play all night. Despite her zero score, Maya's team was encouraging as she prepared to try again. Holding the baton this time, Maya's concentration was broken when she felt a gentle touch on her waist.

"See those arrows on the lane?" Lloyd asked, pointing to the images on the screen.

Maya tried to ignore the placement of Lloyd's hand, and answered, "Yes."

"Before you release, focus on the arrows. Try to get the ball in the center," Lloyd said and backed away, but before Maya positioned herself, he ran back to her side. "And stand straight. You're leaning too much to the right."

As Lloyd suggested, Maya straightened her stance and put the arrows in view. When she released the button this time, the ball rolled straight with full force and knocked down eight pins.

"Lloyd needs to be your coach for the rest of the game," a family friend said as Maya headed back to her seat.

Maya took her seat and Lloyd stood by her. "Thanks for the advice. You're a good coach," she said.

"I'm available anytime," he replied with charm.

Maya played the remainder of her game using Lloyd's advice and had three strikes. From time to time, Lloyd offered tips on ways Maya could improve her game, and she welcomed the attention. And at the end of the game when Lloyd requested that she join him at the bistro-style tables off to the side, she did oblige.

"Can I get you a drink or some food?" he asked when Maya hopped on her stool.

"I'm not really hungry, but if there's any Ginger Ale left, I'll take that," Maya said politely.

Lloyd hadn't been away from the table five seconds before Claudia appeared. "What'd you say to have that man skipping like that?"

"You know he doesn't skip," Maya said and laughed, "and furthermore, he's just getting me a soda. Why is that something to skip about?"

"You can't be that naïve, Maya. You know Lloyd has a thing for you," Claudia told her friend. "You don't see him taking drink orders from anyone else, do you?"

Maya watched Lloyd stroll back toward their table, his old school and smooth stride more apparent. Every time his right foot hit the floor, his body dipped slightly to the side. Although Maya held on to the hope that she and Kenneth would get back together, tonight she entertained the thought of getting to know Lloyd better. "He's just being friendly, Claudia. Is that a crime?"

"Not yet. But I can tell he's into you. I've been watching him," Claudia teased.

Lloyd reached the table with two drinks in hand—Maya's Ginger Ale and a glass of dark liquor for himself. He hopped on the stool and his shiny wing-tipped shoe hit the leg of the table, and brushed against Maya's leg. "Nice party," he told Claudia once he was settled. "I'm glad I made it out this year."

"I told you my husband and I know how to throw a party," Claudia responded. "I hope this means you'll be around for our summer cookouts."

"Only if Maya comes with me," Lloyd answered, and his nerves caused his top lip to twitch.

Claudia gave Maya an I-told-you-so glare, and then looked back at Lloyd. "Well, I can't tell Maya what to do, but I hope you'll come either way." A loud crash upstairs caught Claudia's attention, and she quickly excused herself without waiting for him to answer.

Now that Maya and Lloyd were alone, he moved his stool closer to her. "I think you need a couple lessons in a *real* bowling alley," he said over the music.

Maya swallowed a small amount of her soda before responding. "Why? Are you thinking about starting a league?"

"That's a thought," Lloyd said. "But you'll need private lessons to be on the team."

"I'm not *that* bad," Maya retorted and took another sip of her drink.

"You didn't see what I saw. You're definitely gonna need some extra help. I'd be happy to be your instructor," Lloyd said, and his gold, heavyweight ring hit the rim of his glass as he lifted it to his lips.

"Is this your way of asking me out?" Maya eyed him and asked, more out of curiosity.

Lloyd let out a hearty laugh. "Guilty as charged. I've wanted to take you out for years, but you were *involved*. Since you're a single woman now, this is my chance to let you know how I feel."

Under the dim green light, Maya studied her colleague in more detail. This was the first time she noticed his long lashes and almond-shaped eyes; a combination that suited him well. And it didn't hurt that he filled out his wool sweater nicely. Maya had known Lloyd for several years, but other than his interest in sports, she didn't know much about him. There had been talk in the office about him being a grandfather, but the remarks were always followed by laughter so Maya believed the comments to be a joke. Lloyd didn't look old enough to be a grandfather, but what would it hurt to ask? Maya set her drink on the table and took a deep breath, praying the question wouldn't offend him. "Lloyd, exactly how old are you?"

Lloyd sat up tall. "Does age matter?"

Right away, Maya grew nervous. The fact that he answered her question with a question couldn't be good. "Well," she began and crossed her legs, trying to appear reserved. "It does if you're about to say you're fifty." She couldn't picture herself considering anything other than friendship with a man older than her youngest aunt.

"Whew!" Lloyd replied and pretended to wipe sweat from his forehead. "Lucky for me, I'm forty-nine."

Surprised by his answer, Maya lifted her glass and chewed on a piece of ice. Even with the few gray hairs she detected, Maya would've guessed Lloyd to be in his very early forties. Maya stared at his hands wrapped around his glass. Her mother once told her that a person could tell a lot about another person's life by their hands. The veins on Lloyd's hands were prominent, and his nails looked freshly manicured. And although they appeared to be well taken care of, his hands were large and swollen. Maya could tell that he wasn't a stranger to manual labor.

After the ice in her mouth melted, Maya changed the subject. "So . . . do you have any children?" she inquired. A man of his age was bound to have children, and married at least once.

"I have two beautiful daughters," Lloyd answered proudly.

"So you've been married before?"

Lloyd drank half of his beverage, and then replied, "Yes, but she and I are just parents now. We separated a long time ago and only communicate about our daughters. But enough about that. What about that date? I'd like to take you to a nice restaurant."

"Isn't there a rule against dating a teacher?" Maya half-joked.

"None that I know of, and if there is, I'll quit," responded Lloyd as he finished drinking in one gulp. Maya didn't know how someone could stomach alcohol on the rocks. That had to be bad for his liver.

"Let me sleep on it. Can I get back to you later?" Maya replied, not wanting to be too hasty. What if Kenneth wanted to work things out?

Looking deep into her eyes, Lloyd said, "A good woman is worth waiting for."

For the first time tonight, Maya appreciated the dark lights. She was blushing and was glad Lloyd couldn't tell. Lowering her eyes, Maya glanced at her watch. "It's almost four o'clock," she said and hopped off the stool. "I better go. I have a long drive home." Maya would've spent the night, but she promised to eat breakfast with her aunts in the morning.

Though Lloyd didn't want Maya to leave, he understood and followed her upstairs. While Maya ran up to the guestroom on the second floor to get her duffle bag, Lloyd waited by the coat closet. It didn't take long for Maya to return. When she reached the bottom landing, Lloyd opened the closet door, and Maya took her fur coat off a hanger. "Let me help you with that,"

Lloyd insisted, and as Maya slid one arm down the sleeve of the fur, he sniffed the air. "Do you mind me asking the name of your perfume?"

"Romance, by Ralph Lauren," Maya answered and put on the gloves in her pocket.

"That fragrance smells good on you."

"Thank you," Maya said coyly.

Reaching around her, Lloyd opened the door before Maya could. "Ladies first," he said like a true gentleman.

Maya proceeded outside and quickly turned around to say good-bye, but Lloyd was practically on her heels. "Go back inside," she ordered. "It's too cold to be out here without a coat. You'll catch a cold."

"I just want to make sure you get to your car safely," he replied, happy that she was concerned.

But Maya didn't want him to risk getting a cold. "I'm only across the street. You can watch me through the window."

"Okay," he sighed, and then pulled his business card from his pocket. "When you're ready to take me up on my offer, give me a call."

Maya took the card from his hand and threw it inside her purse. "You're not giving up, huh?"

"Not even for a second."

Maya stared into his inviting eyes and stopped herself from smiling. "Happy New Year, Lloyd.

Enjoy the rest of the party," she said and headed down the walkway to her car.

As promised, Lloyd was watching through the window when Maya got into her car. She waved, and then turned the heat on high. Within seconds the windows fogged and made it difficult to see, but the blast of heat blowing through the vents relaxed Maya and she closed her eyes while the car continued to warm.

A sudden tap on the window startled Maya, and her eyes popped open. Although she thought it might be Lloyd, Maya hesitantly wiped at the window. Maya wiped at the window with her glove, but was stopped by more knocking before she could get a clear view.

"Maya," she heard Claudia shout. "Girl, roll down the window. It's cold out here."

"I looked for you before I left," Maya said as the window lowered.

Standing next to Maya's car, Claudia and Bishop stood coatless in the winter night air. "Sure you did. You've got Lloyd all on the brain," Claudia taunted and looked back at Lloyd still standing at the front door.

"My poor friends didn't have a chance tonight," Bishop commented, covering his wife's tiny frame with his burly arms.

"Just be careful, Maya. Lloyd seems cool, but many office romances don't always end well."

"I just talked to the guy, Claudia," asserted Maya. "Who said anything about a romance?"

Claudia shoved her hands into her pockets. "Well, you do know he's close to your mother's age, right?"

Bishop covered Claudia's mouth. "So what, babe. An older man might be good for her."

"Come on, honey. Maya doesn't want to roll her husband down the aisle," Claudia replied sarcastically.

"You don't know what she wants," Bishop said and laughed. "That might be her thing."

"On that note, I'll see you two later. Love you," Maya replied and zoomed off.

Langston's nose was pressed against the long, narrow window by the front door when Maya parked in the driveway. Maya got out of the car and Langston's furry tail batted at the curtains. It felt good to have someone excited about her coming home; even if it was a cat.

As soon as Maya opened the door, she picked up the hefty cat and nuzzled her nose against his warm fur. Once Langston was content with the attention, Maya gently placed him on the floor and put her coat on the back of the dining room chair. She unzipped her boots and instead of putting them on the steps, she left them in the middle of the living room floor. Since Maya moved back with her parents, she noticed that she hadn't been as anal about certain things— dishes were left in the sink overnight, dirty cups were in almost every room of the house, and her clothes were thrown wherever she took them off. Exhausted, Maya stepped over her boots and walked to the Christmas tree. Her mother used all white lights and gold ribbon instead of garland to decorate the tree this year. Maya liked the new look. Garland always overshadowed the special ornaments.

Maya reached behind the tree and turned off the flashing lights. Before going up to bed, she picked up the water bottle she'd left on the mantle. After guzzling the remaining water, she turned around and laughed aloud, sprinkling the floor with water from her mouth. Langston was under the chair, fighting with one end of Maya's fur coat. If only she had a camera on hand. Maya put the bottle down and ran to rescue her fur. "This isn't your enemy or friend," Maya told him and hung her coat in the closet.

Langston stared at the closet door and wagged his tail rapidly. "I'm not gonna open the door,"

Maya said and grabbed her purse from the table. She started up the stairs and stopped when she realized Langston wasn't behind her. "C'mon, big fella," Maya called in a soft, squeaky tone, and Langston ran up the steps.

Maya felt her way across the dark room to her bed and sat down. Reaching slightly to the left, she turned on her night lamp, and then threw her purse on the nightstand. Lloyd's weathered business card fell to the floor and Maya bent down to pick it up. "I can't believe he's fourteen years older than me," she said aloud as she read the list of coaching services Lloyd advertised on the card. A tiny smile formed and she tossed the card back inside her purse, and then connected her cell phone to its charger. Then, before changing into her pajamas, Maya knelt by the side of her bed. She didn't want to go to sleep without thanking God for allowing her to see Kenneth, and for a pleasant evening with friends, especially Lloyd. In her mind, it was all a sign that the new year was off to a great start.

Langston curled up by her feet and Maya waited for him to settle. Once he was comfortable, she lowered her head and prayed. *Despite my resistance, I had a good night. Thank you for lifting my spirits. And God . . . if Kenneth isn't going to be the man I can be happy with, I'll take someone like Lloyd—mature, established, witty, charming, athletic, wants kids, even if it means we'd have to adopt, and wants to be married. Lord, that's the kind of man I can see myself building a future with.*

After sharing her request for a new relationship with God, Maya decided to write her criteria on a piece of paper. Once she was done, Maya prayed over the list then opened the Bible she kept in the bottom drawer of her nightstand. Remembering a scripture her mother had professionally scripted along the periphery of her home office, Maya turned to the book of Habakkuk and scanned the second and third verses from chapter two. As the scripture stated, Maya had written the vision of her ideal man on paper. Now, all she needed to do was exercise patience.

As she placed the list inside the Bible, Maya had a feeling that God had already sent the man described on the paper. She just had to wait for that ideal man to realize it.

Chapter 10

The first day back to school after a long winter break was just as difficult as the first day of school. Maya had to reprogram her students' behavior and study habits, and by lunchtime she was ready to go home.

Maya sat at her desk and surfed the Internet while she finished her lunch. As part of her New Year's resolution, she needed to find an apartment. It'd been days since she saw Kenneth at church and he still hadn't called, killing her dream of them getting back together. And if they weren't going to be together, Maya was determined to begin a new life without him. She had even called First Lady Williams about becoming a Sunday School teacher. The extra activity would help her stay busy and keep her mind off Kenneth.

Being at home was a nice transition after she left Kenneth, but now it was time for her to live on her own. She needed to have some control over when she cooked meals, did dishes and washed clothes. Her mother was set in her ways, had her own set of rules, and no matter how many times Maya complained, she knew her mother wasn't going to relax her standards.

As she scrolled through a number of apartment listings in Plymouth Meeting, Maya sensed someone standing near the open door. Patrick, who was supposed to be eating lunch, was leaning against the wall, kicking invisible rocks. Maya didn't have to ask why he was there. She could tell from the dejected look on his face that he'd been put out of the lunchroom. "Are we back to the drawing board?" she asked him. Patrick didn't say anything. Maya logged off of the computer and poured a small amount of light dressing over her spinach salad. "You might as well come in and take a seat."

"I'm never gonna get an A," Patrick pouted, and strolled to his desk.

"Well, you've got to learn how to behave in *all* of your classes," Maya replied. "How did you get kicked out of the cafeteria?"

"Mrs. Garrett is on duty today. She picks on me all the time," Patrick complained, and told Maya about the incident that led to his removal.

"Don't let the way someone treats you affect what you're trying to achieve, Patrick," Maya said when he finished talking.

Patrick looked confused, and Maya restated her comment in a different way. "If you think she treats you unfairly, don't challenge her all the time. Just keep your mouth shut, and you won't get put out. Then maybe you'll see that A you want. Don't you agree?"

"I guess," Patrick mumbled.

"In the meantime, you might as well work on some math problems."

As Maya jotted a few multiplication problems in a notebook on Patrick's desk, Claudia entered the classroom. "Talk to Lloyd yet?" she asked, and then covered her mouth when she saw Patrick. "What's he doing here?"

"He's having lunch with his favorite teacher," Maya an-swered and winked at Patrick.

"Well, how much longer is lunch?" Claudia hadn't talked to Maya since the party, and was eager to catch up.

Maya closed the lid to her salad and peeled an orange. "Patrick, why don't you work on your math on the computer while I talk to Mrs. Marshall."

Patrick closed his notebook and carried it to the back of the classroom to the computer station. Impatient, Claudia couldn't wait until Patrick was out of hearing range. She sat in his seat, and tried to whisper. "So," she sang, "have there been any new developments since the party? From Kenneth, or from Lloyd?"

"No," Maya whispered and felt her cheek grow warm. She hadn't talked to Claudia about seeing Kenneth at church, and wasn't sure she wanted to.

"Well, there were a few men inquiring about you after you left."

"Don't get any ideas, Claudia. I'm not interested in anyone right now," she firmly responded, although the thought of dating Lloyd piqued her curiosity.

"Just think about it," Claudia responded. "There's this one guy that I think is perfect for you. He's lives around the corner from—"

"Leave it alone," Maya urged. As much as she preferred to be in a relationship, Maya didn't want the man to be anyone Claudia was familiar with. Claudia was very protective of her at times, and Maya feared her dear friend would eventually overstep her boundaries.

"I thought the man was supposed to find me. Weren't those your genius words of advice?"

"Don't twist my words. Of course the man should find you. I'm just *helping* the man a little."

"You're something else," Maya said and shook her head.

Claudia took an orange slice from a napkin on Maya's desk. "So has Ken called you yet?"

"Nope," Maya answered, unable to look Claudia in the eyes.

Faint noises of children in the hallway grew louder as they neared Maya's door. One of her students poked his head inside the room and Maya was surprised. According to her watch, she didn't have to pick them up for another five minutes. Though she welcomed the interruption, she was confused and walked to the door. She was surprised to see Lloyd standing with her students.

"I thought I'd save you a trip," Lloyd said before Maya could ask what was going on. "I know they're early. I'll stand out here with them while you finish your lunch. They'll be quiet."

"Thanks, but you can leave them with me."

"Are you sure?"

"It's only five minutes," Maya replied and felt Claudia walk up behind her.

"Okay. Enjoy the rest of the day," Lloyd said and left Maya to handle her students.

Maya signaled for the students to enter the classroom, and Claudia leaned close to her ear. "He's not interested in you, huh?" she muttered. "Just so you know, men his age are very persistent when they want something."

"Get out of here," Maya told Claudia playfully, and closed the door when she left.

After work, Maya drove to the LA Fitness on City Line Avenue to meet Gwen. After changing her clothes, Maya put her bag in a locker and headed to the main floor to find Gwen. Maya hadn't seen her sister since Christmas and was looking forward to spending time with her.

"Here I am," Gwen shouted and waved a white towel from a far away treadmill.

Maya jumped on the available machine next to Gwen and started with a slow and steady pace.

"Thanks for watching Langston. I think you spoiled him," Gwen said, as she effortlessly adjusted to the increased speed of the treadmill. "So tell me more about this gym teacher."

Because it'd been months since Maya had been to the gym, it was difficult for her to talk and exercise at the same time, but she filled Gwen in as best she could. By the time her story was done, Gwen had finished her routine.

Gwen dabbed at the sweat on her face and neck with her towel. "So you're going on the date?"

"Claudia thinks it's a bad idea," Maya huffed.

"Who cares what Claudia thinks?" Gwen placed the towel around her neck. "I don't see the harm. You've known the man for many years. And besides all that, it's *just* a date, not an invitation to a wedding chapel."

Maya's session ended and she sat on the side of the treadmill to catch her breath. "She might have a point with this one, Gwen. Did I mention he has kids?"

"That's a problem for you?"

Maya couldn't answer Gwen's question. She'd never dated anyone with children, so she didn't know if it would be a problem for her or not.

"Look at it this way, Maya," Gwen said. "He may not be your next man, but he's someone to help you get over Kenneth. Go on a few dates and have a little fun."

"I'm not going to sweat it. We'll see what happens," Maya replied nonchalantly.

"From the sound of things, he could be what you need to help you move on," Gwen said and waved to someone behind Maya.

Maya turned around and was surprised to see Justin approaching them. He was supposed to be on assignment in Boston. "Back already?" Maya joked.

"No, the gig got canceled," Justin said and grabbed Gwen's hand. "But I stopped by because your sister thinks I'm out of shape."

Gwen giggled and tapped his protruding stomach playfully. "I'm just looking out for you, babe."

Semi-annoyed, Maya looked at the floor. Going to the gym had always been reserved for sisterly bonding. It was the only guaranteed place the two sisters could go without interruptions from their mother, aunts, and friends. Maya was happy that Gwen had found love, but with less than a week remaining before Gwen moved, she was selfish with their limited time together. Embarrassed by her feelings, Maya walked to the water fountain and hoped the lovebirds wouldn't detect her hint of jealousy.

After she'd consumed as much water as she could hold, Maya sluggishly walked back to Gwen and Justin. In the short time that Maya had left them alone, Gwen had assessed Justin's needs and assumed the role of a personal trainer. It didn't take much to convince Maya to join them in the weight room. She just wanted to be near her sister. But as she tried to keep up with the repetitions Gwen suggested, she realized how spoiled her body had gotten the two months she'd been out of the gym. Too often during the exercises, Maya stopped for a drink of water or to ask a question, but Gwen was more focused on how the routine was affecting Justin. And, after fifteen minutes of strenuous exercise and ten minutes of being ignored, Maya grew tired of feeling like the third wheel. She rushed through a last set of leg curls and let Gwen know that she was going home.

"Okay, I'll see you on Thursday in aerobics class," Gwen said, as she spotted Justin while he bench pressed one hundred and fifty pounds.

Upset that Gwen half-paid attention to her, Maya mumbled a good-bye and quickly headed to her locker to get her things. As she walked out of the gym, the cell phone in her bag vibrated against her leg and she fumbled through the bag to answer the call before voice mail kicked in.

"Hi, Ms. Richards. This is Patrick's father. Is this a bad time?" Mr. Gregorio asked.

Maya was surprised to hear his voice. "No," she replied, her voice shaking as the cool air hit her open pores. "I'm actually on my way home."

"I checked my messages and thought I'd better give you a call during my break. I hope you don't mind me calling back on this number."

Maya wanted to inform Mr. Gregorio about his son's behavior, but had forgotten to call him before leaving the school, so she had called him from her cell phone on the way to the gym. "Oh, it's no problem. I was calling to give you an update," she said, and then summarized Patrick's recent behavior.

"I had a feeling something was gonna happen today. He was with his mother for the holidays. She's expecting, and I don't have to tell you that Patrick's not thrilled about the news."

Maya got into her car and barely let it warm up. Eager to get home, she pulled out of the parking lot and turned onto City Line Avenue. "It's not my place, but I can talk to him if you don't mind," Maya offered. She'd never volunteered to interfere in a student's personal life, but felt the call to help. "He's been an only child for a long time, so I can see how this could upset him. I just don't want him to get off track."

"I don't mind at all." Mr. Gregorio sounded pleased. "Maybe you can get through to him better than I can. I'm thinking about putting him in the football league at Monumental. That might be a positive way for him to let out his frustrations."

Maya drove onto the highway and let out a huge sigh when she saw the line of cars ahead of her. At seven o'clock, she hadn't expected to run into heavy traffic.

"Everything okay?" Mr. Gregorio asked, concerned by her moans.

"I can't take this Philly traffic," she complained, embarrassed by her outburst. "When are they going to be done with all this construction on seventy-six?"

"Yeah, that expressway is a nightmare," Mr. Gregorio agreed. "Where are you now?"

Maya strained to see the name of the next exit on the green sign ahead of her. "It looks like I'm coming up on Gladwyne. That is, if I ever make it there," she replied sarcastically.

"You know you can get off and take the side streets. It'll be a lot faster."

Maya was hesitant to get off the highway. "I'm not so sure about that. I've never gotten off there."

Mr. Gregorio seemed surprised. "Aren't you from Philly?"

"Yes," Maya chuckled, "but I didn't travel all over the city. My mother kept me on a short, tight leash when I was young."

"Well, this is your lucky day, Ms. Richards. You're talking to a class A truck driver. I know all the shortcuts. Where are you headed?"

"Norristown," Maya said too fast and realized she shouldn't have told him where she lived. "Well, I'm actually near the King of Prussia Mall." If Mr. Gregorio could get her to the mall, she could find her way home from there.

"Aw, that's easy. I drive up there all the time. Come off at the next exit."

"Don't get me lost. Gas is too high to be playing around," joked Maya.

"Trust me, Ms. Richards," Mr. Gregorio said kindly, and somehow Maya knew that she could. "I can't believe you were born and raised in Philly and don't know how to get around. I'm not even from this country and I know the roads better than you."

Maya laughed as she inched to the Gladwyne exit, calm and unconcerned that it was almost eight o'clock. It took more than twenty minutes to get off the highway, but by talking to Mr. Gregorio, the time had gone by unnoticed. Once she was confident of her detour directions, Maya turned on the radio and enjoyed a smooth ride through the city streets of Philadelphia to her suburban home.

Although Langston had been gone for several days, Maya hadn't adjusted to his absence. She dropped her bags by the living room table and took off her tennis shoes then ran upstairs. Halfway up the steps, Maya heard the television playing in her parents' room and remembered that they'd returned from their trip while she was at work. Quickly, Maya backtracked and grabbed her things from downstairs. She didn't want to aggravate her mother so soon after her vacation.

Trudging back up the stairs, Maya walked down the hall and into her parents' bedroom. Her father was sitting in bed, under a blanket, reading a newspaper. "Hey, Daddy," Maya cheered.

Mr. Richards took off his reading glasses and set his newspaper next to him. "What's going on, Pumpkin?"

"Nothing much," Maya said and kissed her father before sitting on the edge of the bed. "How was Arizona?"

"I think your mother wants to retire there. But I'm not sure I can handle the heat. They say the summers can get up to a hundred and ten degrees."

"Well, you still have a few years until she retires. I'm sure she'll change her mind by then."

Mr. Richards agreed, and then asked, "How was your workout?"

"Tough!" Maya exclaimed. "After the treadmill, Gwen had me lift weights. The girl is a workout nut!"

"You're the nut for letting her talk you into it," Mr. Richards replied and used the remote in his lap to change the channel. "I don't know why you girls have to work out so much. You're fine just the way you are."

"Aww, thank you, Daddy. But I like to eat too much. If I don't go to the gym, I'll triple my pants size. I used to be able to keep up with Gwen, but I don't know what happened," Maya responded and took off the headband holding her hair in place. Maya scratched her sweaty head vigorously. "Where's Mom?"

"She ran to Target."

Although her body was a little tart from the physical exercise, Maya took the opportunity to talk to her father. For the next twenty minutes, they discussed the projects he was working on at church, and his plans to upgrade the house. In turn, Maya shared updates about Kenneth and told her father about Lloyd. "What if the date is a disaster, Daddy?"

"If you're skeptical, Pumpkin, maybe you shouldn't go on the date."

Maya combed through her hair with her fingers and placed the headband back on her head. "I really think it's because I work with him. Don't you think it would be awkward seeing him every day if we didn't enjoy ourselves?"

Mr. Richards shook his head. "That's just an excuse. If you really liked this guy, you'd go whether he worked at Huey or not."

Mr. Richards had a point. Deciding whether or not to go on a date with someone shouldn't be so hard. Maya's cell phone vibrated and she reached inside her tote bag to answer it. "Hello," she said without looking at the screen.

"Hello, Maya," Kenneth said in his intellectual tone.

"Hey, Ken," she answered weakly, in shock that he'd finally called.

"I guess Daddy-Daughter time is over," Mr. Richards said and picked up his paper. Maya flashed a soft smile and headed to her bedroom.

"Are you busy?" Kenneth questioned when he heard Mr. Richards' voice in the background.

"No, I just came in from the gym," Maya replied. "What's up?"

"Do you have time to talk?"

Closing the door behind her, Maya threw her things on the floor. She'd waited a long time to talk to Kenneth. "Yes," Maya said subtly. "I can talk now."

"I don't know where to start," Kenneth began, and then sighed. Maya could tell that the conversation wasn't going to be good. She knew that sound well.

"The beginning is always a good place," Maya nervously stated.

"First of all," Kenneth started, "let me say I'm sorry."

Maya had no control over her emotions. "What's taken you so long to call to say that? I moved out in November, Ken. It's January."

"I know you're upset with me, but believe it or not, I'm upset too," Kenneth said in a reserved manner. "And this is hard for me, so if you don't mind, I'd like to get everything off my chest first. Then you can have the floor."

That was just like Kenneth. He was mentally in a courtroom 24/7. Maya made herself comfortable on the floor and lay flat on her back. "Go ahead, counselor."

Ignoring Maya's sarcasm, Kenneth continued in a serious tone. "It's funny," he said seriously. "I knew you'd get tired of waiting for me to marry you. I just wasn't prepared for it to happen when it did. I was trying to change my feelings about marriage, but I guess I was dragging my feet."

Maya heard her mother come in the house as she listened to Kenneth and hoped she wouldn't come upstairs. She sat straight up and leaned against the wall.

"I can't give you half of me," Kenneth said as Maya listened. "And that's what you'd have if we were to get married tomorrow. Ninety percent of me wants to be with you forever, but ten percent of me isn't ready. You deserve one hundred percent, and I can't give you that right now. This isn't about me not loving you, because I really do. I'm just afraid that if our marriage had to end, I'd lose you forever. I know I should be more positive and have faith, but it's just something about marriage that changes relationships. My family is proof of that."

Maya's heart sank. To hear Kenneth say that he couldn't give her what she wanted was a hard pill to swallow. It didn't matter that her parents were proof that marriage could work. Kenneth's mind was focused on all of the failed marriages he knew about. As difficult as it would be, Maya had to accept that she and Kenneth were over, and she might as well stop praying they'd get back together. As she wiped the tears from her eyes, Maya couldn't believe that her heart had been broken . . . again.

"I wanted to call sooner, but I needed time to try and make sense of everything. I was mad at you for leaving, and then mad at me for not being able to change," Kenneth continued more sincerely. "Then I saw you at church and I realized how much I missed you. I was ready to call you to see if we could work things out, but I got called away on a last minute business trip. I was going to call you as soon as I got home, but then I realized that I wasn't going to change. That's not fair to you. I'm sorry, Maya. But I can't give you what I know God wants you to have."

Maya couldn't believe how easy it was for Kenneth to walk away from the relationship they'd spent years building. He was supposed to beg her to come back home. He was supposed to say that he couldn't stand to be without her. He was supposed to plead for them to work things out. He wasn't supposed to tell her that it was over for good.

"Where's this really coming from, Ken?" There had to be a reason other than his inability to commit. "Is there someone else?"

"This has nothing to do with another woman, babe—" Kenneth realized that he could no longer use that term of endearment with her and corrected himself. "I'm not seeing anyone, Maya."

"So after thirteen years we're back to being friends," Maya stated without expecting a response. But Kenneth had a reply, one that made Maya clutch her chest.

"We can't be friends," he said a little too calmly.

"I can't believe you're saying this to me. How can you just write me off? How can you not give us a chance? How could you—" Unable to hold back her frustrations any longer, Maya was ready to end the call. There was no point in fighting for something only she wanted, and there was certainly no easy way to say good-bye.

So Maya pulled herself together and said, "Ken, I need to go."

Choked up from Maya's barrage of questions, Kenneth's voice cracked when he said good-bye.

Maya threw the phone across the room after Kenneth hung up, and she fell onto the floor. *God, you told me to trust you,* she muttered through her tears. *But right now I need you to take this pain away.*

There was a knock at her door, and as it slowly opened, Mrs. Richards poked her head inside. "You okay, Pumpkin?"

"Ken called," she cried, and without saying another word, buried her face inside her hands and let the tears flow freely.

Mrs. Richards eased down on the floor and scooted next to her daughter. Understanding that this was not the time for a lecture, she rubbed Maya's back gently and sang a medley of gospel hymns until all of her daughter's tears were gone.

Chapter 11

Since Kenneth's call, Maya felt like her life was spiraling downward. Kenneth didn't want to be with her anymore, her living arrangements were stressful, and Gwen was leaving in four days. She was falling behind on work, having trouble sleeping at night, and lately she'd been arriving to work later than usual.

Maya rushed into the main office and grabbed her mail. "Good morning, ladies," she yelled as she passed through. Racing down the hall in new clogs and toting her bag and lunch in her arms, Maya headed to the auditorium to pick up her students. The aides complained to the principal if classes weren't picked up a minute before the scheduled time.

Approaching the auditorium, Maya grew worried when she didn't hear children's voices. It was too quiet. She took a deep breath and opened the door, only to find that her class wasn't there. "Mr. Bradford took them up five minutes ago," the lead-parent volunteer shouted from the stage.

"Thanks," Maya said, worried that the volunteer would tell Mrs. Bridges. Annoyed with herself, Maya climbed the stairs two at a time. Out of breath, she stopped cold when she entered her classroom. The kids were quietly writing in their journals while Lloyd watched over them like a lieutenant. "I apologize for my tardiness," Maya said and sighed.

Lloyd played with the whistle dangling from the chain around his neck. "No problem. Just thought I'd help you out. Have a great day," he replied and walked out the door.

Maya went to her desk and set her belongings in her chair. While she took off her coat, she sensed Patrick staring at her. "Have you finished writing?" she asked him.

"No." Patrick looked down at his blank page, smiling.

"Well, get busy," Maya said, and hung her coat over the back of her chair. She emptied her tote bag and started to place her bag lunch on top of her desk, when she noticed a croissant and Dunkin' Donuts hot tea. Wedged in between the two items, were three sugar packets and an index card. Patrick giggled aloud and she glanced his way. "Get back to work," she said firmly and

Chapter 12

"I can't wear that!" Maya barked at Gwen.

In honor of her sister's date, Gwen made sure she finished her tasks in enough time to help Maya get ready. It was the least she could do after standing Maya up yesterday. "Oh, come on," Gwen snapped back. "There's nothing wrong with showing a little skin."

Maya held up the russet-colored cashmere sweater, and put her hand through the opening running straight down the back. "That's more than a little skin. I might as well wear a bikini top!"

"You should've been in movies," Gwen joked as she applied a coat of bronze eye shadow on Maya's eyelid. "The slit isn't even wide enough to show anything. It just gives the *illusion*. Now hold still!"

"Don't you think the dip in the front is enough illusion? I don't want Lloyd to get the wrong impression."

Gwen stepped back to admire her work. "This is a *date*. Your first date at that," she said and added another layer of eyeliner. "You should only be thinking about getting to know each other. If he expects anything more than that on a first date, then you should move on to the next guy."

"Then I don't need to look like a movie star if I'm only getting to know him," Maya retorted as she leaned in close to the mirror. Though Gwen had applied more makeup than what Maya was accustomed, she had to admit she liked what her sister had done.

"Who says you can't look like a diva? Trust me on this," Gwen said and passed Maya a hand mirror. "How do you like your face?"

"I like it."

"Good. Now put on that sweater."

Carefully, and with Gwen's help, Maya pulled the sweater over her head. The backless bra she had to wear felt weird, and Maya wasn't sure she'd last the whole night without ripping it off. The bra sucked her stomach in to a fault and made her chest sit up too high. The lady at the department store made the product seem like the greatest invention since sliced bread, but Maya begged to differ. She was only a B cup, and would probably make out better not wearing one at all. Maya stepped back in order to get a full view of her sweater and cream skirt attire.

"Not only did I bring you one of my cutest tops to wear . . ." Gwen said and handed Maya her favorite leather Gucci boots. It was the only pair of boots Gwen had spent an enormous amount of money for. ". . . I brought these boots. I think they match perfectly."

Though the boots complimented her outfit well, Maya shook her head. "Oh, no! The last thing I need is to break a heel or drop some food on that good leather. I'd never hear the end of it."

"End of what?" Mrs. Richards questioned as she walked into Maya's room. Neither sister had heard their mother come home. "You're awfully snazzy, Pumpkin. Where are you going?"

"Maya's got a date," Gwen sang and danced around her in a full circle.

"A date?" Mrs. Richards asked. "What in the world happened while I was at church?"

"It's not that serious, Mom. I'm just having dinner with a friend," Maya replied and twisted her skirt to the left so that the small split was exactly in the middle. To avoid telling her parents about going on a date, Maya had hoped to be gone before they came home.

"Not looking like that," Mrs. Richards said and sat on the bed.

"Doesn't she look great?" Gwen affirmed, proud of her contribution to Maya's appearance.

"Put my boots on," Gwen begged. "They've brought me good luck on many occasions." She then reached into a duffle bag and pulled out a medium-sized Gucci handbag. "I even brought the matching purse for you."

Because of time, Maya decided to take her chances with Gwen's special boots. She slid into them easily, then walked back and forth to get used to the new heel. "What do you think, Mom?"

Mrs. Richards grinned from ear to ear. "You look beautiful, just like your momma."

"Am I forgetting anything?" Maya asked as she posed in the mirror.

"You're neck looks bare," responded Gwen, after a quick inspection. "Where's your jewelry?"

Maya pointed to a velvet box on her nightstand and her mother leaped off the bed. "Let me look for something," Mrs. Richards said and searched through the assortment of jewelry.

Staring in the mirror, Maya had flashbacks of her first date with Kenneth. It was natural for her family to turn a small event into a memorable moment. On that night, all of the Richards women were in attendance to help Maya get dressed. It was as if she were going to her second prom and not to dinner with a grown, attractive man. The women made a big fuss over her outfit, each wanting to add their own special flavor, and although Maya pretended to be annoyed, she cherished that night and took their words of encouragement and advice to heart.

"Let's try this one," Mrs. Richards said, and fastened a natural gemstone necklace around Maya's neck. "Perfect!" she exclaimed after examining her daughter.

"I guess I'm ready now that Mom approves," Maya teased.

Gwen pulled a digital camera out of her purse and realized that this could be the last time she helped Maya prepare for a date. "I'm gonna miss these moments."

"You don't have to go to California," Mrs. Richards replied and meant it. "It's not too late to change your mind."

"Let's not go there tonight, Mom. This is Maya's moment," Gwen said as she snapped pictures of Maya combing her hair.

"You brought it up. And now that I think about it, you probably convinced Maya to move out," Mrs. Richards said, and then looked at her firstborn. "Are you still looking for your own place?"

Last week, Maya had decided to find her own place after her mother barged into her bedroom before 8:00 on a Saturday to ask her help clean out the basement. And since Kenneth wasn't interested in rekindling their love, Maya felt it was time to begin a new life. She was going to tell her mother when the time was right, but Mrs. Richards just happened to stumble upon the list of apartments Maya left on her dresser one morning.

"Yes," Maya answered. "I haven't seen anything I like yet though. But don't worry, Mom. I'm not running away from you. I just think I need to live on my own for awhile."

Mrs. Richards couldn't let it go. "It doesn't make sense to me. You're practically living on your own now, *and* you're saving money. What more do you want?"

Mrs. Richards had a point, but living with her parents as a twenty year old was very different from living with them at thirty-six. There were too many rules to follow—emptying the trash every day, cleaning the bathrooms twice a week, and mopping the downstairs floors before going to bed every Sunday evening. Not to mention the fact that Maya couldn't get any schoolwork accomplished until her mother went to bed at night.

"Mom, Maya wants to entertain guests anytime of the day *or night,*" Gwen replied in between taking random pictures of her mother and sister.

"Maya knows she can invite people over," Mrs. Richards said, not fully understanding Gwen's comment.

Both Maya and Gwen stared at each other and laughed. "What about overnight guests?" Gwen asked and adjusted the settings on her camera, as Justin had taught her.

"What's gotten into you?" Mrs. Richards asked Gwen. "I'm not running a prison over here."

Gwen snapped two quick shots of her mother then lowered her camera. "*Male* overnight guests, Mom."

Finally catching on, Mrs. Richards's expression changed. "Don't say things like that, Gwen. Maya's a God-fearing woman." Gwen captured her mother's reaction perfectly on film. Once developed, the photo was going to be priceless.

Maya laughed so hard that her eyes watered. "I'm not leaving for that reason, either," she said to relax her mother's nerves. "I just feel like it's time for me to live on my own."

Although Maya and Gwen were grown women, Mrs. Richards shied away from talking about sex. It was much easier when they were teens, and had no choice but to listen to her lectures. But now that they were experienced women, Mrs. Richards was afraid her daughters might confess things she'd wish they'd kept secret.

"Okay, ladies," Maya said, "as much as I'd like to hang with you tonight, I have to go."

"Give me a few more poses," insisted Gwen. "You never know. If this works out, I could include these first-date pictures in your wedding scrapbook."

"You're going overboard," Maya replied, but posed anyway.

"Is the gentleman coming to get you?" asked Mrs. Richards.

Maya threw several essential items into the purse Gwen let her borrow. "Absolutely not, Mom. It's okay for women to meet their dates these days."

Mrs. Richards looked as if she wanted to give Maya a lecture, but refrained. "Does he at least have a name?"

Maya's cell phone rang, and as she grabbed it from the nightstand, she was glad for the interruption. There was no way she was going to tell her mother more information than what was necessary. "If he sticks around, I'll tell you more," she replied then answered the incoming call. "Hey, Claudia," Maya said in a hurry.

"Hey, lady, what time are you meeting Lloyd?"

Maya leaned over to rub the side of her right foot and winced. Her pinky toe rubbed against the side of the boot, and she prayed the uncomfortable feeling wouldn't last all night. "I'm on my way out the door, Claudia. I'll call you as soon as I get back."

"Okay, but I just have one quick piece of advice," Claudia said, and Maya instantly regretted telling her about the date. "I'm not a fan of office romances—"

"We're just two friends going to dinner," Maya snapped before Claudia could finish.

"If that's the case, then you must be paying for your own meal," Claudia bounced back.

Though Maya intended to pay, she didn't understand Claudia's concern. "What difference does it make who pays? I'm your friend and sometimes I treat you to dinner," Maya replied and heard Gwen grumble off to the side.

"Why can't he pay? He did ask *you* out?" retorted Gwen.

Rather than listen to Gwen and Claudia bicker and put her in a foul mood, Maya cut them both short. "Well, it's six o'clock, so I'm hanging up. I'll give you a call later," she told Claudia and hung up. How dinner was going to be paid for wasn't a concern for her. She just wanted to have a good time.

"Don't pay Claudia any attention. If he wants to pay, let him," asserted Gwen as she put away her camera.

Maya glanced at her image in the mirror one last time, and then headed downstairs with Mrs. Richards and Gwen following close behind her. "Are you coming home tonight?" Mrs. Richards asked when Maya opened the front door.

With a light chuckle, Maya turned to face her mother. "Don't let Gwen get your pressure up. I'll be home in a few hours."

At ease, Mrs. Richards kissed her daughter. "I just wanted to know because I invited your aunts over. They're going to spend the night."

"We're having a slumber party?" Gwen half-joked.

"It's our last night together before you leave, Doodle. I thought it'd be fun," Mrs. Richards remarked. "And we can hear all about Maya's date."

"Great," Maya muttered as she walked to her car.

"Let him pay!" Maya heard Gwen shout before the front door closed.

Circling the top level of the King of Prussia Mall, Maya prayed a space would open up. If not, she'd have to park on the other side of the mega mall and walk nearly a mile back to the restaurant. Her pinky toe was still aggravated in the boot, and Maya preferred not to walk a far distance if she didn't absolutely have to. She drove around the top and bottom levels twice before finding an ideal spot on the side of Macy's, and before getting out of the car, Maya took time to check her hair and makeup in the rearview mirror. She was nervous, but reminded herself that Lloyd was only a friend.

Although her toe burned from the constant friction, Maya walked through the mall without one grimace. The few etiquette classes her mother forced her to take in high school had paid off. She'd learned how to walk with grace and with a smile no matter what the circumstance. When Maya finally reached the Legal Seafood restaurant, she expected to see Lloyd standing in the front waiting for her. There were a number of people waiting to be seated, but Lloyd wasn't one of them. Longing to sit down, she called him and hoped that he wasn't far away.

Lloyd's phone only rang once. "I'm looking at you now," he said before Maya had a chance to speak. "Look at the window."

Turning slightly to her left, Maya caught a glimpse of Lloyd's bedroom eyes and wide grin.

"I'm on my way in," she said and disconnected the call.

Lloyd was standing by the table when Maya walked into the restaurant. Polished and clean-cut in a pair of slacks and thick wool sweater, Lloyd looked completely different from the teacher in sweats Maya was used to seeing during the week.

Happy to see Maya, Lloyd planted a delicate kiss on her cheek, and then helped take off her coat. "You look nice," he complimented, then hung Maya's coat on a nearby hook.

"Thank you," Maya said in return and eased into the booth. "How long have you been here?"

Lloyd waited for Maya to settle before claiming his seat. "I got here early. I wanted to make sure everything was perfect."

"That was awfully kind of you," Maya replied and opened the menu sitting on the table.

"I have a surprise for you," Lloyd said and reached for something next to him. Perplexed, Maya stopped reading the menu and looked up just as Lloyd passed a silver and pink gift bag across the table.

"What's this, Lloyd?" Maya inquired.

"Something I thought you'd like."

Maya pushed the bag toward Lloyd. "I can't accept—"

Lloyd placed his hand on top of Maya's and cut her off mid-sentence. "It's only a small gift. No strings attached," he insisted. "If this is the only night I get to spend with you, I want to make it special. I want you to know what it feels like to be with a *true* gentleman."

Maya stared at the bag, unsure of what to do. "I thought we agreed that this was going to be a friendly dinner."

"It is," Lloyd answered quickly. "Now make an old man happy and take the present."

Hesitantly, Maya grabbed the bag and leaned back. She moved the sparkly tissue paper aside and slowly removed a three ounce package containing Romance perfume. Maya was speechless. She couldn't believe that he remembered her favorite fragrance. Blushing, she put the package back and set the gift bag next to her. "Thank you. That was really sweet. But no more surprises, okay?"

Seeing that Maya was pleased with her gift, Lloyd's lip twitched mildly as he stared at her. For a man so strong and confident, Maya thought his nervous reaction was cute.

"You know what you want to eat?" Maya asked in an effort to divert his attention.

"I have an idea. But take your time. And please get whatever you want."

Figuring this wasn't a good time to discuss who was paying for dinner, Maya relaxed as she browsed the menu, and let the evening run its course on its own schedule.

Over dinner, Maya let her guard down as she and Lloyd talked in great deal about their childhood, past relationships, and reasons for becoming teachers. For Maya, the motivation to teach was inherent, while Lloyd fell into education after he wasn't recruited by the NFL. In college, Lloyd was one of the star players, but shamefully admitted that he didn't have the drive or stamina needed to compete in the professional league.

"I coach many different sports," he informed Maya, as he finished his tuna steak.

"Really?" Maya said and cut a piece of her large scallop. "That's pretty neat. Which sports?"

Lloyd swallowed the piece of steak in his mouth. "Since I have two daughters, I have to stick to what they like; mostly basketball and volleyball. Last year I coached the softball team, but that was too stressful for my girls, so we gave it up."

"I'm sure your daughters love having you as a coach."

"I wouldn't say that," Lloyd asserted. "I'm a fierce competitor. I love to win, and I push my team to do their best. Sometimes the girls won't speak to me for days because I worked them too hard."

"Still," said Maya, glad that the evening had progressed into a more relaxed atmosphere, "just having you around has to be good for them. Some kids don't have that."

Earnestly, Lloyd replied, "I try to be a good father."

"And what about their mother?" inquired Maya. "If you don't mind me asking, do you still have feelings for each other?"

"You can ask me anything, Maya," Lloyd replied and his lip twitched again. Maya had brought up a sensitive topic, but Lloyd continued to talk. "I think we'll always love each other, but we've learned the hard way, I'm afraid, that we're better off being friends. Some days run smoothly. *Most* days she's screaming at me for something I didn't do, or should've done for our kids. I do my part as their father. I keep them every other weekend. I give her money every month and buy them clothes all the time," he continued sincerely. "But nothing I do is ever good enough for her. And she bad mouths me in front of my girls."

Growing up in a two-parent home, Maya couldn't relate to Lloyd's struggles. If her parents had ever argued, she'd never witnessed it, and she certainly never heard them speak negatively of one another in her presence. She could only imagine how Lloyd's children felt, and could tell by his pulsating temples and nervous twitch, the subject bothered him.

Drawn to Lloyd's dedication to his daughters, Maya tried to lighten the mood. "How old are your girls?"

Lloyd reached for his wallet and pulled out a picture of his children. In the picture, his daughters posed next to one another on a volleyball court, both holding a customized pink and white volleyball. "Lanecia," he said and pointed to his oldest daughter, "she's sixteen and reminds me of that every day. She can be a firecracker, but I don't mind. I was like that too. She channels her aggression into sports, and I believe that makes her a great player."

"She has your smile."

"That's about it. Everything else she got from her mother," he replied, and then pointed to his youngest child. "Now Lauren," he beamed, "she's every bit of me. She'll be seven next week."

Maya admired the picture, and for a brief moment thought about Kenneth and what their children would've looked like. "She's adorable, Lloyd. They both are."

"Maybe you'll meet them one day," he said, and before Maya could respond the waiter approached their table.

"Are you finished with dinner?" the waiter asked.

"I'd like a to-go bag," Maya said and glanced at her watch. Where did the time go? She couldn't believe that she'd been sitting in the restaurant for almost four hours. And even though it was late, Maya knew her mother was still wide awake. "I'm having a nice time, but I better go. It's getting late," Maya said after the waiter left the table.

Lloyd seemed disappointed. "Already?"

"I know, but I'm teaching my first Sunday School class in the morning. Do you go to church?"

Lloyd nodded. "My girls and I go to White Rock over on Fifty-third and Chestnut."

"Reverend Shaw's church. I've been there a few times. My family and I attend Monumental. We've been there since I was ten."

The waiter returned with Maya's leftovers and the check enclosed in a thin, leather case. He put everything down, and then took a pen from his shirt pocket. "No rush," he said, and walked away.

Maya took a deep breath as Lloyd calmly reviewed the bill. The night had been a success and she didn't want to ruin the evening by offering to pay for her dinner. "Lloyd, I can cover my food," she blurted.

"I can't allow that."

"Really, I can handle it."

"If it's going to bother you, you can pay for our next *friendly* dinner."

"You're more stubborn than I am. If there is a second dinner, you have to promise to let me pay."

Lloyd gazed into Maya's eyes, and lovingly replied, "I promise." Lloyd pulled out an American Express card and placed it inside the case. "Well, I guess I have to call it a night since I can't compete with God."

"You sure can't," Maya responded with a smile. "But remember you promised to let me pay for dinner next time."

"How about dinner *and* a movie next Saturday?"

Against her better judgment, Maya agreed to a second date. It wasn't that she didn't enjoy his company, because she did, and whatever reservations she had in the beginning were squashed. It was Lloyd's timing that Maya was concerned about. She wasn't really over Kenneth, and her life was very unstable. It wouldn't be fair to bring Lloyd into her hectic world, but if he were willing to be patient, Maya was willing to give their newfound friendship a try.

Because he found a parking space a few feet away from the restaurant, Lloyd insisted he drive Maya to her car. Considering the long walk in thirty-degree weather in boots that hurt, Maya consented without a fuss. They walked the short distance to Lloyd's cherry-colored Escalade, and like the gentleman he'd proven to be thus far, he held the car door open until she was safely inside. While Maya waited for him to walk around to the driver's side, she heard what sounded like a ringing cell phone coming from the glove compartment.

By the time Lloyd hopped into the car, the ringing had stopped. "I think you have a missed call," Maya informed him, but Lloyd didn't seem concerned.

"At this time of night, it's probably my daughter. She thinks I'm her personal taxi," Lloyd stated and started the car. Heat blowing through the vents warmed the large truck in less than a minute, and before Lloyd put the car in reverse, his cell phone rang again.

"You sure you don't want to get that? It could be important."

Lloyd admired Maya's thoughtfulness, but didn't change his mind. "I'll give her a call once our date is officially over. This is your time, love."

While Lloyd's attention was refreshing, Maya didn't want to interfere with his relationship with his daughter. "Are you sure?" she questioned, hoping Lloyd would give in and open the glove compartment.

Lloyd reached across the car and touched Maya's hand. "I'm sure. I know my daughter. We go through this every weekend."

Though Maya smiled, it was hard for her to let it go. With children, one could never assume they always cried wolf. Uneasy, Maya sat back and directed Lloyd to her parking space, and when he parked the ringing started again.

Without looking at her, Lloyd knew Maya was staring at him. "All right, sweetheart. You win," he said and opened the glove compartment. But when he answered, the person on the end had hung up. Lloyd shook his head and scrolled through his phone. He leaned close to Maya and showed her the screen. "See, I told you it was Lanecia," he said as if Maya knew his daughter's number.

Afraid that she appeared suspicious, Maya pushed the phone away. "I wasn't trying to be in your business or anything."

"I know," Lloyd responded warmly, and the phone rang again. This time, he answered. "Yes," he sang into the phone. Maya could hear that his daughter was upset, but Lloyd remained reserved. "I'll be there in twenty minutes, sweetheart," he told her in the same stern voice he used with misbehaving students, and then hung up. "I'm sorry you had to hear that," he told Maya, and put the phone on the dashboard. "Lanecia thinks I'm supposed to drop everything for her."

Maya chuckled softly and grabbed the door handle. "Well, you better go or you'll have to deal with a teenage attitude."

"I think you're right," confessed Lloyd. "But don't move yet. Let me get the door for you." Lloyd ran to the passenger side, and when he opened the door, a chill swept through the car and up Maya's skirt, causing her to shiver. Lloyd grabbed Maya's hand and helped her out of the car. "Do you have your key ready? You shouldn't search for it in the cold." Maya pulled a key ring from her coat pocket, and Lloyd smiled as she waved it in front of him. "See, I knew you were a smart woman," he said, and helped her out of the car.

Good-bye was the one part of the date Maya hadn't thought about until now. Was saying thank you enough, or was he expecting a kiss? Maya decided to take a chance with the thank you. "I had a really nice time, Lloyd. Thanks for everything," she said, and loosely wrapped her arm around him.

Lloyd placed both arms around her, and squeezed tight. "You're more than welcome, love. But I better go."

Lloyd pulled back a little, and then leaned in close to Maya's face, only inches away from her lips. Nervous, Maya stepped back. She wasn't ready for anything more than a peck on the cheek. "Have a safe drive home," she said and unlocked her car door.

While Lloyd waited for Maya to settle inside, his phone rang again. "My daughter is spoiled," he announced almost apologetically.

"Why don't you go," Maya commanded. "I think our date is officially over now. I'll see you on Monday." Lloyd blew Maya a kiss, and then headed back to his car.

Through the mildly fogged window, Maya could see Lloyd talking on the phone. Though she couldn't read his lips, Lloyd's hand gestures let her know that he wasn't happy. Wherever his daughter was, she was really ready to go.

Maya navigated through the parking lot with Lloyd trailing behind her, and eased into the left lane of the mall exit. From her rearview mirror, Maya could see that he was still talking on the phone and prayed everything was all right.

As she made a left onto the street, she yawned. It had been a long day. If Maya hadn't promised to observe a Sunday School class, she would've missed church altogether and slept in late. And, no matter how tired, Maya knew there were four eager people awaiting her arrival at home. There was no way she was going to sleep without first telling Gwen, her mother, and aunts all about her date with Lloyd.

Chapter 13

To eliminate an emotional scene at the airport, Maya's father had convinced the Richards women to say their good-byes at home, and after a hearty breakfast, Mr. Richards took Gwen to the airport alone. It was better that way. Maya would've taken the day off from work to keep her mother company, but decided that keeping busy was the only way to forget about Gwen leaving. Besides, Maya wanted to see Lloyd.

Maya emptied the paper chocolates she spent all night cutting onto the floor in front of her classroom door. She needed to finish the February bulletin board outside her classroom door by the end of the day. This was the first time in all the years Maya had been teaching, that she was late putting her board together. Mrs. Bridges had given her an extension, but after today, a pink slip would be placed in her file if the board wasn't completed. Between the break-up with Kenneth, Gwen's relocation, her current living arrangements, and a growing interest in Lloyd, she'd never been so distracted. Lesson plans used to be written a week in advance and now they were a couple days behind. Assignments were normally graded the same day they were completed, and now Maya found that she was nearly a week late in getting them back to her students.

Maya covered the board with red craft paper and handwrote, "Math is like a box of chocolates. You never know what problem you'll have to solve," in fancy black script. She stapled the paper chocolates haphazardly on the bulletin board, and under each wrapper glued several word problems written by her students. As people passed the board, they could lift the wrapper of a chocolate candy and solve the problem underneath. At the end of the month, those who submitted correct answers would be eligible to win a box of real chocolates.

Working diligently, Maya hadn't heard Mrs. Bridges walk up behind her. "You're so creative," the principal said, and Maya nearly dropped the stapler in her hand.

Maya hadn't expected Mrs. Bridges to check up on her so early in the morning. "Thank you. I was inspired by *Forrest Gump*," she replied, glad that her boss approved.

"That was a good movie. Long, but good," Mrs. Bridges said and read a few of the problems on the board. "I stopped by to let you know that I like your idea for a math afterschool program. Write up a proposal, and I'll get back to you as soon as I can."

"I'll get it to you by the end of the week," Maya promised.

Mrs. Bridges stood back and admired Maya's talent. "Keep up the good work, Ms. Richards. You're doing a wonderful job with these kids."

As Maya watched her principal walk down the hall, she tried to contain her excitement. Mrs. Bridges was an excellent principal, and many students, parents, and staff members had a lot of respect for her, but she wasn't one to freely share a compliment.

Back at work, Maya heard someone in the stairwell, humming a Marvin Gaye classic and hoped it was Lloyd. When he emerged through the doors in a new designer sweatsuit and holding a Styrofoam cup, Maya was glad it was him. The sweatsuit made him look at least fifteen years younger, and Maya couldn't help but stare as he strolled toward her.

Lloyd waited until he was close to her before speaking. It wasn't that he was trying to hide his affection for Maya. He didn't care if the world knew, but he did care that Maya preferred her personal life to be kept private. "Good morning, beautiful," he whispered and winked his right eye.

Maya stapled the last problem on the board, and then cleaned up the materials she'd tossed about the floor. "Did you sleep well?" she asked with a grin. Since their date, Maya and Lloyd talked on the phone every night past midnight; the latest she'd been up on a weeknight since graduate school.

Lloyd flashed a crooked grin. "Seeing you is all I need to boost my adrenaline for the day."

To keep Lloyd from seeing her blush, Maya went inside the classroom and set the leftover material in her hand on a small table by the chalkboard. Lloyd followed Maya into the classroom and placed the cup in his hand on her desk. "I thought you'd like some hot tea," he said.

"You're so thoughtful," Maya said, and then checked the sweetness of her tea. *Almost perfect*.

"So . . . Valentine's Day is less than a month away," Lloyd stated as he sat atop Patrick's desk. "You have any plans?"

Maya hadn't thought that far ahead. Holidays didn't have the same meaning for her anymore. She wrapped her hands around the warm cup and looked at Lloyd. Stray gray hairs in his long lashes and mustache seemed more prominent than before, but he still had the body of a young man. "Do you have something in mind?" Maybe spending that special day with him would help erase thoughts of Kenneth for good.

"Just leave the day open for me. Can you do that?"

Maya sipped her mint-flavored tea. "I sure can." It was time to begin new traditions.

At three o'clock, Maya dismissed her students, and then headed to the gym to find Lloyd. He usually came to her classroom after dismissal to say good-bye, but Maya wanted to take the initiative this afternoon. She was having a good day and wanted to share a bit of her happiness with him. But when Maya reached his office, it was empty.

After what felt like five minutes of waiting for him to return, Maya looked inside his office. His coat was hanging from a closet doorknob and his computer was on, so he was definitely in the building. *Maybe I should go back to my room. He could be waiting for me there.* Before leaving, Maya scanned his desk for something to write on. Without being too invasive, she pushed some of the papers clouding his desk aside and noticed a notepad underneath a stack of invoices. She eased the notepad from under the pile, and a heart-shaped note floated to the floor. Careful not to read the writing on the paper, Maya leaned down to pick it up and set it back on Lloyd's desk. As she searched for something to write with, Maya's eyes gravitated to the note. In a female's writing, there was a list of hardware items and a brief message: *Home Depot is having a sale*. Maya wondered who had written the note and how long it had been hidden on his desk.

Maya spotted a pencil holder behind the computer and used one of the pencils inside it to scribble a message for Lloyd on a piece of scrap paper. She taped it on his computer, then stared at the heart-shaped note again. For a second, she rationalized that his oldest daughter may have written it. But how many teenagers care about a sale at Home Depot? Maya convinced herself that the note was written awhile ago and moved it under a pile of papers, where she thought it originally belonged, then left his office.

"Maya," Claudia called as she passed the main office. "Where have you been? I was just in your room five minutes ago," she said and pulled her knit hat down to cover her ears.

Though Maya suspected Claudia knew she was coming from the gym, she didn't want to confirm it. Lately, Claudia had been acting weird about the amount of time Maya spent with Lloyd and not with her. "We must've missed each other."

"I guess," Claudia agreed and buttoned her pea coat. "I'm on my way to the dentist, but I wanted to tell you that Bishop wants me to take that aerobics class with you. He's going to pick up the kids twice a week. So let's talk about it tonight . . . or tomorrow. Whatever will work for you."

That was good news. Going to the gym was more motivating for Maya if she had a partner to share her goals with. "I'll call tonight. I have to tell Bishop thank you," Maya replied, ignoring the insinuation that she didn't have time to talk on the phone anymore. While Maya and Lloyd talked every night, that didn't take away from time spent with friends and family. Besides, Claudia was often too busy with her family during the times Maya wanted to talk to her.

"Don't thank him yet. He's gonna have to come up with hair money every week since he thinks I belong in a gym," Claudia said and strutted out the door.

Chuckling to herself, Maya quickly walked upstairs, hoping to find Lloyd sitting in Patrick's chair. But she was disappointed. There was no indication that Lloyd had been there. Hurriedly, she gathered her things and took the elevator back to the first floor. Before leaving the building, she walked by his office again. This time the lights were off and the door was closed. Perplexed, Maya pulled out her cell phone and dialed his number, but the call went straight to voice mail. Maya left him a message and as she walked to her car, prayed nothing bad had happened. It wasn't like him to leave without saying good-bye.

The only bonus to Gwen's relocation for Maya was coming home to Langston every day. Like he'd done during the Christmas holiday, Langston sat next to the front window, waiting for Maya to come home. "There's my handsome baby," Maya cooed when she walked into the house and Langston rubbed against her legs. Leaning down, Maya scratched the top of his head and Langston flopped to his side so that she could rub his stomach. "You're so spoiled," she told him, using both hands to massage the backs of his ears.

Familiar voices coming from the basement reminded Maya that Gwen had left her to deal with their mother and aunts alone. Somehow that didn't seem fair. As she took off her coat, Langston circled her feet and let out a strong meow, letting Maya know that he was hungry. Instead of going downstairs to chat with the women, Maya went to the kitchen and put a few hard treats inside Langston's snack bowl. The treats always tied him over until his scheduled six o'clock dinner. Maya put the cat treats away then poured herself a small glass of homemade lemonade. On the stove, a large pot of beef, green peppers, and onions cooked slowly in a dark brown sauce. Unable to resist the savory aroma, she opened the lid and pulled out a short strip of beef. Maya wasn't a fan of red meat because it took too long to completely digest in her system, but always made an exception for her mother's pepper steak. "Mmm," she moaned when the tenderloin touched her tongue.

While Maya chewed the meat in her mouth, the special Isley Brothers's ringtone she'd assigned to Lloyd's number sounded in the next room. She hurried out of the kitchen and took the phone out of her tote bag. "Hello."

"Hey, lady," Lloyd replied as if nothing was wrong.

Lloyd's "disappearing act" shouldn't have bothered her, but in an odd way, it did. "Is everything okay? Did something happen to your kids?"

"I'm sorry, Maya. I did get your message, but time got away from me."

"I was concerned," stated Maya. "You usually come into my room before leaving."

Lloyd chuckled slyly. "You're getting used to me, huh? That's a good sign."

Heavy footsteps coming from the basement signaled that Mrs. Richards and her sisters were on their way upstairs. "Let me give you a call later," she whispered, and Lloyd opposed.

"My brother hurt himself at work," he blurted, desperate to keep Maya on the line. "I had to rush over to Pennsylvania hospital. I'm sorry if I disappointed you."

Maya was impressed with Lloyd's dedication to his family. Had the situation been reversed, she would've dropped everything to be by her sister's side as well. "No need to be sorry. Family should come first."

"This won't happen again. I hope you're not upset with me."

"Honestly, Lloyd. It's okay. But can I call you back? My aunts are here and I should probably talk to them," Maya said, as her mother and aunts climbed the stairs.

Not wanting to let her go, Lloyd ignored Maya's attempt to hang up. "I was invited to a cabaret on Friday. If I buy two tickets, will you be my special date? I know we made plans for Saturday, but I'd like to hang with you on Friday too . . . if that's all right."

"There's the mystery woman," announced Aunt Bess when she made it to the kitchen.

Mrs. Richards lightly tapped her daughter's bottom as she passed by. "And she's on that phone again."

"I wonder with *whom?*" Aunt Bess teased, and then helped Aunt Mary sit in the kitchen chair.

Before they had a chance to embarrass her further, Maya blew each of the women a kiss and eased into the next room, and so that they couldn't hear her conversation, lowered her voice. "Sorry about that, but you said the cabaret is this Friday? As in two days from now?"

"I know it's short notice, but a good buddy of mine told me about it today," Lloyd responded. Then nervously, he asked, "Do you have other plans?"

The question wasn't whether or not she had plans. Eating dinner at a restaurant and going to the movies where it was just the two of them was one thing. Going to a cabaret where they'd have to interact with his friends was something different. What would the people there think about an almost fifty-year-old man toting around a younger woman?

Maya sat on the couch and stared out of the patio window as she weighed her options. If she didn't go to the cabaret, she'd be running errands for her mother, or marking papers, or watching movies with her parents. Maya sighed. Accepting Lloyd's invitations should've been easy. Not only did she like Lloyd, but Maya had prayed for someone special in her life.

"Dinner's ready, Maya!" Mrs. Richards shouted from the kitchen.

Through the trees in the backyard, two puppies chased one another as their owner captured their fun on film. Maya wished her life was as carefree as the two puppies. "I'd love to go," Maya finally answered and stood to her feet. Dancing with an old man had to be better than sitting at home on a Friday night.

Chapter 14

Light snow flurries fell from the sky as Maya walked down the street leading to a popular nightclub in the Mount Airy section of the city. Per Lloyd's instructions, Maya stopped by the storefront window and waited for him to come get her. To keep them from going numb in her suede pumps, Maya moved her feet from side to side and shoved her hands inside her pockets. She'd called Lloyd less than two minutes ago to let him know she was outside, and if he didn't come out of the club soon, she was sure to get frostbite. Staring up into the night sky, Maya let a few soft flakes drift onto her face, and oddly it had a calming effect on her spirit.

Tired of waiting, Maya joined the fast-moving line at the club entrance. At this point, she didn't care about the cost of the ticket. She just wanted to get inside the warm building.

"You have a ticket?" the burly bouncer asked when it was Maya's turn in line. With arms the size of melons, he looked like a weight-lifting champion.

Maya took a twenty-dollar bill from her purse. "How much—"

"I have the beautiful lady's ticket," Lloyd yelled from across the room. He strolled to the door in his Fedora and alligator shoes and stood by the bouncer, grinning from ear to ear. "Here you go, young man," he said and handed him a folded ticket.

The bouncer stamped the ticket then looked at Maya with a slight smirk. "I need to see some ID."

Maya was surprised. She hadn't been carded in at least three years, and as she searched through her purse Lloyd grabbed her waist, making it obvious to everyone she was with him. Maya gave the bouncer her license and he studied every detail carefully before giving it back.

"I feel like the luckiest man in the club tonight," Lloyd said as he escorted Maya to the coat check. "How was your drive in?"

Maya didn't feel as lucky as Lloyd, but tried to relax. "The roads were slick, but I managed," she replied, and followed him down a narrow hall. Along the way, she glimpsed at a banner hanging across the wall that read: *Happy 50th Birthday, Alvin!* and prayed she wouldn't be the only person under forty in attendance.

"Next time, I'm coming to get you. I was raised to pick up the woman I'm taking on a date."

"We live in opposite ends of the city. It's only fair that I meet you halfway."

"I know you can take care of yourself. But sometimes, it's okay to let a man take care of you. You don't have to do *everything* on your own."

Maya realized that she may have come off brash, and lightened her tone. "Sorry, some habits are hard to break."

Lloyd helped Maya take off her coat, and when he saw her strapless dress, his eyes lit up. "You look nice."

"Thank you," she said coyly and turned away from him.

While Lloyd stepped away to check her coat, Maya admired the architecture of the building. The modern nightclub was nothing like what she'd imagined. Its tin ceilings, maple floors, and brick walls gave the club a casual, yet sophisticated ambience. Looking around, Maya sensed people standing near the bar area, watching her every move. Women in semi-formal gowns and glittery dresses stared in her direction, envious of her youth, and gray-bearded men dressed in silk suits gazed at her with alluring eyes. Suddenly, Maya felt more like a trophy than a date.

Returning to Maya's side, Lloyd grabbed her hand and proudly led her further down the hall. And as they passed a small crowd of people, Lloyd greeted them with a tilt of his hat and a subtle smile. Feeling self-conscious, Maya stared at the floor until she was in the clear.

Before reaching the open area, Lloyd walked up to a minibar station and took out his wallet. "Can I get you a drink?" he asked Maya.

After considering the current weather conditions, Maya thought it best she drink light. "Just a Ginger Ale and cranberry juice."

"I'll have another glass of Hennessey," Lloyd told a friendly bartender, and then requested Maya's nonalcoholic beverage.

As they waited for their drinks, "Got to Give It Up," an old Marvin Gaye song, came on and people gravitated to the dance floor, shaking and bopping to the catchy beat. Lloyd couldn't wait to follow them, and as soon as the bartender finished their drinks, he placed a tip on the counter and danced his way to the tables in the back of the large room. He set both drinks on the table, and then held out the chair for Maya. "I'm so glad you're here," Lloyd said when he sat down.

"Thanks for inviting me," Maya responded politely. The jury was still out on whether or not she was glad to be there.

Lloyd removed his hat and let it hang on his right knee. As he consumed moderate amounts of his drink, he bopped in his seat and sang the lyrics of each song the DJ played. Watching him move, Maya forgot that Lloyd was almost fifty. "I'm honored. It's not every day you come across an intelligent *and* beautiful woman such as yourself. I mean, you have so much dedication for your students, especially that one kid."

"Do you mean Patrick?"

"The one and only. Not many teachers would deal with him the way you do."

Maya agreed that Patrick was turning into a special project; one that she was actually beginning to enjoy.

Lloyd slid his chair closer to Maya and touched her hand. "Kenneth is a fool. If given the chance, I promise you I won't take you for granted. I'll treat you like the queen you are. Young guys don't know how to treat a real woman."

Maya watched Lloyd finish his drink in one gulp, and wondered if he were being sincere, or if the alcohol was prompting him to say things he didn't really mean. "We'll see how you feel tomorrow," she stated and took a small sip of her mixed drink.

"How can you say that, Maya?" Lloyd asked softly, visibly hurt by her words. "I've been attracted to you since the first day you walked into the school. I'm too old to play games," he said and delicately rubbed her hand.

A young couple seated at a nearby table eyed Maya curiously, and she eased her hand from under Lloyd's grasp then sat back in her chair. It was possible the couple was staring at the dozens of people on the dance floor, but Maya had a feeling that wasn't the case. "I guess time will tell," she told Lloyd. "Just remember that the heart can be a fragile organ. I'd hate for you to pump me up, and then toy with my emotions later."

Lloyd moved forward in his chair and gently kissed Maya on the cheek. "You can relax, love. Those days are *long* gone for me."

When Lloyd sat back down, Maya caught a glimpse of the strained look on the young couple's face. "Do you know everyone here?"

"Just about. I grew up with a couple of these old guys. Why?"

"I have a feeling they're not used to outsiders." Either that or, for some reason, they had a problem with her being there with Lloyd.

"I wouldn't worry about these folks. You'll meet everyone over time, and once they get used to you, they'll see how special you are." Lloyd stood up and extended his arm. "Now, c'mon and dance with me. Let me check out your moves."

Lloyd's words didn't raise Maya's comfort level much, but she tried to relax. She'd forgotten how difficult dating could be. Maya figured Lloyd's friends were probably observing her tonight, and analyzing her every move. If that was the case, Maya wasn't going to give them anything negative to report. She grabbed Lloyd's hand and walked beside him to the center of the room, and for the next fifteen minutes, followed Lloyd's lead as he twirled, dipped, and moved to the music smoothly and without stopping to catch his breath.

Maya tried to match Lloyd's vigor, but midway through the fourth song, Lloyd was still going strong like the Energizer Bunny, and her feet could no longer withstand the pressure. "Can we take a break?" Before Lloyd had a chance to respond, she headed off the dance floor.

On the way back, Lloyd picked up speed when they approached the table where Lloyd's brother and his date were waiting. "I want you to meet my brother," he announced with excitement. "Maya, this is Robert."

Taller and thinner than his older brother, Robert shared Lloyd's oval-shaped head and eyes. His nose was slightly larger, but there was no mistake that the two were related. "It's nice to finally meet you," he said and reached for her hand. "Lloyd speaks very highly of you."

"Nice meeting you too," Maya replied, shaking his hand timidly. "How are you feeling?"

A confused glare crossed Robert's face, and Lloyd quickly interjected. "I told Maya about your fall on the job."

"Oh, yeah," Robert said. "I work for a printing company and I'm always hurting myself. Two months ago, my finger got caught in one of the machines. I didn't break it, but I sure bruised it real good," he joked. "I fell this time and hurt my back. The fall sounded worse than the actual pain."

"Glad to hear you're feeling better," Maya replied, then looked at Robert's date sitting quietly at the table. "Hello, I'm Maya," she said and offered to shake her hand, but the woman didn't move.

Robert stood behind his date's chair. "This is my lady, Tanya," he said and rubbed her shoulders.

Tanya looked up from the Coors Light bottle she was holding, and with a straight face mumbled, "Hello," then looked back down at her beer. Either Tanya was shy or unaccustomed to the courteous way to meet new people.

"Well, I'm starving," Lloyd said, ignoring Tanya's coarse mood. "Maya, can I get you something to eat?"

While Maya understood that Lloyd was trying to be a gentleman, the thought of leaving her alone with Tanya was a little frightening. She didn't seem the least bit interested in getting to know Maya.

"Yeah, babe," Robert said. "I'll go get us some of that jerk chicken."

Tanya nodded and Maya smiled as she slowly took her seat. "I'm not very hungry," she told Lloyd, in hopes that he'd hurry back, and then braced herself to be alone with Tanya.

Several minutes passed without an exchange of words or look to acknowledge Maya's presence after the men left. There wasn't a great deal of liquid in the bottle Tanya was nursing, but she sipped on it steadily to avoid talking. Maya couldn't stand the silence between them and decided to take the initiative. "That's a really pretty blouse," she said, hoping Tanya would at least accept the compliment about her multi-layered shirt.

"Thank you," Tanya replied dryly, and scooped up a handful of peanuts from a dish on the table.

"I'm surprised Robert wanted to come out and dance after his fall," Maya said in an attempt to start another conversation.

Tanya threw a few peanuts into her mouth and chewed them. "He took a few Tylenol before we left," she responded without looking directly at Maya.

Tired of trying to be nice, Maya gave up. Had she known about the cabaret a week ago, she would've invited Claudia and Bishop. The happy couple would've twirled around the room most of the night and been much better company.

"You miss me?" Lloyd asked when he returned to the table with two hefty plates of food.

Maya stared deep into his eyes and thought, *You have no idea how much.*

The DJ played "Before I Let Go," the ultimate Frankie Beverly old school dance tune, as everyone picked through the last of the food on their plates. Robert wiped his mouth with a napkin then jumped to his feet and dragged Tanya along with him to the dance floor.

"Don't hurt her, Robert!" Lloyd yelled, tapping the floor with his foot.

Tanya turned around with a tiny streak of amusement in her eyes. "Don't worry about me. You better hope *I* don't hurt *him*," she said and continued dancing behind her man.

"I'll be right back," Lloyd told Maya and headed in the direction of the men's room. As he walked away, Maya saw him pull his cell phone out of his pocket, and figured he needed to check on his eldest daughter. She turned to face the dance floor and studied Robert as he showed Tanya a move Maya had seen her students try during recess. For a man that had hurt his back, Robert moved around smoothly and without missing a beat.

Once the song ended, the lights came on and the DJ grabbed the microphone. "Okay, party people, it's midnight and officially Alvin's birthday." The DJ played with a few buttons on his machine, and then continued. "Alvin, my man, happy fiftieth. You don't look a day over forty-nine." The crowd laughed as Alvin made his way to the front of the room. "Now, let's celebrate with the birthday song."

Immediately after the traditional happy birthday song, the crowd went into Stevie Wonder's rhythmic version. Alvin, the guest of honor, reminded Maya of comedian and actor Bill Cosby as he danced across the floor. His limbs barely moved, but Maya could tell he was having a great time.

While the guests cheered for Alvin, Maya felt someone grab her by the waist. "That'll be me next year," Lloyd whispered in her ear, and Maya's smile slowly subsided. If she and Lloyd were in a relationship next year, she'd have to plan his fiftieth party. The thought was unsettling.

As Lloyd rocked her back and forth to the music, Maya had visions of taking him to doctor appointments, pushing him in a wheelchair, and visiting him in a nursing home. *What am I doing?* she questioned, and just when she was about to abandon thoughts of beginning a relationship with him, the disco music resumed, and full of energy, Lloyd danced circles around her. Clearly, Lloyd was more than the average middle-aged man, and as he whisked Maya around the room, she believed that he could live to be a hundred and still have the agility of a young man.

Maya pushed through two more songs with her aching feet, and then told Lloyd that she had to leave. It was late and she feared the roads would be icy. "It's best I leave now, while I still have *some* energy."

"This is why I wanted to drive," Lloyd whined and stopped dancing. "But I guess I understand. I'm just glad you came."

Maya smiled with appreciation and grabbed Lloyd's hand. "I better say good-bye to Robert and Tanya," she said, and as she started to walk off the dance floor, Lloyd pulled her close and with great passion, kissed her. Taken off-guard, Maya forgot that they were standing near the center of the dance floor, and freely succumbed to Lloyd's control.

"Wow," Maya said once she regained her composure. Unlike most of the night, the kiss wasn't awkward. It was affectionate and endearing, and it satisfied her craving for affection. Although he was almost fifty, and sometimes dressed and talked like an old man, he certainly didn't kiss like one.

When Maya made it home, she walked into the house expecting to see Langston, but he wasn't by the door. "Langston," she called softly, but he didn't surface or make a sound. *That's odd,* Maya thought, and walked up to the lamp in the corner of the living room. Her mother had left it on. As she reached behind the base of the lamp to turn it off, Maya noticed a handwritten note on the stand and picked it up.

> *Maya,*
> *Langston left a hairball on the couch in the basement.*
> *You need to clean it up. I locked him in your room, so he wouldn't do anymore damage.*
> *Mom*

Having no idea how long Langston had been shut inside her bedroom, Maya balled up the note and quietly ran upstairs to check on her feline friend. *What if he had to go to the bathroom?* she thought, praying he hadn't used an empty corner as his personal litter box.

Maya opened the door and sighed with relief. Her mother had brought Langston's litter box up from the basement. Langston jumped off the bed and ran to Maya's side and his sharp claws pricked her skin, tearing tiny holes in her sheer stockings. "Hey fella," she whispered and picked him up before his nails drew blood. "I'm sorry I stayed out late. But no more hairballs, Lanky. Mom is gonna kick us out before we find a new home." And, as if he understood, Langston let out a mellow meow and jumped out of her arms.

An unfamiliar stench caught Maya's attention and she walked toward the corner of the room to be sure Langston hadn't sprayed outside of his box. Maya knew Langston's litter box couldn't stay in her bedroom all night without the tough scent settling into her belongings. So after changing into her flannel pajamas, Maya took the box back down to the basement and cleaned Langston's hairball.

On the way back to her bedroom, Maya thought about Lloyd and her cheeks warmed. Every time she came up with reasons not to like him, he did something to change her mind. Like that kiss. Either she'd forgotten what it felt like to be kissed, or Lloyd should have his technique prototyped. Before getting into bed, Maya took out her Bible and reexamined the list she'd created awhile ago about her ideal man. Lloyd had met all the requirements. *Lord, is Lloyd the one?* she queried, and then knelt by the side of her bed with the paper in hand. As she prayed for an answer, Maya realized that her list was not yet complete. While it was fresh on her mind, Maya grabbed a pen from her nightstand and added to the list:

> *must treat me like a queen*
> *can't be selfish*
> *and should go to church.*

Maya folded the list, and as she continued to pray by the side of her bed, realized that Lloyd might be her ideal man after all. But it was still too soon for her to be absolutely sure, and trusted that God would reveal the truth in time.

Chapter 15

Weaving in and out of the heavy weekend traffic, Maya raced through the city to get to the hair salon. Almost twenty minutes late, she prayed Janelle, her stylist, wasn't already backed up with heads to do. If she were, Maya would have to sit around and hope someone called to cancel their appointment, so she could take their slot.

It was her fault that she was running late, though Maya blamed her tardiness on traffic. The truth was that Maya and Lloyd had been talking on the phone and she lost track of time. This was the first Saturday in the last few weeks that she and Lloyd didn't have plans to be together, so they talked for an hour this morning before he had to run off to a volleyball game in South Philly. Rather than go with him, Maya decided to spend time in the hair salon with her best friend.

"Where've you been? Claudia's been looking for you," asked Janelle, when Maya opened the salon door.

"Where is she?" Maya queried, glad that the salon wasn't packed and she could still get her hair done.

Janelle sprayed her spiked hair, and then nodded toward the back of the salon where the shampoo bowls were stationed. "She's getting her highlights touched up. What are you getting done today?"

"Just wash and curl," Maya said and hung her coat in the closet. As she leisurely headed to the back, Maya let out a deep sigh and prepared to answer questions about why she was late.

Claudia was sitting in front of a shampoo bowl, reading a romance novel when Maya poked her head in the room. Small strips of foil used to constrict hair color to a specific area stood straight in different directions, making her look like a blonde Martian.

"Hey, Claudia," Maya said meekly.

When Claudia saw Maya she dropped her book in her lap. "Let me guess. You're late because you were with Lloyd."

"Not exactly," Maya replied and eased into an empty chair along the wall. "We were on the phone."

"He seems to be the only person you have time for these days."

Maya detected a hint of sarcasm in her state-ment. "That's not fair, Claudia. You're not always available when I need someone to talk to. I understand that you have a family. Why can't you understand that I'm getting to know Lloyd?"

"I'm glad you're getting to know him. But why should that interfere with our friendship? I know that we're both mature adults with other obligations, but I rarely ever talk to you at work anymore. We don't even have a chance to really talk at the gym."

"You're exaggerating," Maya fired back. But as she thought about it further, Maya had to admit Claudia was right. As much as she tried to avoid Lloyd at school, ironically, they shared the same prep period and lunch schedule, so he found ways to be in her presence whenever students weren't around. And with both of their busy schedules, Maya and Lloyd had set specific times to be together. Wednesday and Friday evenings were dedicated to late night dinners, and weekends were reserved for other fun dating activities. They also met afterschool a few times a week at different coffeehouses until Maya had to leave for the gym, and Lloyd had to leave for volleyball practice. Now that Maya thought about it, it was a miracle she had time for anything else.

"I'm exaggerating?" Claudia asked and rolled her eyes. "When was the last time you saw my kids?"

Again, Claudia was right. Maya used to see Claudia's children at least once a week, and at the moment, couldn't recall when she'd seen them last. "I can hang out with you guys today. I just need to stop by the mall to get Lloyd's Valentine's Day present. He's with his daughters all day, so my day is fairly flexible."

"Oh, I see how things work now," Claudia responded, but this time with a grin. "My family and I have been bumped. But it's okay. I'm taking them ice skating tonight *if* you can join us."

Relieved that her friend had loosened up, Maya felt it was safe to relax and drop her guard. "I can, and I will, and no one's gonna stop me."

With that discussion out of the way, the two friends caught up on gossip and funny stories about their families. In the middle of a story about her mother-in-law, Claudia stopped talking when Lloyd unexpectedly appeared in the shampoo room. "You just can't leave her side, can you, Lloyd?" Claudia asked him with candor.

Maya turned around in disbelief. "What are you doing here? I thought you had a game today."

"The game was cancelled and my girls wanted to go to the Gallery," Lloyd explained and sat in any seat, "and since I was in the neighborhood, I thought I'd surprise you."

"I think it's safe to say she's surprised," Claudia added, and reopened her book.

While Maya was happy to see him, she prayed he wasn't planning to stay long. Especially after the talk she had with Claudia this morning, Maya wanted to devote the day to her best friend.

"How long are you going to be?" Lloyd tried to whisper. "Maybe I can drop my daughters off at Robert's and we can—"

"Maya has plans with me today, Lloyd," Claudia remarked, half-joking. "You can let her loose for *one* day, can't you?"

Maya turned her back to Claudia and lowered her voice, though out the tiny room the slightest whisper could be heard. "Why don't I give you a call later on tonight?"

Lloyd gave Maya a look that said he understood and stood up. "Okay," he complied and kissed Maya on the lips. "Guess I'll do a little shopping with my girls today." And despite her distance, Lloyd faced Claudia and said good-bye before he left the room.

Maya didn't have to see Claudia's face to know that she was frowning. She didn't want to start an argument, but Maya was curious to know why Claudia treated Lloyd so coldly; especially since they'd always gotten along at work. "You could've been a little nicer," she said coolly. "I thought you liked Lloyd."

"He's cool as a teacher. I'm not sure about anything more than that. You two have been together a lot in such a short time. Kenneth didn't monopolize your time as much as Lloyd."

"We're getting to know each other," retorted Maya. "You do remember the *praise stage* you made up?"

The "praise stage" was the part in a new relationship when a new couple showered one another with compliments, and couldn't stand to leave each other's side. There were no arguments, disagreements, or attitudes exchanged during this stage. The couple was constantly on their best behavior.

Defeated, Claudia continued to read. "I miss my friend, that's all. We didn't have this problem when you were with Ken."

"Ken worked around the clock." Maya playfully snapped. "But you're still my friend. Just give me time to get to know a *new* friend."

Janelle stepped into the room and fingered through Maya's hair. "I see someone has a new man. Kenneth is really history, huh?"

Maya tried not to blush in Claudia's presence. "He's just a good friend."

"Well," Janelle said, and walked over to Claudia to check her highlights, "that *good* friend paid for your hair before he left." Claudia shot Maya an infamous glare. "Five more minutes for you, Claudia," Janelle said. "Maya, I'll have someone shampoo you in a minute."

Claudia placed a bookmark inside the book she was reading, then placed it inside her handbag. She wanted to give Maya her full attention. "Is there something you need to tell me?"

"Something like what?" Maya responded, confused by the question.

"Did you sleep with him?"

"Did I what?" she snapped, obviously offended.

"Don't blow a fuse, Maya. I'm just asking. If the two of you are *only* friends, I'm not sure why he's doing all these things for you. First, it was the perfume, now he's paying for your hair. You don't think that's a bit overboard?"

"Why is it that if a man does nice things for a woman he wants to sleep with her?" argued Maya, although she wasn't thrilled with what Lloyd had done, either. She had asked him not to buy her any more gifts. "I don't think he's looking for anything in return, Claudia. He doesn't appear to be that kind of man."

"You're being naive," Claudia replied quickly, "but I pray you're right this time. I've seen a few men like him. He's trying too hard to impress you, Maya, and that's something you should pay close attention to. You've only been seeing each other for a month."

"It's been almost forty days," informed Maya. "Wasn't it the Israelites that reached the Promised Land after forty days? Maybe Lloyd and I are going to have a good ending too."

"It was forty years," Claudia corrected. "And I wouldn't use the Israelites as a reference. They complained the whole time God tried to help them, thus what could've happened in eleven days took forty years. *And,*" Claudia was taking Maya's lightheartedness too seriously, "when God delivered them, they repeated the *same* mistakes again. Is that *really* what you want to pattern your friendship with Lloyd after?"

One of Janelle's shampoo girls came into the room and the two friends were silent.

"You can sit at the middle bowl," the shampoo girl directed Maya.

Maya did as she was told, and before the warm water touched her scalp, she turned to Claudia and said, "I think we need to change the subject."

"I agree," Claudia responded blithely. And for the rest of the morning, neither friend brought up Lloyd's name.

***

After Maya's hair was shampooed and conditioned, she sat under a hot hair dryer while Janelle finished styling Claudia's hair. As the hot air blew on Maya's head, she prayed that her best friend would eventually embrace Lloyd as more than just a colleague. As she drifted off to sleep, the addictive groove of "Sexy Back" by Justin Timberlake sounded from Maya's cell phone, already in her hand, and she hit the talk button before the music annoyed the ladies sitting near her. "Hey, Gwen," she said softly.

"Hey, sis," Gwen sang cheerfully into the phone. "How's Langston?"

"He's very happy, and so am I." Maya beamed, glad to hear Gwen's voice. "What's up with you?"

"I'm on my way to Justin's. One of his cameraman friends invited us to an early lunch. How are things with you? Still seeing Lloyd?"

"Well," began Maya, "as a matter of fact, we're fine. Did I tell you I went to a fiftieth birthday cabaret with him?"

"So you've been hanging with the old folks?" Gwen laughed.

"You should've seen Lloyd dance circles around me," Maya told her, and then thought about the kiss. "He has more stamina than I do."

"Don't tell me you couldn't keep up with your old man," Gwen teased.

"I had on the wrong shoes," Maya replied playfully and Gwen giggled harder.

The constant flow of heat from the dryer burned Maya's hand and she turned it off. She moved from under the dryer and fingered through her hair. In her opinion, her hair felt dry, so she got up and sat on the other side of the room.

"Things must be getting pretty serious," Gwen said when she stopped laughing.

"Not yet," Maya tried to convince herself; although she had to admit there was a strong chance they were heading in that direction. "But let me tell you about the night." Maya turned her back to the other women sitting in the room, and lowered her voice as she told Gwen everything about that evening, including Tanya's cold personality.

"Don't worry about her. Tanya is probably friends with Lloyd's ex and just needs time to get used to you. Women can be funny like that sometimes."

"At least the brother liked me."

"I'm glad to hear that you and Lloyd are progressing. But are you sure you're not using him as a substitute for Kenneth? You haven't been single a good six months yet."

Maya let Gwen's question settle in her spirit. When Kenneth confirmed that their relationship was over, Maya fought hard to push memories of him out of her mind. It was better that way. And when Lloyd came along, forgetting about being in love with Kenneth altogether became easy.

"I'm over Kenneth. Lloyd is really a nice guy. He's been very respectful, and we seem to be on the same page; even about marriage. We used to talk on the phone a lot, but we noticed that the late nights were causing us to drag during the day, so we try to say good night by ten now."

"He gets off the phone early because he's almost fifty." Gwen giggled. "He needs to get *all* of his rest, like most old men do."

Maya couldn't help but laugh. "I'll tell you one thing, Lloyd is very attentive. If men don't understand women until they pass forty, then that's the man I want to be with."

"Justin's not forty and he's very good to me. You just need a mature man, Maya. But it sounds like you're enjoying yourself, and that's all that matters right now. How's the apartment search going?"

"I saw a couple in Plymouth Meeting that were okay. I might choose one of them if I don't find something I like soon."

"You need to rent something that's more than just okay, Maya. Keep looking. You can't settle for *good enough*. If you're going to lock yourself into a lease you might as well love what you're paying for every month."

Heeding the wisdom of her younger sister, Maya sighed. "You're right. I guess I'm tired of looking. I wish your old apartment was still vacant. I called last week, but nothing's available until the summer. I don't think I can wait that long."

"I hear you, but don't get tired. That's when you'll do something you'll regret later. And, do you *really* want to be so close to Mom?"

Sometimes Maya wondered if God made a mistake creating her before Gwen. It was clear that Gwen acted more like the older sister. "You're right again."

"Well, I'd keep looking in the city if I were you. The farther you are from Norristown, the better. You don't want Mom popping up on you all the time."

"You're up, Maya!" Janelle called from the door, and Maya wrapped up her call with Gwen. She wished she had more time to talk because she knew it would be a week before Gwen had a chance to call her again. Maya especially wanted to get her take on Claudia's recent behavior. But that conversation would have to wait until the next time.

As Maya headed to Janelle's chair, she looked at Claudia sitting by the window with bright highlights, and newly shaved brows, and prayed their day would end better than it had started.

Chapter 16

In a red velvet sweater and cream pants, Ms. Covington struted into Maya's classroom, wheeling an oversized arrangement of roses on a cart. "Happy Valentine's Day, Ms. Richards," Ms. Covington sang and rolled the cart next to Maya's desk. "I wonder who these are from," she continued, suggesting she already knew the answer.

"I bet I know," Patrick shouted from his seat.

A few students giggled and Maya tapped her desk with a ruler. "Get back to work," she said and the students immediately settled down. Looking at the huge bouquet of roses, Maya rearranged a few items on her desk to make room for her gift. Maya loved surprises, but she'd begged Lloyd not to do anything. Although he was okay with their special friendship, Maya didn't want to put it on display.

The arrangement was too heavy for one person to carry, so Maya helped Ms. Covington place the roses perfectly in the middle of her desk. Ms. Covington sniffed the fresh-cut roses. "I didn't read the card, and I'd understand if you don't want to—"

"I'll read it later," Maya replied and swiftly removed the card from the bundle. Ms. Covington had probably told half the school about the roses before they made it to her classroom.

"There must be a hundred roses in there," blurted Patrick.

"I thought I told you to get back to work," Maya scolded, unable to take her eyes off the roses.

"These kids are so nosy," Ms. Covington mumbled under her breath, then before she rolled the cart to the door, turned and said, "By the way, the home and school association is selling silk roses today. I'll be making my rounds this afternoon," she told the children, then looked at Maya. "Make sure you stop by the office before you go home."

"Okay," Maya agreed, but she didn't mean it. Fueling Ms. Covington's gossip train was the last thing Maya wanted to do.

Once the secretary was gone, Maya sat down and hid behind her floral surprise. She removed the small envelope and made sure her students weren't watching her, especially Patrick. "Patrick will collect your papers in two minutes," Maya said, so that the students would concentrate on finishing their work and not on what she was doing. When Maya was sure the children weren't looking at her, she read the card.

> *You've brightened up my life in a way words cannot express.*
> *Thanks for putting a smile on an old man's face every day.*
> *Lloyd*

Maya read the card at least five times before putting it back inside the envelope. In just a short amount of time, Lloyd had managed to repair the damage Kenneth had done to her heart. Maya wanted to tell Claudia about the roses during lunch, but since their talk at the hair salon, the two friends hadn't mentioned Lloyd's name. It was days like this that Maya wished her sister hadn't moved so far away. Even if Gwen didn't like Lloyd, she would've admired Maya's roses.

Patrick tapped Maya's hand and whispered, "We have a guest."

Maya lifted her head above the long-stemmed roses as Mrs. Bridges walked inside the classroom and Maya jumped up.

Casually, the principal strolled around the room, and out of all the students to observe, stopped at Julian's desk. Maya prayed he was on task and had finished most of his assignment. "What are you working on?" Mrs. Bridges asked him, and Maya nervously awaited his response.

"I'm writing a story about trading and bartering. The men at this store," Julian said, pointing to two men from the colonial era in his social studies book, "are the characters in my story."

Mrs. Bridges nodded in approval. "Very good," she said, and then asked volunteers to share their stories. Surprisingly, more than half of the children raised their hands. "Thanks for sharing," Mrs. Bridges said after the fourth child read their story. "I'm very impressed. Your teacher must be doing a great job."

Maya let her students know that she was pleased with a slight smile, then walked around her desk and stood next to Mrs. Bridges. "Proofread your work while I talk to Mrs. Bridges," she told the class. Her palms were sweaty. Unannounced visits were never random for Mrs. Bridges. If she showed up to her class, there was a reason.

"I read your idea for an afterschool math program," Mrs. Bridges said. "Stop by my office next week and we'll work out the details."

"We're late for art class," Julian shouted.

Maya gave him a disapproving stare. She didn't know he liked art enough to fear being late a few minutes.

"Don't worry, Ms. Richards. I'll talk to you later," Mrs. Bridges said, unaffected by Julian's outburst.

Embarrassed, Maya had the students leave their papers on their desks and line up at the door. And as they marched upstairs to art class, Maya made a note to speak to Julian about classroom etiquette.

Instead of going to see Claudia, Maya went back to her classroom and finished her half-eaten turkey sandwich from lunch. As she ate, she thumbed through apartment listings in the *Inquirer*, but none seemed to meet all of her standards. A modern one-bedroom, complete with a dishwasher, washer and dryer, and under eight hundred a month, utilities included, shouldn't have been difficult to find.

"I hear the ladies on the first floor are jealous of your roses," Lloyd said, interrupting Maya's search.

Maya looked up from the newspaper then wiped her mouth with a napkin. "Guess I have you to thank for that."

"I hope you like them," Lloyd said, and his upper lip twitched; something Maya learned happened whenever he was nervous.

"I love them, Lloyd," Maya replied, hoping her friendly tone would relax him. "But you didn't have to buy so many. I'm sure these cost a small fortune."

"There's no limit when it comes to you, Maya," Lloyd said and invited himself inside the room. "Besides, I had to do better than your last man."

"So this is a competition?" For a moment, Maya feared the conversation she had with Claudia in the salon was true.

"Not at all. I just want you to see that I can take care of you better than he did," Lloyd responded, losing some of his enthusiasm.

"Just be yourself. There's no need for you to try and outshine anyone. I like you just the way you are," Maya told him, a little relieved. She wrapped up the remains of her sandwich and threw it in the trash. "I thought we were exchanging gifts after work," she said and sealed the lid of the salad bowl.

"Please forgive me. I wanted our first holiday together to be special."

Conscious of her tone, Maya spoke delicately. She didn't want Lloyd to think she was disappointed. "I understand, but we agreed not to do anything at work."

"Sometimes I get too excited. But this isn't your big gift. You'll get the other one later."

Maya thought about the silk tie and box of chocolate turtles she purchased. Lloyd had well-surpassed the amount she'd spent on his gift with the roses alone. "I don't need another thing, Lloyd. You've done enough. I mean that."

"That's what I like about you. You're so humble. I wish all women were as appreciative as you."

A familiar pair of sneakers appeared behind Lloyd and Maya got out of her chair. "Patrick?" she said, and Lloyd turned around. Holding a silk rose in one hand, Patrick looked down at his feet. "Why can't you stay in art class the entire time? Every week we go through this," Maya complained. "What's the problem, Patrick?"

"Valentine's Day is stupid!" Patrick hollered and threw the rose across the room.

"Now hold on, son," Lloyd said. "You have to—"

"It's okay, Mr. Bradford. He'll calm down in a minute," Maya guaranteed him, and prayed she was right. She'd never seen Patrick this angry. "Do I need to call Mrs. Marshall?" she asked a frowning Patrick, but he didn't answer. Ready to reprimand him, Maya closed her mouth when she saw tears rolling down his cheeks. Whatever happened must've been serious to make him produce tears. "Lloyd," Maya began and faced him, "do you mind getting my kids from art class?"

Lloyd didn't want to leave, but agreed to do what Maya requested. "Get yourself together, sweetheart," Maya said when Lloyd was gone, and wrapped her arms around Patrick. "Your classmates will be here in a few minutes. Do you want to tell me what's bothering you?"

Patrick wiped his face until it was dry. "My mom was supposed to come get me today," he said glumly.

"How do you know she's not coming? The day's not over yet."

"I bought a rose from Ms. Covington," Patrick said, and his tears resurfaced, "and she told me that my mom called."

It hurt Maya's heart to see him in such pain. Having shared every holiday with her mother, Maya didn't know what to say to make Patrick feel better. Telling him that everything was going to be all right didn't seem like the appropriate choice of words at the time.

"I told you she didn't love me," Patrick cried out, and Maya almost let a few tears of her own escape.

Afraid to say anything, especially without knowing all the facts, Maya decided to let him cry. And as Patrick stained her arm with his tears, Maya debated whether or not she should mention what happened to his father.

"Your classmates should be here soon, Patrick," Maya said a minute later, "so try and get yourself together. It might help if you write your feelings in your journal."

For once, Patrick didn't challenge Maya's request to write down his feelings. He pulled away from his teacher and walked across the room to pick up the rose he'd thrown. Before going to his assigned seat, he handed the gift he'd purchased for his mother to Maya. "This is for you," Patrick said. "I don't want my mother to have it anymore."

Maya was hesitant to take the rose. "You might see your mother later today, Patrick. Why don't you hold on to this."

"I'd rather give it to you," he replied adamantly.

Hearing the students at the door, Maya accepted the rose, mostly to make him happy. "Thank you," she said and set the gift on top of a bookcase behind her chair.

After all the trouble Patrick had caused since he arrived at the school, in that moment, Maya believed that she'd finally connected with him. Patrick could've given the rose to a student, or left it to rot in the back of the room. The fact that he chose to give it to Maya spoke volumes.

Once Patrick was settled at his desk, Maya walked to the door and motioned for her students to come inside. She was glad there was only twenty minutes before dismissal. "Work with a partner and quickly review your spelling words," she announced as the children walked inside the room. After the last child entered, Maya turned to Lloyd. "Thanks . . . for everything."

"Anytime," Lloyd whispered and winked his eye. Then, with his smooth stroll, he left to return to the gym.

After dismissal, Maya tried to rush through the main office unnoticed, but failed. Ms. Covington had been waiting for her. "Your secret admirer left a goody bag in your mailbox," she said. "I think I have an idea who it is, but if you tell me, I don't have to guess."

Maya shook her head. Lloyd insisted on doing things his way. What happened to exchanging gifts over dinner? Maya walked to her mailbox and removed a tall and thin red fluorescent bag. "You mean you didn't see who put this in here?"

Maya joked, though she hoped Lloyd exercised some discretion. Ms. Covington was like a private detective; determined and persistent to find out the facts. But if she were going to learn the truth this time, she wasn't going to get the information from Maya.

"I can't believe it myself. Nothing gets by me," Ms. Covington replied, and came from around her desk. "What'd you get?"

Maya stuck her hand inside the bag and felt a silky garment. *Lloyd didn't get me a pair of underwear, did he?* Maya thought to herself, and quickly removed her hand. She folded the bag and stuck it under her arm. "For my eyes only," she told the nosy secretary in a playful manner and headed out the office.

Back inside her classroom, Maya closed the door and set the bag on a desk. If there was a pair of underwear inside, she and Lloyd needed to have a serious talk. But before she could panic, she opened the bag and slowly pulled out the soft garment.

Whew! Maya sighed when she realized the gift was a beautiful silk dress. Though the fuchsia and purple paisley print was appealing, Maya planned to talk to Lloyd about his stubbornness. *How much did this cost?* she questioned as she studied the features of the dress.

With mixed emotions, Maya opened the Hallmark card that accompanied her gift. Expecting to read heartfelt poetry that captured his feelings about her, Maya was surprised to find a handwritten note.

Let's meet at Starbucks after work. I need to pick up my daughters.

I'll make up our dinner plans this weekend. I'm a great cook.

The door opened and Maya stuffed the dress back inside the bag. "Hey, Claudia," she said when her friend walked in.

"How are you? I haven't seen you all day," Claudia replied. "I heard Patrick had another incident."

Maya walked to her desk and put the card and gift inside her tote bag. "Yes, he's upset with his mother."

Though she wanted to hear the details, Claudia looked at the roses on Maya's desk. "Need I ask who these are from?" she asked snidely.

"Aren't they beautiful?" Maya asked, ignoring Claudia's sarcasm.

"A little massive," Claudia responded with a twisted lip, "but I suppose they are nice."

"Have a seat," Maya said. Before the conversation turned sour, Maya wanted to tell her about Patrick's day. Claudia wasn't in a mood to talk about Lloyd, either, so she sat down and listened to Maya.

"Well, God protects babies and fools. I pray God will protect his tender heart," Claudia stated when Maya was done. "Some women don't realize how much they hurt their children. And to think, there are so many women who'd give their right kidney to have a child of their own."

"Which reminds me," Maya said. "I need to call Mr. Gregorio." Maya also needed to meet Lloyd in fifteen minutes, but she kept that information to herself. Though it was Valentine's Day, she had a feeling Claudia wouldn't have understood.

"You go ahead and have your phone conference," Claudia said. "I have a few calls to make myself."

As Maya watched Claudia leave, a wave of sadness overcame her. This was the first time they hadn't shared their gift ideas and plans for their significant others. In the past, Claudia, who was excited about holidays she didn't even celebrate, could barely wait to tell Maya about the activities she planned for her children or how they decorated her house. Maya felt slighted, but pretended that it didn't matter.

Before calling Mr. Gregorio on her cell phone, Maya sent Lloyd a text to confirm their meeting time and place. As she dialed Mr. Gregorio's number, she prayed he hadn't left for work.

"Uh-oh," Mr. Gregorio exclaimed when he answered the phone. "What's my son done now, Ms. Richards?"

Maya was surprised that he recognized her number. "Hi, Mr. Gregorio. It's not what you think. I wanted to tell you about something that happened this afternoon." For the next twenty-five minutes, Maya told Mr. Gregorio about Patrick's outburst, and in return, he shared detailed information about Patrick's mother. Maya gained a better understanding of their mother-son relationship. "He's been working so hard. I'd hate for him to backslide," Maya said when he finished. "Is there anything I can do to help?"

"I signed him up for the basketball league at church. His first basketball game is on Saturday. I hope that helps him," he replied and paused briefly before continuing. "His mother is supposed to come, but in case she doesn't . . . I was wondering if you'd mind coming to the game. If she doesn't show up, at least you'll be there. I'm sure Patrick would like that."

Though Maya had a rule about supporting her students outside of the academic realm, she shocked herself and answered without hesitation. "I have some apartments to look at in the morning, but what time is the game?" she asked, then remembered that Lloyd invited her to dinner and prayed there wouldn't be a conflict of time. When Mr. Gregorio explained that the game started at noon, Maya sighed with relief.

"I didn't know you were looking for a place. A guy I work with just got married and is looking for someone to rent his townhouse in Lansdowne, not too far from Yeadon. It's a real nice place. If you like, I can take you by there after the game. I think you'll like it."

Desperate for a place to stay, Maya replied, "Sure, why not? What do I have to lose?"

"Good. I'll see about getting the key from my friend."

"Well, I better get going," Maya told Mr. Gregorio as she looked at the clock. Lloyd had to leave Starbucks by 5:30.

"Thanks, Ms. Richards," he said. "And Happy Valentine's Day."

There was something enchanting about the way Mr. Gregorio spoke those words. "Same to you," Maya replied and hung up.

Maya faced the wall as she put on her coat, and looked at the rose Patrick had given her. She removed it from the bookcase and quickly surveyed the room for a special place to display it, and settled on taping it to the chalkboard. That way, Patrick could see it every time he looked at the board and know that his teacher really appreciated his gift; even if it weren't initially intended for her.

On her way out the door, Maya prayed that Patrick would have a good night, and that Lloyd didn't have any more surprises up his sleeve, because all she had to give him was a silk tie and a box of chocolate turtles.

Chapter 17

Walking close to his teacher, Patrick skipped out of the recreation center where his basketball game was played. A newcomer to Monumental Baptist's youth league, he was lucky to have had the chance to play most of the game. And Maya was glad his team had won. After his disappointment on Friday when his mother did not show, Patrick held on to the hope that she would make it to his first game. But she never came. When Maya arrived ten minutes earlier than anticipated, she found Patrick stationed by the main doors, refusing to leave until it was time to warm up. It took almost the entire first quarter before the frown on his face completely disappeared.

"Thanks for coming," a triumphant Patrick exclaimed as he walked down the street beside his teacher.

"I wouldn't have traded it for the world," Maya said and hugged the miniature champion.

Maya stopped at her car and searched the small crowd leaving the center and wondered where Mr. Gregorio had gone. On the way out of the building, he fell behind to talk to Patrick's coach, but now he was nowhere in sight. Wherever he was, Maya hoped he wasn't going to be much longer. Though the temperature wasn't below freezing, her nose was numb from the cold, and she needed to look at the rental property in Lansdowne before heading to Lloyd's for dinner.

Oblivious to the cold weather, Patrick replayed the highlights of his game as they waited for his father, and after an abbreviated account of the first-half, Maya heard someone call Patrick's name. Within seconds, a woman with a belly as long and swollen as a ripe watermelon charged down the street toward them, repeatedly shouting his name. Mr. Gregorio chased after the woman, trying to get a hold of her arm, but the pregnant woman yanked her body away every time he caught up with her.

"Lena!" Mr. Gregorio yelled. "Lena, hold up! You can't keep doing this to him."

"That's my mom," Patrick said nonchalantly. The excited child that stood before Maya only seconds ago was gone. "She must've forgotten what time my game started."

"Better late than never, right?" Maya said, trying to shed a positive light on the situation.

Patrick shrugged his shoulders and waited for his mother to reach him.

"Hey, baby. Sorry I'm late, but I'm here now," his mother said and picked at his small afro with her hand. Patrick's mother turned slightly, and quickly analyzed Maya from head to toe. "Hello, I'm Patrick's mother. And you are?"

Hoping to avoid further embarrassment, Mr. Gregorio intervened. "This is Ms. Richards, Patrick's teacher."

Focusing on her son again, Patrick's mother kissed his forehead. "Want to go to Red Lobster?"

"We already have plans," Mr. Gregorio replied dryly. "Why don't you try again next week?"

"I'm here now," Patrick's mother snapped and held her belly.

Used to his parents' squabbles, Patrick stood between them. "I wanna go. Mom might not be able to make it next week," he told his father.

There was an awkward moment of silence—Patrick's mother realizing she'd hurt her son, and Mr. Gregorio realizing he shouldn't stand in the way of her attempt to reconcile. "Okay," Mr. Gregorio said reluctantly, "but have him home by nine."

"Oh, so now I have a time limit with *my* son?" Patrick's mother put her arm around him, and as she walked away, shouted, "I'll call you when I'm ready to drop him off!"

Mr. Gregorio watched them walk down the street and get into an old Ford Taurus. "I'm sorry you had to see that," Mr. Gregorio said as he watched them drive off into the distance. "Next week she'll forget she even has a son."

Not sure what to say, Maya sensed that Mr. Gregorio needed a friend. "Just be the best father you can be. Everything else will fall into place."

Almost immediately, the strong muscles in Mr. Gregorio's face relaxed. "You're right. Now let's go get you a place to live before your cheeks turn red," he said and grinned. "Since I know how great you are with directions, you wanna follow me?"

Maya playfully rolled her eyes. "Do I *really* need to answer that question?"

"I'll make sure I drive slow enough for you," he teased as Maya got into her car.

Mr. Gregorio flashed his signature smile, showing off his straight white teeth. "Give me a minute to drive my car around the corner."

Maya nodded, and as he walked down the street, her eyes were drawn to his urban stroll. *The man even walks sexy,* she thought, and immediately looked down at her cup holder. It was unprofessional to think of her student's father in that way. Besides, Lloyd was just as attractive . . . just many years older.

The light on her cell phone flashed and Maya removed it from her cup holder. She had seven missed calls. Maya would almost bet they were all from Lloyd. She hadn't spoken to him since she'd wasted two hours looking at apartments in Montgomery County. That was at 10:30 this morning. It was now a quarter to four and dinner was supposed to start at five. By the time she made it home to shower and change, the earliest she'd be able to make it to Southwest Philly would be 7:30.

Expecting to see his number, Maya scrolled through her missed calls, but only one was from Lloyd. The rest were from an unknown number. "I hope telemarketers haven't put my number on some kind of list," she grumbled, and then texted Lloyd to let him know she was going to be late. While she waited for him to respond, Mr. Gregorio's Honda Accord pulled alongside her car. She thought about calling Lloyd, but there was a law against using cell phones while driving. In addition, it would've been rude to make Mr. Gregorio wait. So she put her phone back in the cup holder and hoped the text she sent would suffice.

Avoiding the highway, Mr. Gregorio and Maya traveled to Lansdowne through the city streets and areas Maya never knew existed. With its tree-lined streets and obvious interest in the arts and cultural activity, Maya couldn't believe that she lived so close to such a unique neighborhood. In an odd way, she found the small suburb appealing.

Mr. Gregorio turned onto a small residential street not far from the main road, and Maya instantly fell in love with the well-kept Victorian-style homes along the street. There weren't many places to park, but Mr. Gregorio let Maya have the space closest to the house. It took three attempts before she successfully parallel parked, and when Maya got out of her car, Mr. Gregorio was laughing at her from across the street.

"How did you pass your driving test?" he joked with his winning smile.

"So I need a little work," she replied and followed him to a redbrick house three houses from the corner. The porch of the rental property was small, but Maya could picture herself sitting in a chair and sipping a cool glass of ice tea on a warm summer day. Without seeing the inside of the house, she already felt at home.

"I used to hang out here when my friend was single. We have so many memories here." Realizing that he may have said too much, Mr. Gregorio unlocked the door and pushed it open. "Not any wild memories. The kind good friends—"

Maya cut him off before he caught himself in a web of lies. "This was the bachelor pad, huh?"

Mr. Gregorio chuckled softly. "We used to play cards, but this hasn't been a hang out spot in over three years."

"Let me guess, your friend got married and the wife shut all that down."

Laughing harder, Mr. Gregorio walked into the living room. "Isn't that how it always happens?"

"Men would be clueless without a woman. I'm sure your friend is a happier man now."

Mr. Gregorio looked directly at her with a subtle twinkle in his soft brown eyes. "On most days, but don't you think a woman needs a man too?"

Maya looked away from him. There was something captivating about his eyes. "Yes, we do need each other, and the world would be a better place if everyone believed that."

"Well, check out the place. I'll wait here for you," he said and sat on a folding chair by the fireplace.

"I won't be long," she said, reminding herself that Lloyd was waiting on her.

"Take your time," Mr. Gregorio said and took a BlackBerry from his pocket. "Holler if you need me."

As Maya toured the three-bedroom house, she wrote notes on a notepad she had in her purse. The house was near perfect. Compared to the apartment she'd shared with Kenneth, the house was a mini mansion. Maya had finally found a place that met her standards.

"What do you think?" Mr. Gregorio asked when she was done touring the house.

"I think this a very nice place," Maya replied and stood in the middle of the living room. She'd already envisioned what the house would look like once her paintings and sculptures were in place. "I'm almost afraid to ask, but how much is the rent?" A place this nice had to be more then she planned to pay for an apartment.

Mr. Gregorio reached into his pocket and handed Maya a folded paper clipping. "I printed this off for you. All the info you need is on there."

Maya scanned the information and stopped when she read: $1,200 a month.

"My buddy might be able to knock off a couple hundred, if you're interested," he said as if he could read Maya's thoughts. "His wife is eager to rent the place out, and I already gave you a strong recommendation."

Twelve hundred was a great deal of money, but Maya could afford it. She was able to save a considerable amount of money when she lived with Kenneth. "This is a great place, but let me review my budget before I make a final decision."

"Fair enough. My friend's number is on that paper when you're ready or if you have any questions. Is that cool?"

"It's more than cool, Mr. Gregorio. I'll give him a call next week." She didn't have to look over her budget or waste time viewing another apartment. The townhouse was perfect. And even if Mr. Gregorio's friend didn't lower the rent, Maya was going to sign the lease.

Maya crossed the Gray's Ferry Bridge then drove a few blocks to Woodland Avenue and made a left. The streetlights on the block were dim, so she had to drive slow enough to read the house numbers. Unlike the homes in Lansdowne, the houses on Woodland Avenue seemed more compact. At the corner, a group of men, smoking and drinking from brown paper bags, eyed her car suspiciously and Maya loosened her grip on the steering wheel so they wouldn't think she was lost or nervous.

Maya checked the address on the paper she'd written the directions on. She was definitely on the right street. Continuing down the block, it was easy to identify Lloyd's house. The light from inside was bright and lit up the tiny numbers stuck to the brick wall. Instead of driving around the corner, Maya put the car in reverse and backed up until she saw an open parking space. Parallel parking on the left side of the street was always challenging, but she took a deep breath and made it into the snug space after one try.

Uncomfortable in her fancy high-heeled pumps and three-quarter-length leather coat, Maya made sure her coat was buttoned when she got out of the car. As Maya rushed to Lloyd's door, the men down the street whistled at her and she quickly pressed the doorbell. She pushed the bell so fast that she nicked the side of her hand on a loose wire hanging from the screen door. Wincing quietly, she looked through the spaces of blinds on the window.

After standing in the cold for what felt like two minutes, Maya looked through the front window. The lights and the television in the living room were on, but she didn't see anyone. In case Lloyd hadn't heard the bell the first time, Maya pressed it again. Still, there wasn't any action. *Where is he?* Lloyd knew Maya was in the vicinity, and should've been waiting for her by the door.

A little annoyed, Maya knocked on the door with her fist, and seconds later, Robert ran down the steps from the second floor. Dressed in jeans and a ribbed turtleneck sweater, he opened the door and removed a toothpick from his mouth. "Hey, Maya. Our bell broke last week. Have you been outside long?" he asked when he saw Maya's knees shaking.

"I get cold fast." Maya quickly entered the house. Realistically, her being cold wasn't Robert's fault. Had Maya worn warmer clothes or a longer coat, her knees wouldn't have been knocking together.

Looking around the house, it was clear the brothers lived in a bachelor pad. Plastic cups were lined behind a plant on the mantle, sports and men's magazines rested at the foot of a worn reclining chair, and the house plant on top of a wooden bookshelf looked as if it hadn't been watered in weeks. The faux stucco walls were bare and chipped in several places, and the dingy vinyl blinds desperately needed to be replaced.

"My brother must really like you. He hasn't cooked a real meal for anyone in a long time. Can I take your coat?"

Slowly, Maya unbuttoned her coat, unveiling the halter dress Lloyd bought. She hadn't expected Robert to be home, and was uncomfortable in her handkerchief dress. Like a good brother, Robert did his best not to stare, but Maya caught him examining her when she completely removed her coat. "Is Lloyd still cooking?" On cue, Lloyd appeared in an apron and chef's hat.

"I thought I heard your voice," Lloyd said cheerfully, and relieved. Maya handed him her coat.

"It was good to see you again," Robert said, then backed into the next room and removed a coat from the back of a chair. "Save some food me for me," he begged and walked out the front door.

"I thought you'd never get here," he stated, then grabbed Maya by the waist and spun her around gradually. "You look lovely. I love this dress. You're like an angel."

Blushing, Maya moved away from him. She had yet to get use to his constant flattery and charm. "Well, you better take your eyes off me. I'm ready to eat."

"Okay, beautiful. Have a seat. Give me five minutes to set up."

When Lloyd left the room, Maya sat on the edge of a caramel-colored sofa and casually observed her surroundings. In the center of an antique china cabinet, graduation pictures of

Lloyd and Robert were prominently displayed next to what looked like an old black and white picture of their parents. Maya leaned on the arm of the sofa and crossed her legs, shaking her foot rhythmically to the light jazz playing in the next room, and within seconds she dozed off.

Awakened by Lloyd's strong hands on her shoulder, Maya had temporarily forgotten that she was at his place. "Long day?" he asked, no longer dressed in his cooking gear.

Slightly embarrassed, Maya yawned. "I guess so."

Lloyd helped Maya up from the sofa and guided her to a cluttered dining room. "I hope you still have that appetite," Lloyd said, and pulled out a chair as far as it could go without bumping into the cabinet behind it.

Overlooking the fact that the table was too large for the room, Maya slid onto the plastic-covered seat. "I sure do."

In the center of the table, a collection of un-scented candles burned slowly next to a colorful bouquet of flowers. The arrangement was like a spread from an exquisite food magazine. On each placemat were healthy portions of a Salisbury steak, baby baked potatoes, and spinach. Maya closed her eyes and savored each individual spice with pleasure. The room may have been cramped, but Maya was impressed by Lloyd's dinner presentation.

Lloyd sat down across from her and poured each of them a glass of red wine. "I hope everything is to your liking. I haven't cooked this much since I left the Marines."

"When were you in the Marines?" Maya stared at the full glass of wine. She'd never had more than a half glass of champagne.

Lloyd peeled the melted wax from the sides of the candles on the table and wrapped it in a napkin. "I wasn't a soldier. I worked as a chef after I wasn't picked up by the NFL. Then after Lanecia was born I decided to become a teacher." He put the napkin on the long table behind him. "But enough about that. Eat up. I want you to grade my cooking skills."

"I'm a tough grader," replied Maya, ready to sink her teeth into the steak. "Are you gonna bless the food, or should I?"

Lloyd stretched his hands across the table and Maya grabbed them. As he blessed the food, he rubbed Maya's petite hands, and before saying, "Amen," thanked God for sending him an angel.

After dinner, Maya and Lloyd sat on opposite ends of the couch, watching the Blockbuster rental, *Once*. The scene was like a picture from the life she once shared with Kenneth.

"Do you have a blanket handy?" Maya asked midway through the movie.

"I'd much rather cover your shoulders with my arms."

Maya almost insisted he give her a blanket, but considering the fact that he'd been a gentleman from the very beginning, she nervously inched over to him and nestled comfortably under his arm. By the end of the movie, Maya was so relaxed that she'd fallen to sleep.

When she woke up, the room was dark and she was wrapped in Lloyd's arms. She figured Lloyd had turned the television off when the movie ended and fallen asleep too. Though Maya could've driven home, she felt a bit woozy from the wine and decided to rest another hour before attempting to leave.

Maya kicked off her shoes and shifted her weight to get more comfortable, and without realizing it, placed her arm around Lloyd's waist, causing him to reposition himself as well. It didn't take long for Maya to doze off again, and for a moment, the gentle brush up and down her arm felt like a dream. In response to the touch, she rubbed Lloyd's stomach delicately, and soon the two were engaged in a passionate kiss. One thing led to another, and before long, Lloyd had taken off his pants. It was then that Maya realized she wasn't dreaming, yet as she watched Lloyd open the condom he conveniently had in his pants pocket, she didn't tell him to stop.

When they were done making love, Maya leaned back into Lloyd's arms and stared at the cracks in the ceiling while Lloyd played with the tiny beads on her dress. They lay silently in the dark—Maya in shock, and Lloyd breathing heavy from their round of passion.

Lloyd brushed Maya's arm with the tips of his fingers. "What are you thinking?"

"I can't believe what just happened."

"I know. It was great, wasn't it?"

Maya sat up and pulled her dress down. "It's not every day that I have sex with a man who isn't mine. Did you spike the wine?" she joked half-heartedly. She was usually more responsible, especially when it came to intimacy. How could she have sex with Lloyd, a man she'd been dating less than two months? It was close to a year before she and Kenneth spent an entire night together. Blaming alcohol for her lack of control would've been easy, but if Maya were being honest, she had to admit that she'd been longing for affection.

Lloyd turned Maya's face so that he was look-ing into her eyes. "I'm not in this for games, Maya. I'm crazy about you. And I am your man if you'll have me. I wouldn't pursue you as hard as I've been if I didn't want you to be my woman." Lloyd kissed her shoulder gently. "So stop wor-rying."

Only Maya couldn't help but worry. "How are you so sure about your feelings, Lloyd? I know we've known each other for a while, but that's as coworkers. That doesn't mean—"

Lloyd placed his finger over Maya's lips. "When I saw you for the very first time, God told me that you were going to be my wife one day. I just had to be patient. So don't worry about what happened here tonight. It was meant to be."

Instantly, Proverbs 18:22 came to mind. *He who finds a wife finds a good thing and obtains favor from the Lord*. Maya's mother had written that scripture on an index card and taped it to her vanity when she moved back home. It was supposed to encourage Maya every morning. "God's going to send someone special to you, Pumpkin," Mrs. Richards recited every morning before she left for work.

Have my prayers for a husband come true? At church, she'd heard testimonies from couples who knew who they were going to marry the second they laid eyes on them. Though Maya knew not to question God, Maya wasn't sure she believed in love at first sight. Love, in her opinion, happened over time, and after being exposed to the mood changes, faults, and strengths of a significant other.

"This isn't the way I wanted our first time to be. Sex on the couch is for high school kids."

Lloyd laughed aloud. "It was the heat of the moment. We'll prepare better for the next time. Or, we could go upstairs and—" Maya heard keys at the door and jumped to her feet. "Relax, babe. It's only Robert," said Lloyd, as if lying half-naked on the couch was all right.

Ignoring him, Maya quickly slid into her underwear laying on the arm of the couch. "Where's your bathroom?" she asked and put on her shoes.

Lloyd pointed upstairs and put his pants back on. "I'm sorry. I thought he was staying at Tanya's tonight."

"No problem." Maya ran upstairs. Inside the bathroom, she found a fresh rag in the linen closet and freshened up, and when she was done, she sat on the toilet. She'd never done anything like this before. Not even in high school or college.

Through the thin walls, Maya could hear the brothers talking downstairs. She couldn't make out the words clearly, but she wondered if Robert knew what she and his brother had done. How could she go downstairs and pretend that nothing had happened? Embarrassed and ashamed of her actions, Maya walked to the mirror and tried to calm down. Whether she liked it or not, she had to go back downstairs.

Maya smoothed her hair with her fingers to make herself more presentable, and to help her relax. *God, please tell me that I haven't made a mistake,* she prayed, and then realized that Lloyd had gone to great lengths to create a perfect evening. Lloyd hadn't done anything to make her feel like his intentions were false. And although the relationship was moving faster than she could handle, she'd slept with him. It was too late to slow things down now.

Once Maya was ready, she went back downstairs. Lloyd was still sitting in the same position, only with the remote in his hand. "I better get going," she told him and went to the closet to get her coat.

"You sure you don't want to stay the night? Robert went back to Tanya's house."

"I can't stay. My mo—" Maya began and caught herself. Although Lloyd knew she lived with her parents, using that as an excuse at thirty-six seemed strange. "I have Sunday School in the morning." Suddenly the idea of teaching a bunch of five year olds a lesson about sin felt wrong.

Lloyd didn't want her to leave, but understood. "Next time, you need to pack an overnight bag," he said, then put on his coat so he could walk Maya to her car. "Make sure you call me when you're home safe."

Maya dropped her coat on the dining room table when she walked into her house. Her parents had gone to Virginia for the weekend, so there would be no one to yell at her in the morning. She tucked her purse under her arm, and then trudged up the stairs, gradually removing an item of clothing. And like a loyal companion, Langston followed her. By the time she reached her bedroom, she was down to just her underwear. As soon as Maya fell on the bed, Langston jumped onto her stomach.

"Hey, little guy." She rubbed beneath his fluffy chin. With her free hand, Maya went inside her purse and took out her cell phone. If she didn't tell someone about her night, she wouldn't get an ounce of sleep. Maya sat up and sent Gwen a text: Lloyd and I did it . . .

And before Maya could put the phone on the nightstand Gwen called.

"You slept with the old man?" shouted Gwen over a noisy crowd.

The jazz playing in the background was too loud, so Maya held her phone an inch away from her ear. "Is this the only way I can get you to call me back on a Saturday night?" She hadn't talked to Gwen in three days.

"I only have a few minutes before Justin comes back with our drinks. So be quick. How was he?"

"I can't kiss and tell. But guess what?"

"You did something bigger than have sex with Grandpa?"

Ignoring her sister's taunts, Maya continued to talk as she prepared for a shower. "That *grandpa* is my man, now," she said, needing feedback from her sister to somehow validate what she'd done.

"Wow! You must've put it on him. I guess you really like this guy, huh?"

"It all happened so fast actually. We were watching a movie, and the next thing I know—"

"His hand was on your thigh, right?" Gwen couldn't stop laughing.

"You think we did it too soon?"

"It doesn't matter what I think, Maya. Are you okay with what happened?"

Maya was silent. Even with Lloyd trying to comfort her, there was something keeping Maya from being at peace with the intimate act.

"Look, Maya, you can't beat yourself up over something you can't change. You like him, right?"

"Yes." That she knew for sure.

"So are you bothered that you slept with him too soon, or that you're in a relationship?"

Finding it hard to speak, Maya moaned to indicate that she didn't know the answer to Gwen's question.

"You need to be able to answer that, sis. And you really need to share your feelings with Lloyd. If you don't, it could complicate things later."

"I know."

"Well, Justin's back, so I need to go. But make sure you call me after church. You are still going to church in the morning, right?"

"Yes, Sunday School is depending on me," Maya answered, then released Gwen, so she could enjoy her evening.

Before saying her prayers and showering, Maya dialed Lloyd's number. She wanted him to know that she'd made it home safely, but the call went straight to voice mail. It wasn't like Lloyd to not answer his phone, especially when she called. Maya hung up and counted to ten before dialing his number again, only to get the same result. Rather than think the worst, she left a message. It was possible that she'd worn her old man out and he was sound asleep.

Chapter 18

One by one, Maya's Sunday School group exited the classroom. While the last four children waited for their parents to pick them up, Maya stacked the folding chairs against the wall. Claudia entertained the five year olds to pass time, singing catchy, hip songs about Jesus. Maya was glad Claudia offered to help her teach this morning. She was dragging and needed her extra energy.

"Good morning," First Lady Williams said when she entered the room. The children jumped with excitement in her presence, especially Victoria, the first lady's daughter.

"Look, Mommy!" Victoria shouted and ran to her mother.

"What did you learn today?" the first lady asked the remaining children as she glanced through the folder Victoria gave her.

Immediately, Victoria took charge, and with a fiery personality looked at her classmates. "A good decision is when you listen to your teacher. A good decision gets a—" Victoria motioned for them to respond. There was no question that she was going to follow in her father's footsteps. In unison, the children pointed their thumbs toward the ceiling. "Not listening to your parents is a bad decision," continued Victoria. "That gets what?" The children giggled as they made a *wa-wa* sound and pointed their thumbs toward the floor.

"Very cute," First Lady Williams said with a smile.

"We even did skits, Mommy," Victoria added. "I was on the bad decision team. I can show you tonight, okay?"

"Sounds like you all had a lot of fun," the first lady said and faced Maya. "You have a gift, Ms. Richards. Thanks for blessing this ministry. See you upstairs."

"Well," Claudia said when the first lady was gone. "That must make you feel good."

Maya stacked the last folding chair then leaned against the tall file cabinet. "It does feel good to be acknowledged by the lady of the house."

"That was a good lesson. I think I'm going to use it with my *repeat offenders* at school," Claudia kidded.

Purposely avoiding eye contact, Maya chuckled under her breath. She walked to the corner of the room and took a broom from a closet. A woman in her early forties poked her head inside the room, and then quickly realized she was in the wrong place.

Claudia pulled out her makeup case and touched up her lipstick once the children had gone. "You want to tell me what's on your mind?"

Maya swept tiny pieces of paper into one pile. "Nothing. Why? What's up with you?"

"You barely talked to me all morning, Maya. I think I've known you long enough to know when something's wrong."

Maya wanted her best friend to know about last night, but feared what her reaction would be.

The woman who had peeped in earlier passed the classroom again, and Maya headed to the door. "I wonder if she's lost."

Claudia stepped in front of her friend. "Don't change the subject. I'm sure someone else can help her. Is everything all right with you?"

Maya smiled, pretending all was well. "I'm fine." She placed the broom back inside the closet.

Claudia didn't buy Maya's act. "I'm not gonna leave you alone until you tell me the truth, so you might as well spill the beans."

Knowing Claudia wouldn't let up, Maya took a deep breath. "Lloyd and I are official." Maya waited for a response, but Claudia said nothing. "Lloyd and I are a couple," she repeated louder.

Claudia took a brush from her purse and fixed her hair until it was tangle-free. "That's nice."

Expecting an explosive reaction, Maya was surprised by Claudia's calmness and decided to push the envelope even further. "We had sex last night."

Claudia kept her cool. She put her brush back inside her purse. "You *really* like him?" she queried, then put on her suit jacket, which was hanging on the back of the door.

"Obviously," Maya replied with confidence. She didn't want Claudia to sense any reservations. "But why don't you like him? It has to be something more than his age or that we work together."

"It's not his age that concerns me anymore. An older man may actually be good for you. It's just that this isn't like you, Maya. I mean, what do you *really* know about this man? Have you met his children? Do you know *why* he and his wife got divorced? Are you even sure they're divorced?"

"Relax, Claudia. Lloyd and I are still getting to know each other, but . . ." Maya sighed before continuing. She knew Claudia wasn't going to like what she was about to say. "I've been praying for someone, and I think Lloyd may be God's answer to my prayer."

"You prayed for a man who would sleep with you after dating for only a month?" Claudia snapped.

"Are you really gonna lecture *me* about that?" Claudia's past wasn't exactly a model of perfection.

"I'm not ashamed of being a teen mother," Claudia bounced back. "I wish I knew Jesus in high school. But you're a grown woman; a saved grown woman at that, talking in church on Sunday morning about having sex."

Annoyed, Maya felt betrayed. Best friends were supposed to be supportive, whether they agreed with one another or not. "Be happy for me!"

Claudia rolled her eyes. She didn't want to argue in church. "If you're happy, I'll try to be. Just don't expect me to bite my tongue if I think he's taking advantage of you."

From experience, Maya knew that Claudia couldn't promise anything more than what she said. "I guess I'll have to accept that."

"I hope you took notes from your lesson today," Claudia said and turned off the lights.

"Making good decisions doesn't only apply to children."

"Look, service is about to start, so let's just drop it." When Maya stepped out of the room, she bumped into the unknown woman from earlier. "Can I help you find something?"

"I'm sorry." She reminded Maya of the comedian Sherri Shepherd—short and top heavy with thin legs. "I'm trying to find the ladies' room."

"Have you been looking all this time?" Maya inquired.

"Oh, no, I was looking for someone. I found her, but now I'm in need of a bathroom."

"If you walk to the end of this hallway, the bathroom is the last door on the left."

"Thank you," the woman replied, and headed down the hall.

Maya and Claudia made sure the woman made it to the bathroom, and then went upstairs to the sanctuary. "I'll see you after service," Maya said, and the two friends parted ways—Claudia to the far right, and Maya to the fifth row from the pulpit.

The choir began a remixed version of "Call Him Up" as Maya sat in her assigned seat next to Aunt Mary. She listened to the Young Adult choir and connected to every word. By the end of the song, she decided that Claudia's feelings about Lloyd weren't going to be a concern. It didn't matter that Claudia wasn't fond of him. Lloyd was her new man and, if God approved, that's all that mattered. Claudia would just have to get used to that.

Chapter 19

A teardrop rolled off of Maya's nose and she opened her eyes. "Are you crying?" she asked Lloyd.

Lloyd rolled off of Maya and lay on his back. "I don't know what I've done to deserve you."

It was Friday, almost three weeks from the first night they made love, and Lloyd had gone through great lengths to prove that Maya was his woman. Between her math program, Sunday School class, and his coaching responsibilities, their days to be together were limited. But Lloyd made sure he kept their coffeehouse and weeknight commitments. Weekends depended on basketball schedules, but they made sure to fit in quality time, even if it was for an hour.

Maya climbed on top of Lloyd and wiped his cheeks with her hands. "Guess we have God to thank for bringing us together." She tenderly kissed the tip of his nose.

"I think I'm in love."

Maya shifted her eyes from Lloyd's and focused on the curled hairs on his chest. She couldn't bring herself to say she loved him too. It was the end of March, but it was still too soon for love.

"I know you don't love me. But lucky for you, I'm a patient man."

Maya rolled off of him and lay on her side. "I care about you a lot, but give me some time, Lloyd. When I do say it, you'll know I really mean it."

"Don't worry. I know you'll say the words one day," Lloyd replied, more so to encourage himself.

Maya sensed that their touching moment had been spoiled, and leaned up a little in order to see the digital clock below the television. "It's ten-fifteen already?" she bellowed and jumped out of bed.

"Can't you stay the night?"

"You know I can't do that." Maya rushed to put on her clothes, which were thrown about the floor.

"You're an adult, Maya. Your mother understands that."

Maya searched for her shoes under the bed. "You don't know my mother."

"Baby, please. I want you to stay with me tonight."

"I'm moving in two weeks." Maya sat on the edge of the bed. She put one foot inside her leather mule, and then faced Lloyd. "You can't wait until then?"

Lloyd poked out his lips and seductively stroked Maya's arm. "I need you tonight."

Maya sighed. It was too late to call her mother, so Maya called her sister instead. Mrs. Richards had taught her daughters that it was important someone always knew where they were. Though Lloyd wasn't a stranger to Maya, he was to her mother and to Gwen. After she got off the phone, Maya put it on the nightstand, took off her clothes, and crawled back into bed with her man. "I'll stay, but I *have* to leave by six.

At the sound of Maya's cell phone, Lloyd moaned and pressed his body into her side. Planning to turn the ringer off, Maya reached for the phone and checked the caller ID. At such an early hour, she figured it was her mother. But when Maya saw Mr. Gregorio's number, she instantly remembered that it was Saturday, Patrick's basketball game day. Maya hadn't missed any of his games since he joined the team, and she wasn't about to disappoint him today. "Hello." She tried to sound fully awake, but she didn't fool Mr. Gregorio.

"Hey, Ms. Richards. Did I wake you?"

Maya cleared her throat and sat up. "I'm glad you called. I might've slept through the morning."

"You must've been partying last night."

"I was playing Spades with my friends," Maya said in an attempt to be funny. He knew Maya was a homebody. Mr. Gregorio was the one to play cards until wee hours in the morning.

Mr. Gregorio burst into laughter. "You're funny, but I play for fun now with the men's ministry and not for money. We're trying to keep the guys off the streets on Saturday nights."

Maya felt foolish for making fun of his playing cards hobby. "That sounds cool. I was actually watching movies," she corrected, and placed her feet on the cold floor.

"Well, I didn't mean to wake you. Patrick mentioned that he forgot to tell you that his game was going to be at Sharon Baptist this morning. I hope you can still make it."

Hearing a male voice through the phone, Lloyd opened his eyes and mumbled words Maya couldn't understand. She ignored him and asked Mr. Gregorio if the game started at the same time.

"Probably closer to eleven. Those guys never start on time."

Maya attempted to get out of bed, but Lloyd grabbed her waist and she fell backward, nearly losing control of her phone. "Okay," she said, holding the phone tight to her ear. "I might be a little late, but I'll be there."

Before hanging up, Mr. Gregorio mentioned the rental property in Lansdowne. "I heard you signed the lease."

Upset that Maya wasn't paying attention to him, Lloyd threw the covers off of his body. Maya motioned for him to be patient. "Yes, your friend took off two hundred dollars. Thanks for telling me about the place."

"No, problem. Consider it repayment for all you do with my son. I believe you're his angel."

An angel? Though Lloyd had often referred to Maya as an angel, hearing Mr. Gregorio call her one had a different effect. She knew she was gifted to be a teacher, but Mr. Gregorio implied something much deeper.

"Well, I better get moving. I have to pick up my sister. She wants to go to the game too."

Maya said good-bye then hit the end call button, and for several seconds she stared at her phone. Mr. Gregorio had touched her spirit.

Lloyd noticed that her mind was somewhere else. "What's up, babe?"

Snapping back into reality, Maya stood up and faced Lloyd. "Nothing, I just forgot about Patrick's game. I better go or I'll be late."

"If I didn't know any better, I'd believe Patrick was your son." Lloyd eased out of the bed. "My game isn't until seven, so I can go with you this time."

"You can't go, Lloyd." Maya put on her clothes. "There will be kids from school there. You don't want them to start spreading rumors about us, do you?"

"The kids already suspect something," Lloyd pointed out, and Maya looked shocked. "Oh, c'mon, Maya. We're together all the time."

"Then we need to stop being together so much. What if Mrs. Bridges finds out?"

"Look, nobody has mentioned anything so far, so it's not a problem. But if you're worried, I can sit far away from you. Although, Patrick's dad needs to see us together."

"Mr. Gregorio isn't worried about me." Maya was startled by Lloyd's jealous remark. "And regardless of that, where's the trust in me?"

"I trust you, but I don't trust men."

Maya took a comb and headband from her purse and fixed her hair. "As long as you trust me, we're good. So chill out and get back in bed." Pouting like a child who'd been placed on punishment, Lloyd was disappointed, but got back into bed.

"Hey, I was thinking," Maya said before leaving. "Can you come to my church on Sunday?"

The invitation seemed to perk up Lloyd. "Will I get to meet your family?"

"Only if you show up."

"Oh, I'll show up." Lloyd beamed. "Are we still on for the art exhibit tonight?"

Maya walked back to the bed and kissed him good-bye. "I'll call you on my way there."

On the way downstairs, Maya didn't see Tanya resting on the couch, until she coughed. "Good morning," Maya said, hoping Tanya was in a friendlier mood.

"Hey," Tanya muttered, and fixed the scarf on her head. "I didn't know you stayed the night."

"Lloyd and I fell asleep watching movies," Maya explained as she buttoned her coat. For some reason, Tanya made her feel more nervous than her own mother.

Tanya stared at Maya with an unnerving smirk on her face. "I better finish breakfast," she spouted and dragged herself back to the kitchen.

Maya didn't know what Tanya's problem was with her, but she couldn't harp on it this morning. She had a basketball game to get to.

***

Maya's hand trembled when she put the key inside the lock. Her parents were early risers, so Maya knew they were awake and probably halfway through breakfast. Taking a deep breath, Maya closed her eyes. *I'm grown,* she reminded herself and pushed the door open.

The house was quiet and Langston wasn't at the door to meet her. Something was off, but Maya didn't have time to conduct a thorough investigation. She only hoped Langston hadn't thrown up another hairball. Scurrying up to her bedroom, she was happy to see Langston lying across the bed, apparently in a deep sleep. From the patches of hair on her comforter, Maya guessed that he slept there all night. "Hey, Lank," she whispered, but Langston didn't move, not even a mellow meow. "Mad at me?" Maya asked and rubbed behind his ears. Langston barely opened his eyes, and Maya knew that meant he was mad. "I missed you too, big fella," she cooed and rubbed his stomach until he purred. It was then that Maya knew all was forgiven.

After taking care of Langston, Maya kicked off her shoes and went to her closet to search for a comfortable outfit. Settling on a stylish pair of jeans and an old college sweatshirt, Maya tossed them over her forearm. She shut the closet door and gasped. Mrs. Richards was sitting on her bed dressed in her gardening clothes. That would explain why Maya hadn't seen her when she came in. Every year, before the start of spring, Mrs. Richards was the first person in the neighborhood to evaluate and assess the needs of her garden. "Good morning, Mom."

"Good morning to you too," Mrs. Richards said as she picked individual cat hairs from Maya's comforter. "Your father and I were worried about you all night. I didn't know if you were in an accident or had gotten into some other trouble. I called your sister and I know she knew where you were, but didn't want to tell me." She shooed Langston off of the bed. "You could've called to let me know you weren't coming home."

Maya lay her clothes at the bottom of the bed and away from the cat hairs. "You don't have to call around for me, Mom, I'm not sixteen anymore."

"I didn't have this problem when you were sixteen." Mrs. Richards rolled the cat hairs into one tiny ball and set it on her lap. "Since you live here, it would be a great courtesy if you called when you're staying out all night. Or at least answer my call when I call your cell phone."

"You called?" Maya checked the phone in her purse for missed calls. Maya wanted to prove her mother wrong, but when she scrolled through the call list, there were several calls from her mother, as well as three from an unfamiliar number. Maya couldn't explain why she hadn't heard the phone ringing. It was likely she and Lloyd were too busy making love. How could she tell her mother that? "I'll call next time, okay?" Maya set the phone on her bed.

"That's all I'm asking, Pumpkin." Mrs. Richards stared at her daughter as if she knew the real reason why Maya hadn't answered her phone. "Who is this mystery man, anyway? I should at least know the name of the man keeping my daughter out all night."

"You'll meet him tomorrow at church. Now can I go shower? I need to get to Patrick's game."

"You just got home, Pumpkin. Now you're running out again?"

"I'll be home to—" Maya stopped herself before she made a promise she couldn't keep. Later tonight, she planned to meet Lloyd at the African American museum downtown. "We'll do something after church tomorrow, okay?" Maya sensed her mother missed having her around on a regular basis.

"I might have plans tomorrow." Mrs. Richards put on her garden hat and left the bedroom.

After a quick shower, Maya dressed and practically ran out of the house. If traffic was on her side, she'd only miss the first ten minutes of Patrick's game.

"Morning, Pumpkin," Mr. Richards called from the end of the driveway. Maya was in such a hurry that she hadn't seen him.

"What are you doing out, Daddy?" She opened her car door. Although the worst of the winter cold had past, fifty-seven degrees was still too cold for her father to be walking in. Since his heart attack, Mr. Richards tried to exercise on a regular basis, sometimes to the extreme.

Mr. Richards lifted his Dunkin Donuts coffee. "I needed to walk this morning."

Dunkin Donuts had to be a mile away, roundtrip. "Okay, but now go inside and rest for a bit." She got inside the car.

Mr. Richards held the car door, preventing Maya from closing it. "I know you're about to run off, but can I talk to you a minute?"

"Sure, Daddy." She was afraid that he wanted to discuss what happened last night. Maya's palms moistened and her heart rate accelerated with anticipation of what he had to say. Mr. Richards usually shied away from lecturing his children. That was Mrs. Richards's job. But when he did find it necessary to speak up, it was really serious. And even at thirty-six, that frightened Maya.

"I won't be long, but I need to say what's on my mind. I've been watching you the last few weeks. You've been moving in and out of here like a whirlwind and you haven't had time for your aunts or your mother lately. Now, I know you're a grown woman, but I'm still your father. I don't want you to get so caught up in someone or something that you forget who you are and that you have a family that loves you. We want to see you more than just at church."

Maya blinked several times to keep from crying. Though Mr. Richards didn't say it, Maya knew he blamed Lloyd for recent actions.

"I'm not chastising you, Pumpkin." I only want you to be careful. You can only move so fast for so long. Eventually, you slow down and fall hard." Mr. Richards reached inside Maya's car and squeezed her shoulders. "I don't want you to fall hard, Pumpkin, that's all."

"I know, Daddy." Maya wiped a tear from the side of her eye. "I'll make some changes."

"Okay, Pumpkin. I love you." Mr. Richards shut the car door. "Will I see you later?"

"I'll be home after the game," Maya told her father and meant it. She didn't know how Lloyd would react when she canceled their plans, but there was no way she was going to disappoint her father. And considering that she invited Lloyd to church on Sunday, Maya didn't want her parents, especially her father, to dislike Lloyd before getting to know him.

As Maya pulled off, she realized that there was one more requirement for her ideal man list and she made a mental note to add "is liked by my family and friends" when she made it home after the game.

Chapter 20

Sandwiched between her mother and Aunt Bess while trying not to appear anxious, Maya questioned whether or not Lloyd was going to make it to church. Service was due to start in fifteen minutes and Lloyd hadn't even called. This wasn't the first impression Maya wanted her family to have of him, especially after the talk she had with her father. When Maya talked to Lloyd last night, he was upset that she had to cancel their date, but promised that he'd be at church.

Sensing Maya's uneasiness, Aunt Bess touched her niece's hand. "Michael said traffic on seventy-six was heavy this morning."

Heavy traffic was not an acceptable excuse for Lloyd's tardiness. Lloyd didn't have to get on the highway. Once he crossed the Gray's Ferry Bridge, it was a straight drive down Spruce Street. "Maybe he's lost," Maya rationalized, though she didn't believe that. Monumental wasn't a difficult place to find. But no matter what the reason, unless he was seriously injured, Lloyd should've at least called.

Praise and worship started and Mrs. Richards gave Maya "the eye" as she stood up. Maya could only imagine what she was thinking. *Lloyd better have a great excuse.* She crossed her legs as she sat through praise and worship in a foul mood.

By the end of the announcements, Maya was past the stage of embarrassment. She was livid. How could he do this to her? As subtle as she could, Maya glanced at her watch, and then stood up. "I'll be back." Maya wanted to call Lloyd again. It would be the tenth time in less than an hour.

Maya eased down the aisle, and before she reached the end, recognized Lloyd among the latecomers entering the sanctuary. Not only had he arrived late, he'd arrived in style. In his trenchcoat, clean-shaven head and fresh-cut goatee, Lloyd favored the famous black detective, John Shaft. "That's him." Maya tapped her aunt's shoulder. "The one in the black leather."

Mrs. Richards stopped singing and looked behind her to get a better view. "How old is he? He looks like he should be dating Bess."

"Bess is taken," Michael teased and held Aunt Bess's hand.

Ignoring her mother, Maya waved to get Lloyd's attention, and when he reached the fifth row, motioned for him to sit in between her and Aunt Bess. As Lloyd settled, Maya quickly introduced him.

"Sorry I'm late," Lloyd said in a hushed tone. "I had to drop my daughters off at White Rock."

"No problem," Maya fibbed. She'd at least cooled off enough to enjoy the sermon. "You're just in time." She pointed to Pastor Williams walking to the pulpit.

Already energized, Pastor Williams positioned himself as he sang a medley of praise songs. "I was prepared to preach a message about deliverance, but last night I received a call—" The pastor stopped mid-sentence and broke out in a praise dance.

Following behind him, with lifted hands, the first lady repeatedly shouted, "Thank you!" The congregation had no idea why Pastor Williams was praising God, but several members joined in the victory dance too.

"I got a call last night from the owner of the store next to our church." The pastor was still moving his feet and on the brink of another dance. "Now saints . . . we've been searching for a decent building for a school and have been turned down more times than I can count. But last night, God performed a miracle."

In between shouts, Pastor Williams explained that the owner of the hardware store next to the church was moving his business to a different part of the city. He couldn't afford to maintain two stores, so he offered the church a huge discount to purchase the property. Once the legal papers were signed and renovations completed, the church would've only paid half of what they had budgeted for. "After five long years of praying and waiting on God, our dream finally came to pass."

The congregation exploded into an uproar of praises, and when the atmosphere calmed, Pastor Williams preached about the miracles of God and the importance of patience. "Faith without boundaries!" he shouted. "It's time for the church to stop complaining and wait on the Lord. There is no limit to what God can do. We need to trust that our dreams will come to pass in due season. Trust Him with your *whole* heart. I promise you, saints, God will never fail you."

Maya didn't have to ask Lloyd if he were enjoying the service. Occasionally she'd hear him yell, "Amen," or "Preach on preacher!" He didn't appear bothered that he was under Mrs. Richards's watchful and keen eye.

Near the end of the sermon, Pastor Williams sprinted across the pulpit and Lloyd jumped up and began speaking in tongues. Maya was startled. She'd never been with a man so emotionally in tune with God, and yet, as Lloyd uttered words Maya couldn't translate, she smiled and sat back in her seat. There was something attractive about a man who wasn't too proud to praise the Lord.

After the benediction, Mrs. Richards barely stepped a foot into the lobby before she barraged Lloyd with questions. "My daughter's been keeping you a secret. I know that you're a gym teacher at Huey. Are you from Philly? Did you go to college in the area?"

Mr. Richards touched his wife's arm, and guided her away from the sanctuary doors. "That's enough with the questions, honey. Let the man get to know the family."

"That's okay. I'd be the same way with my daughters."

"You have children?" Mrs. Richards asked, and then stared at Maya.

Afraid that her mother was intimidating him, Maya answered, "He has two beautiful girls."

"Lanecia is sixteen and Lauren is seven," Lloyd added, unmoved by Mrs. Richards's interrogation.

"So you've been married before?" continued Mrs. Richards.

"Yes . . . but only once."

Before Mrs. Richards could finish her inspection, First Lady Williams walked over to them, and Maya was relieved. It was the only way to silence her mother.

Enamored by the first lady's presence, Lloyd talked nonstop about the service and how it touched his spirit. The first lady listened intently, pleased that he had enjoyed his visit. "I hope you'll come back. My husband is filled with inspiring messages," she told him, then looked at Mrs. Richards. "That sure is a sharp peach suit."

Mrs. Richards casually twirled around so that everyone could capture the full effect of her double-pleated skirt. "Thank you. I got it on sale at Macy's last month."

"Well, you sure made a great choice," First Lady Williams said, then pulled Maya close. "Before I go, I have to tell you that Maya is an amazing Sunday School teacher. As a matter of fact, last night I prayed for a curriculum team for the new school, and Maya's name immediately came to mind." The first lady faced Maya and held her hand. "We could really use your talent."

"I'm sure she'll love to be a part of the team," Mrs. Richards chimed in, and Maya shot her a cold look. Where was she going to find time to commit to *another* project?

The first lady sensed Maya's hesitation and decided not to press the issue. "Pray about it, Maya, and come to my office when you're ready. I'd love to share the vision with you."

Maya felt that she had no choice but to respond favorably. "Okay. I'll call and schedule a time soon."

As soon as the first lady walked away, Mrs. Richards resumed her questioning. "Did I hear you say that you attend White Rock?"

"Yes, Ma'am."

"I know a few of the members. Do you know Brother Baldwin? He's a deacon."

Lloyd tried to place the name, but was coming up short. "I don't think I—"

Since Lloyd was having trouble, Mrs. Richards was ready with another name. "What about—"

"What about dinner? How does Red Lobster sound?" Maya interrupted. If she hadn't, Lloyd would've been answering questions until everyone had left the church.

"We have to take a rain check, Pumpkin. We're meeting a friend in Sharon Hill for brunch," Aunt Bess replied.

"What a shame," added Mrs. Richards. "I really wanted to spend more time with Lloyd."

"Don't worry, Mrs. Richards. This isn't the last time you'll see me. As a matter of fact, I'm gonna help Maya move next Saturday."

"Good," Mrs. Richards said, and then put on a flowery hat that matched the belt to her suit. "Guess I'll see you then."

After Maya kissed her family good-bye, Lloyd looked at his watch. "Before we leave, I need to call my daughters to make sure their mother is still going to pick them up. I'll just be a moment."

"Okay, I'll be in the bookstore when you're done." Maya walked across the parquet floor to the church bookstore.

As Maya browsed the new releases, she heard familiar voices behind her and turned around. Standing in the children's section were Claudia and her family. Before going over to them, Maya observed the way they interacted as a family, and wondered if God would ever bless her with a husband and children. The way Claudia's son hopped all over Bishop reminded Maya of the days she and Gwen used to play with her father. It would be a shame if she never had a chance to create similar memories with a family of her own.

"There's Aunt Maya," Claudia's youngest daughter called, and pointed in her direction.

Maya put the book she was holding back on the shelf and walked over to Claudia's family. "Hey, I thought you were going to early service?"

"That was the plan," Claudia said with a smug look, "but *someone* had trouble getting up this morning."

"Please don't get her started, Maya," Bishop replied. "She was the one who forgot to set the alarm clock."

"What would you two do without each other," Maya said, admiring their playful banter.

"I'd be lost," Claudia responded and grabbed her husband's hand.

"There you are," Lloyd bellowed, and Maya turned to face him. "I've been looking all over for you." Lloyd placed his arm around Maya's waist then pleasantly greeted Claudia and her husband.

To Maya's surprise, Claudia remained cordial and introduced Lloyd to her family. Right away, Maya thanked God for answering her prayer. Maybe Claudia had had a change of heart about Lloyd.

"Well," Claudia said, after a brief conversation about the sermon, "we need to hit the road. We're on our way to my mother's for dinner."

Claudia helped her son with his coat, and then looked at Lloyd. "Hope to see you next week."

Though Maya was happy about Claudia's behavior, she felt weird as she followed her family outside. They used to spend Sundays together after church, and Maya couldn't pinpoint when or why that had stopped; especially because she and Lloyd rarely saw each other on Sundays. Whatever the reason, Maya hoped things would soon change back to the way they were.

"So what do you think about my parents?" Maya asked Lloyd, after separating from Claudia and her crew.

Lloyd grinned confidently. "They were tough, but I think they like me."

Chapter 21

"Is Lloyd coming?" Mrs. Richards asked as she flipped the bacon on the frying pan. She'd been up since 5:30, preparing a huge southern-style breakfast in honor of Maya's moving day.

Maya hadn't spoken to Lloyd since last night, but he assured her that he'd be there. She removed a clean fork from the drying rack and took a forkful of home fries from a skillet on the stove. "He'll be here." She stuffed the seasoned potatoes inside her mouth.

Seated at the kitchen table, Aunt Mary pulled plump red grapes from their stems and tossed them into a large bowl. Maya walked to the table and put a handful of grapes in her hand. "You're gonna eat all the food," Aunt Mary said and smacked Maya's hand, just as she used to when she was young.

"I'm sorry, Auntie. Everything just looks so tasty," Maya replied and put two grapes in her mouth. As with most things, Mrs. Richards had gone overboard. The kitchen table was filled with food—bacon, eggs, grits, pancakes, biscuits, sausage, fresh fruit, and a couple pork chops. "Mom, you're really doing too much. People are going to be too tired to work."

"Breakfast jumpstarts the metabolism. We're going to need all the energy we can get this morning," Mrs. Richards explained. "Besides, I have to do something to keep my mind off of you leaving."

"I'm only going to Lansdowne. It's not California."

"Don't remind me," Mrs. Richards said and turned off the stove.

While Aunt Mary wasn't looking, Maya snuck a sausage link from a plate, and then kissed her mother. "Thank you. It's too much food, but you're the best."

Maya walked into the living room filled with boxes and checked her phone. There wasn't a call from Lloyd, so she assumed he was on his way. Mr. Gregorio, however, had sent her a text.

Good luck w/ ur move 2day. Let me no if u need my help.
Maya texted back: I'm good. But thx 4 offer.

She set her phone atop one of the boxes in the room and looked around. Maya never imagined that she'd one day live alone, but was looking forward to exploring her independence. Although her parents didn't want her to leave, they donated aged yet well-maintained furniture they were planning to replace within a few months. Maya scanned the room one last time to be sure all her boxes were accounted for, and noticed Langston sleeping on top of a pile of boxes. "Soon we'll be in our own home," she whispered, and as if he understood, Langston lifted his head and purred.

Maya's cell phone beeped and she thought it might be Lloyd or Mr. Gregorio returning a text. But when she looked at the screen, it was actually picture mail from a number she didn't recognize. Curious, she downloaded the image, and when it opened she was even more confused. Someone had sent a picture of Maya and Lloyd at the cabaret they attended, kissing on the dance floor. Several questions came to mind. Who would send it? Why would they send it? And how did they get her number?

Maya called the number back, but received an automated voice mail message. She looked at the picture again, and wondered if Lloyd had asked someone to send it. He wasn't technology savvy, nor did his cell phone have a camera.

"Breakfast is getting cold," Mrs. Richards yelled from the kitchen. "We can't wait for Lloyd any longer."

Maya saved the picture, with the intention of discussing it with Lloyd later, right after she talked to him about being late.

When Maya and Claudia pulled up to her new home, the men were unloading the U-Haul truck. Maya sighed at the sight of Michael and her father struggling to get a loveseat into the house. She felt guilty. *Maybe I should've accepted Mr. Gregorio's offer.* Although Mr. Richards thought he was Superman, Maya was concerned about all of the strenuous exercise. The plan had been to have five men—Mr. Bridges, Michael, Bishop, Eddie, and Lloyd—load and unload the truck, while the women, unpacked all the boxes and decorated Maya's new home. With one man short, Maya decided to help the men as best she could. And when she was done, she had a broken nail, sore back, and slight headache. Not to mention the tight curls she started with before breakfast had fallen.

With everyone against Lloyd, Maya had no one to vent her frustrations to. Claudia was too critical, her mother too dramatic, and her aunts indifferent, and Gwen in another time zone. So Maya drifted through the morning, pretending not to see the murmurs or the disgruntled looks on their faces.

"Kenneth wouldn't have stood you up like this," Claudia said as Maya parked the car.

Maya didn't respond, but she was rethinking Mr. Gregorio's offer to help. Aggravated, she got out of the car and rushed to her father's side. "Let Eddie and Bishop handle the heavy furniture, Daddy."

Mr. Richards set his end of the loveseat on the porch and caught his breath. Michael dropped his end too. "I can handle this, Pumpkin. It'll take longer, but I can get this old chair into the house."

"There are plenty of boxes you can carry, Daddy. Mom will never forgive me if she has to doctor you all night. So please lay off the furniture."

Mr. Richards hesitantly gave in to his daughter's request and abandoned the loveseat to find something light to carry in the U-Haul. Maya stayed on the porch until Eddie and Michael carried the loveseat inside, and her father grabbed a smaller box. Though she'd rather keep a close eye on her father, Maya knew that if she didn't go inside the house, her mother would arrange the furniture and organize the cabinets to *her* liking.

At 1:52 P.M., all of the grueling work had been completed. The men had retreated to the living room, where they watched ESPN and enjoyed an extra-large pizza. Mrs. Richards and her sisters stayed in the kitchen and browsed vacation magazines.

To keep her mind off of Lloyd, Maya kept busy by organizing her bedroom. As much as she liked Lloyd, his disregard in this matter troubled her. His recent behavior didn't add up to the gentleman he professed to be, for the most part, had been.

"These sheets are so soft," Claudia said as she smoothed out the wrinkles of a new set of baby blue sheets. Langston thought she'd given him an invitation to play and jumped onto the bed. He played with the subtle ripples, and Claudia tried to shoo him away. But Langston fell back and batted at her hand as his tail thumped hard on the mattress.

"Just pick him up," Maya instructed. "He thinks you're playing with him."

Claudia tried to catch Langston, but he scurried across the fresh sheets, completely messing up the work she'd already done. The scene was like a comedy act and Maya giggled. "Don't be afraid, Claudia. He doesn't go for blood."

But Claudia was still hesitant. She feared the cat might scratch her, and after several attempts Claudia gave up and fell onto the bed. "Girl, he's too fast for me."

Laughing harder, Maya walked to the bed and pulled Langston from under a pillow. He playfully nipped her hand and Maya almost dropped him. She'd never seen him so excited. Langston jumped off the bed and ran across the room, finding a safe place under a chair.

The two friends couldn't stop laughing, and for Maya, the release felt good. As the laughter wound down, Maya figured it was a good time to talk about the picture mail she received. "So something strange happened today."

Claudia fluffed the pillow beneath her head. "Does it involve Lloyd or explain why he's not here?"

"Are you gonna jump all over Lloyd before I even tell you what happened?" Maya asked, and turned over on her stomach.

"Okay, I'm sorry. I'm all ears."

As she told Claudia what happened, Maya walked to the dresser and grabbed her phone. She showed Claudia the picture of her and Lloyd on the dance floor, gazing into each other's eyes, then asked, "Who would've done this?"

Claudia sat up and stared off to the side, like she was analyzing the details of a mystery. "Has he called yet?"

"No, and I guess he's not coming."

"Humph! And you don't recognize the number?"

Maya sat on the edge of the bed, afraid of what Claudia had surmised. "Not at all."

Claudia curled her lips and tapped the side of her leg with her finger; something Maya had seen Claudia do many times when she was weighing the consequences of speaking her mind. When Claudia had come to a decision, she folded her hands across her stomach and took a deep breath. "I promised Bishop I'd be silent, but I feel a strain in our friendship because of Lloyd and have to speak. You're my best friend, Maya, and regardless of what I feel, I don't want him to come between us. So as long as he's making you happy, I'll be cool."

While Maya appreciated Claudia's confession, she sensed that her friend was holding something back. "Please, Claudia. If there's something else on your mind, say it. I want to know what you're thinking."

"Well," Claudia said, and talked slow, "something doesn't feel right. Are you sure he's not involved with another woman?"

Maya wanted to tell Claudia that her suspicions were wrong. There was no way, with his busy schedule, that Lloyd had time to court someone other than Maya. Just as she was about to speak, Maya heard a doorbell ring. "Was that my bell?" Maya stretched her neck toward the door.

"Yes, and I bet it's Lloyd," Claudia said and looked at her watch. "And he's only five hours late."

Maya hit Claudia with one of her pillows. "We'll finish this talk later," she replied, and then charged downstairs. By the time she reached the bottom stair, Maya realized she hadn't moved fast enough. Eddie had beaten her to the door.

"You've missed all the hard work, dawg," Maya heard Eddie say when she reached the door. "But I'm sure there's still something you can do."

Uneasy, Lloyd stuttered heavily as he tried to explain his absence. Maya pushed Eddie out of the vestibule and pulled Lloyd inside the house. "My cousin's just kidding."

"Don't be mad at me, Maya. The kids' mother found out I was seeing someone special and—"

Maya raised her hand inches away from his face. "I've heard enough. I just hope you handled whatever the problem was so that this won't happen again. This is the *second* time you showed up late. How do you think that makes you look?"

Lloyd lowered his head. "I'm sorry, sweetheart."

As upset as Maya was, she couldn't stay mad at anyone for an extended period of time. She was going to forgive him, but she wanted Lloyd to think about his actions a little longer before letting him know. "Well, I suggest you go and speak to my family."

Without delay, Lloyd did as Maya asked. On his way out of the vestibule, he passed Claudia and mumbled a soft hello without looking her in the eyes. "He's guilty about something," Claudia observed, but Maya pretended not to hear the comment.

Maya tried to leave the vestibule, but Claudia blocked her in the tiny space. "So what's his story?"

Feeling claustrophobic, Maya figured she better respond. Claudia could be stubborn and aggressive when she wanted answers. "He mentioned something about problems with his girls' mother."

Being familiar with Lloyd's situation from personal experience, Claudia gave Maya advice.

"You need to nip that in the bud. If you don't, this drama may never end."

"I know." Maya sighed and pushed her way out of the tight space.

It took almost an hour for the family to warm up to Lloyd, but after devouring two large pizzas and Mrs. Richards's homemade lemon cake, the mood lightened and Lloyd had blended in. There was even a moment when Lloyd and Mr. Richards stepped onto the porch to discuss the latest in sports.

It was getting late, and for some reason, Lloyd felt compelled to apologize in front of everyone for being late. Maya tried to silence him, but Lloyd was determined to explain himself. "My daughters wanted to spend the day with me, and when I told them I had plans, their mother made them feel like I was choosing Maya over them."

"*Your daughters* held you up," Claudia retorted, implying that his children were not the problem.

Bishop delicately hit Claudia's leg. "Leave it alone, honey."

A room that once bustled with conversation and laughter suddenly became silent. *Why couldn't he have just kept quiet!*

"Well, it's been fun, Maya," Bishop said and stood up, pulling on Claudia to get up off the floor as well. "Congrats on the move, but we better get home and relieve my mother of baby-sitting duty."

"We better get going too," Mrs. Richards chimed in, and then looked at Lloyd. "Will we be seeing you in church tomorrow?"

"Yes, ma'am, and I'll be on time," he joked, but Mrs. Richards didn't find it funny. Neither did Maya.

Maya helped everyone with their coats and walked them outside. Before pulling off, Mrs. Richards hopped out of the car she was in and climbed up the steps, leading to Maya's porch. "What'd you forget?" queried Maya.

"I forgot to kiss you good night." Mrs. Richards looked inside the house to make sure Lloyd wasn't standing by the open door. When she was sure all was clear, Mrs. Richards gave Maya a hug. "You don't have to settle for anything, Pumpkin. If he's going to be around, you need to get him in shape." Mrs. Richards pulled away slowly, and then kissed Maya's cheek. "Don't stay up too late." She headed back to the car.

As Maya watched her family drive away, flashbacks of the day she moved in with Kenneth came to mind. Her mother's insight proved to be true then, and Maya worried that she'd be right once again.

Back inside the house, Maya locked up and wondered when Lloyd was going to leave. It was late, and she had to teach Sunday School in the morning. When she walked into the living room, Lloyd was stretched out along the sofa, barefoot and half-asleep. *Why is he so tired?* Maya used one of his shoes to hit his leg.

Startled by the touch, Lloyd slowly opened his eyes and sat up. "How long was I asleep?"

"I have no idea, Lloyd." Maya dropped his shoe before sitting in the loveseat on the other side of the room. She wanted to talk to Lloyd about all that happened, but there was so much to say, that Maya wasn't sure where to begin.

Lloyd seemed perplexed by the distance Maya placed between them. "Why so far away?" Maya didn't answer. Instead, she changed the channel to one of her favorite late-night detective shows. "You can't just pretend I'm not here, Maya. I know you're mad, but I prom—"

"No more excuses, Lloyd, please." Maya turned up the volume.

Lloyd sat through two commercials, hoping Maya's mood would change. But when it became clear that she didn't want to be bothered, Lloyd stood up and walked into the next room. "I think I have something to put a smile on your face."

When Lloyd returned, he placed several small envelopes in Maya's lap. "A little housewarming gift." He tried to kiss her, but Maya stopped him with her hand. Feeling rejected, Lloyd squeezed into the space next to Maya and rested his head on the back of the loveseat. Maya wasn't moved by his frustration, and simply out of curiosity, she opened each of the five envelopes, each containing a $100 gift certificate from Macy's. *Five hundred dollars?* Most girlfriends would've applauded their man's generosity. But Maya wasn't impressed. She put the cards on an end table. "I would've preferred having you here to actually help me move today. That would've been the perfect gift."

Lloyd sat up. That wasn't the response he had expected. "I'm sorry I disappointed you, but are you gonna be mad at me *all* night?"

Maya turned off the television and faced Lloyd. "We need to talk. Do you not want my family to like you?"

"Of course I do," Lloyd answered, upset that he'd disappointed Maya again.

"Don't give me that tone. Your actions say different, and quite frankly, I'm tired of it. I'm tired of having to come up with excuses, and looking like a fool."

"I know I messed up. But please forgive me."

Maya got up and walked to the mantle to get her cell phone. She scrolled through her mail, and expanded the picture of them at the cabaret. She held the phone in front of him. "What about this picture?" Lloyd looked as if he'd seen a ghost. "Who sent this to me? And how did they get my number?"

Speechless, Lloyd stared at Maya. The small twitches of his lip indicated that he was nervous . . . or trying to come up with a good lie. Since Claudia alluded to the fact that there may be another woman in his life, Maya couldn't get the thought out of her mind. "Tell me something, Lloyd, why would someone send me this picture?"

"You know what?" Lloyd cracked a smile. "I bet that's the picture Robert took that night. I can't believe he's just sending that to you. What number was it sent from?"

Maya checked the details of the picture mail and read the number to Lloyd. Though she wasn't completely satisfied with his answer, Maya had no proof to challenge him otherwise.

"Yep, that's his number."

Not sure what to say next, Maya sat down and turned the television back on. "How long are you staying? You told my mother you'd be at church, and I think you should get a good night's rest, so you don't disappoint us *again*."

"Well, I was thinking I could stay the night. My overnight bag is in the car."

While Maya would've preferred he go home, she really didn't want to spend the first night in her new place alone. And she definitely didn't want to risk Lloyd showing up to church late, or not at all. "I'm going up to bed."

Lloyd tried his best not to smile. He planted a kiss on Maya's forehead and ran out to the car to get his things. Before he returned, Maya closed her eyes and prayed. *Please let Claudia's assumption be wrong. But if she is right, please open my eyes to clearly see the truth.*

Chapter 22

"There's a spider by your hand!" Patrick shouted from his seat.

Maya thought he was trying to distract her from writing an assignment on the board, but when she looked, there was a black spider on the metal rim. Although she wasn't afraid of insects, the sight of the fat-bellied creature made her cringe. Maya slowly backed away from the board. "Get it outside!" Several of the students in Maya's afterschool math program snickered as Patrick strolled to the board. Just as he stretched his hand toward the spider, Maya pulled him back. "Don't touch that with your hand!" She was careful not to alarm the children, though she realized some of the boys found the scene amusing.

Patrick looked at her with a smirk on his face. "I'm not afraid. It's *just* a bug."

"Bugs bite." Maya grabbed a scrap sheet of paper from her desk. As she handed Patrick the paper, Maya caught a better glimpse of the spider. It only had seven legs. She moved closer to the board and blew hard on its long, hairy legs, and it didn't budge. Not even a little. In case her suspicions were wrong, Maya carefully touched the spider and the students burst into laughter. Soft and furry, the rubber spider was a good real-life imitation.

Patrick doubled over in laughter, and on his cue, the children shouted, "April Fool's Day!"

"We got you!" Patrick said and pointed at his teacher in jest.

Maya moved Patrick aside and removed the fake spider from the board, then threw it onto his desk. "I'm gonna get you all. I'm taking five minutes off of your recess tomorrow," Maya said and walked back to the board.

"Aww," moaned Patrick, "it was only a joke."

"I told you it was a bad idea," Julian groaned from the back of the room.

Maya listened to the young mathematicians grumble within their groups, and after writing the last problem, Maya faced them with a serious expression. The children anticipated a lecture for what they'd done, but Maya cracked a tiny smile and calmly said, "April Fool's back at ya!"

"Ms. Richards," Ciona whined, and slowly the other eleven children relaxed.

Although Maya was more laid back with her afterschool group, the children knew not to push the envelope too far. "I allow one prank a year, so . . . now that that's out of the way, let's talk about division."

The children moved to the front of the room and listened intently as Maya discussed a new strategy for solving division problems quickly. Once she was sure the children had grasped the concept, Maya divided them into three groups and gave them time to apply the skill while playing several rounds of Challenge 24®. As they played, Maya put a stack of papers inside her tote bag and noticed that her cell phone light was blinking. She wasn't used to getting calls during the day, and curiously, Maya scrolled through the call log. Someone from an unfamiliar number had called over ten times in the last two hours.

With fifteen minutes left, there wasn't time to call the number back, so she set the phone on her desk and observed the children, rewarding the winner of each round with a gold star. It was a simple reward, but the children worked hard for their stars. Proud of the group she formed, Maya had turned children skeptical about their mathematical gifts into a fierce group of competitors. In only a few weeks, the team had won five of their six games against other area schools.

"It's almost four o'clock," Ciona said after winning her third game. "Should I collect the boards?"

That's strange. Lloyd usually stopped by on his way home. It was how she knew it was time to leave. "Sure, Ciona, but wait until the others finish." Maya went to her desk. As she put on her coat, Maya saw the light on her phone blinking again. The mystery number had called five more times, and this time, the caller left a message. Maya looked at the twelve children. As usual, Ciona had everything under control, so while they prepared to leave, Maya checked her voice mail. There were three messages. She pressed the button and listened to the first one.

"This is Queenie Bradford. I was looking through my March cell phone bill and your number appeared one hundred and forty-three times. I don't recognize this number, and I'm being charged for going over my minutes, so can you please give me a call?" Maya's hands shook as she saved the message. The next one played automatically. "This is Queenie again, Lloyd's wife. I checked my January *and* February statements online and see that you and my husband have been talking to each other every day for hours at a time. I think you need to call me back." Maya fell back into her chair as she listened to the angry woman. She saved the second message then listened to the last one. "Okay, look. I'm not gonna play games with you. I know who you are, Ms. Maya Richards, and I think you know about me. I suggest you give me a call today, so we can get this mess straight. I'm gonna call until you answer this phone, so be a woman and face me. I won't let you destroy my family." Queenie hung up.

Maya's skin turned pale. How could Lloyd have a wife? He was with her all the time and she'd been to his house. They'd spent the night at each other's homes. If Lloyd was married, wouldn't there be a trace of a woman's presence in his home? His scattered tardiness was sketchy lately, but sketchy enough to have a wife?

"Are you okay?" Patrick asked his teacher and Maya jumped up. She'd forgotten the children were there.

"Yes, I'm fine." She tried to make sense of the messages. Was this another April Fool's joke? And if it were, who would do such a thing?

The phone lit up again, and Maya saw that Queenie was calling. Her fingers hit the talk button before she could convince herself otherwise. "Hello," Maya said in a professional manner.

"Is this Maya Richards?" the woman asked in a powerful voice.

"This is she." Maya wondered how Queenie knew her full name.

"How long have you been seeing *my husband?*"

Stunned, Maya looked at the children patiently waiting in line and covered the phone with her hand. "Go ahead downstairs. And go straight out the side door. No playing in the hall." As they marched out of the room, Maya prayed no one would see or hear them leaving without adult supervision. She sat on her desk and took a deep breath. "I'm sorry, but I think you have the wrong number," Maya said, praying that was the case.

"Let's not play games here. I've known about you for some time. I know about the cabaret, the flowers he sent you for Valentine's Day, and the dinner at Legal Seafood. I know that he's been going to church with you. I even know that you've been going to Robert's house to be with him. I know all about you, *Ms. Richards.* Including what you look like. How'd you like that picture Tanya sent you?"

Robert's house? Tanya sent the picture? Maya was finding it hard to breathe. What had she gotten herself into? She didn't want to believe the woman on the phone, but Queenie knew far too much for her words to be a lie. "I'm sorry." Maya clutched her phone with both hands to keep it steady. She was shaking uncontrollably. "Are we talking about the same Lloyd Bradford?"

"You're a college-educated woman, so don't try to act dumb," Queenie replied adamantly. Before Maya could get in another word, Queenie continued. "I didn't say anything because Lloyd kept denying it, but he's such a *liar*. But I saw the gift card receipt from Macy's this morning and decided it was time to take matters into my own hands. You should be ashamed of yourself. Is this how Christians act at your church?"

Maya was tired of Queenie's verbal abuse. "Wait a minute; the Lloyd Bradford I know is divorced."

"Is that what he told you? You've got to be smarter than that. Lloyd is a professional liar, and he's obviously pulled one over on you. He's been able to sneak around with you because I work the night shift at a nursing home. And he's been telling me that he coaches a team at your church. But I know that's a lie 'cause I called the church."

"But are you *still* married?" Maya was clearly in denial.

The questioned aggravated Queenie even more. "Look, we've been married for *eleven* years and have *two* children. And until he started pulling these mystery missions and make-believe coaching jobs, we were a happy family."

The last thing Maya wanted to do was ruin someone's happy home. "I really didn't know Lloyd was married," was all she could part her lips to say.

"What did you think was going on? Haven't you wondered why he doesn't show up sometimes? I don't just let him leave whenever he wants to. Lloyd told me it was over between you two, and I wanted to believe him because I love him. But I'm not a stupid or naive woman, Ms. Richards. I didn't go to college like you, but I have common sense. I know when something ain't right with *my* man."

After being scolded by a grown woman, Maya rubbed her temples. "Why doesn't he wear a ring?" she asked aloud, though she didn't mean to.

For the first time in the conversation, Queenie choked over her words. "He has one. I can't believe he's doing this to our family."

Though the facts were clear, Maya found it hard to believe that a woman would know about her husband's affair and do nothing about it early on. Queenie didn't seem like the kind of woman who could sit by idly without saying anything.

Rather than listen to more of her rampage, Maya wanted to get off the phone. There wasn't anything more they had to say to one another. Lloyd was the one who had explaining to do. "If Lloyd is in fact your husband, you don't have to worry about me any longer." She tried to hang up, but Queenie started to cry.

"Lloyd *is* married. I know he's a charming man and that you have feelings for him, but he *is* married. And I'd appreciate it if you'd leave our family alone."

The sting of Queenie's words struck a chord through Maya's heart and she hung up.

After gathering her things, Maya ran downstairs to look for Lloyd. But when she reached the gym the lights were off. *Where could he be?* She glanced at her watch. It was only 4:12. Unless Lloyd left the building with Maya, he rarely left before 4:30. She looked around the empty gym as if he were hiding in the darkened room, and remembered the last and only time he'd disappeared without saying good-bye. He'd said that Robert hurt his back at work, but later that week, his brother had danced the night away at a cabaret.

Maya's face warmed and she leaned against the wall to keep from falling. The more Maya thought about Lloyd's behavior, the more she realized that he had lied to her on several occasions. And the part that aggravated Maya the most was that she hadn't challenged him once. How could she have missed signs that were so obvious to everyone else?

Storming out of the gym, Maya didn't see Claudia standing in the hall. "Maya!" Claudia called a few times, each shout louder than the last. Maya stopped walking and turned around. The dazed look on her face told Claudia that something was seriously wrong. "What's going on?"

"Nothing," Maya said as calmly as she could, and as she buttoned her jacket, the bag on her shoulder fell on the floor. Maya bent down, and with shaky hands, picked up the few pens and papers that had fallen out.

Claudia lowered herself and covered Maya's hands with hers. "You sure you're okay?"

Maya stood up. "I'm sure."

Claudia's expression let Maya know that she wasn't buying her response. But as promised, she held her tongue from saying anything negative. "Are we still on for the gym?"

"Can we skip class today?" Maya fumbled through her purse for her car keys. "I have something important to take care of."

Claudia eyed Maya suspiciously. "No, I've lost eight pounds so far. I don't want to mess up my groove."

"Then you'll have to go without me." Maya was unaware of her sharp tone.

"Hold on, Maya, I don't deserve this attitude. Is everything with you and Lloyd all right?"

"We're fine." There was no need in telling Claudia what happened until she had all the facts; facts she needed to find out from Lloyd. "I'll call you tonight."

Maya wanted to call Lloyd when she got home, but feared Queenie would answer his phone. And because she'd had enough of Queenie for one day, Maya sat in bed for several hours, waiting for him to call.

At 8:43 that night, Lloyd still hadn't called. Maya got out of bed and headed to the bathroom. Maybe a warm bath was what she needed. Halfway down the hall, Maya realized she'd forgotten her phone, and went back to her bedroom to get it. In case Lloyd did call, she didn't want to miss it.

In the bathroom, Maya rubbed facial cleanser on her face and stared in the mirror, letting the creamy substance marinate her skin for the suggested three minutes. "What is it about me that keeps attracting the wrong men?" she asked aloud, looking herself in the eyes. Her high school sweetheart broke up with her when she was a sophomore in college, citing that they "grew apart." Kenneth was afraid of marriage, and Lloyd was a married man. "How could they be so mean to me?" She broke down into tears. *Why me, God? Why me?*

Langston came into the bathroom and jumped on top of the counter. Feeling his warm fur rub against her hand brought a smile to Maya's face. Figuring she'd been crying longer than three minutes, Maya ran warm water, and then wiped the thick cleanser off her face. She continued to stare at herself in the mirror until the phone broke her concentration. From the general ringtone, Maya knew it wasn't Lloyd, but prayed it wasn't Queenie. She was in a fragile state and needed a break from Queenie's abrasive attitude.

Slowly, Maya lifted her phone and was relieved to see Mr. Gregorio's number. *I need to give him a ringtone.* Though she wasn't in a mood to talk, she answered in case he wanted to talk about Patrick. "Hey, Mr. Gregorio."

"Hey, lady. And I think it's safe for you to call me Solomon, don't you? I actually talk to you more than I talk to my own sister."

After thinking about what he had said, Maya realized he was right. Especially since Gwen had moved and Claudia became distant, besides Lloyd, Mr. Gregorio had filled a gap of friendship that Maya needed. "You're right, *Solomon*. I guess it's safe for you to call me Maya too." She smiled.

"Patrick told me about the spider today." Mr. Gregorio laughed as if he'd been there.

Maya chuckled. "Yes, he thought it was funny. He's lucky I'm not afraid of them."

"You okay? You don't sound like yourself."

Maya let out a huge sigh and sat on the lid of the toilet. "Nothing I care to talk about."

"Are you sure? I'm a great listener."

"Maybe another time." Maya wasn't ready to talk to him about Lloyd.

"Well, situations have a way of working themselves out. Try not to stress over whatever it is. Pastor would remind you that God is in control. So since pastor isn't here, I'm gonna encourage you." In his finest impression of Pastor Williams, Mr. Gregorio tried to lift Maya's spirits. "God is able to do the impossible. So don't waste your time worrying about tomorrow. God has already made a way for you."

A faint smile crossed her face. "That was good, Mr. Greg—I mean, Solomon. And it helped."

"Don't worry. I've learned that God gives us the strength we need when we need it most. But I think I know something that may help."

"Please do tell. I need all the positive energy I can get."

"Why don't you come out to the outreach center on Saturday night and play cards with us. I don't just enjoy the ministry because I love cards, the fellowship with the young cats remind me that my life could've gone down a different path. The ministry helps me appreciate God's grace and that makes it easier to deal with the challenges that come my way." Mr. Gregorio took a deep breath. "But I don't mean to preach to you."

"Trust me, Solomon; you've blessed me more than you know. You've helped me put things into perspective. So I'll definitely come out one night."

"Well, glad that I could be of some help. Get some rest now and I'll check on you tomorrow."

When Maya hung up, she looked toward heaven. *Why couldn't I have met a nice man like him?* For a fleeting moment, Maya imagined how different her life would've been if she were in a relationship with Mr. Gregorio. But before her imagination fully developed she switched gears. Mr. Gregorio seemed like a good man and he was turning out to be a good friend. She didn't want to ruin that. Besides, if they were together, it was just a matter of time before he devastated her, just as the others had. If it weren't for her father, Maya would've lost all hope that a good, decent, and honest man existed.

It was after nine o'clock and Lloyd still hadn't called. Remembering that Queenie worked a late shift, Maya took a chance and sent him a text. There was a lot that she wanted to say, but summed up her feelings in one sentence: My heart is broken.

For someone who claimed to be in love and adored her every move, how could Lloyd not call to at least apologize? Maya sat on the toilet lid for another five minutes before giving up hope that he'd return her message. She went back to her bedroom and connected the phone to its charger. As she settled in bed, with Langston curled at her side, Maya said a quick prayer then turned off the light. Seconds later, the phone beeped and Maya shifted to read the incoming message.

He broke mine 2. Don't let him ruin ur life
the way he's ruined mine. Queenie

As Maya had guessed, Queenie had seized
Lloyd's cell phone. Before she allowed her emotions to rise again, she turned off the ringer and
reached for the Bible behind her nightlight. Maya
turned the pages until she came across the list
she created some time ago. There was no need
to turn on the light again. She'd memorized all
the traits and characteristics she wanted in her
"ideal" man. *This is ridiculous,* she mumbled,
and then slowly ripped the paper into tiny pieces.
She'd given up on finding love, so there was no
need to pray over a list anymore.

Maya nibbled on a small piece of meatloaf
she made two nights ago, and paged through an
Essence magazine while her students were in art
class. It had been almost twenty-four hours and
Lloyd still hadn't tried to contact her. In case
he called, Maya kept her phone on vibrate. She
knew it was wishful thinking, but she wanted
to be available whenever he got up the nerve to
finally call. Maya knew he had come to work, and
it was ironic that they hadn't bumped into each
other once. When they were going strong, it was

hard to keep Lloyd away for more than an hour at a time.

A pair of familiar sneakers appeared in Maya's peripheral view and she dropped her fork. "What happened this time?"

Patrick frowned and immediately explained why Mrs. Garrett made him leave her classroom. Halfway through his explanation, Maya stood up and headed to the door. "I've had enough of this. C'mon, Patrick, you're going back to art class."

Briskly, Maya walked up to the third floor as Patrick silently followed. When Maya opened the art room door, the mild chatter in the room ceased. "Go take a seat." Without hesitation Patrick did as he was told.

Maya looked at Mrs. Garret, sitting behind her desk, wearing an expression a grandmother used when a child got out of line. "Can I talk to you outside for a minute?"

Mrs. Garrett processed Maya's request, then took her time walking to the door. She partially closed the door behind her. "What's this about?"

"I don't know what you have against Patrick, but it doesn't make sense that he gets kicked out of class *every* week."

"He's not asked to leave every week."

"Just about. It's not fair that I have to give up my prep time to watch him. All of the other teachers deal with his behavior, which has improved dramatically since the beginning of the school year, by the way. Why can't you do the same? It's only forty minutes of your time." The classroom door next to the art class closed and Maya stopped talking.

Mrs. Garrett stared at Maya blankly. "Are you done?"

Although Maya was aware that she'd taken her frustrations about Lloyd out on Mrs. Garrett, she meant them. Under different circumstances, she would've expressed them in a more professional way. "I'm done." Instead of telling Maya what was on her mind, Mrs. Garrett went back inside the classroom.

Suddenly embarrassed, Maya headed to the stairwell, and as she passed the classroom next to Mrs. Garrett's, the teacher inside opened her door and whispered, "You go, girl."

Pretending not to hear the remark, Maya continued walking. What she'd done shouldn't have been looked upon as a badge of honor.

Various colleagues flashed Maya a victorious grin at the end of the day when they passed her in the hallway, but she couldn't accept their praise. Though Mrs. Garrett wasn't a favorite amongst the staff, she didn't deserve Maya's tongue-lashing.

Maya's cell phone vibrated against her chair, and although she was hoping to receive a call, the noise caught her off guard. Without getting her hopes up, Maya removed the phone from her bag and checked the message.

Don't mean 2 bug u. Can u tell me if Lloyd tried to contact u 2day?

"Ms. Richards, are you there?" Maya heard through the classroom intercom.

Maya rolled her eyes and quickly erased the text. When was *Lloyd* going to text her? "I'm here," she answered, recognizing her principal's voice.

"Can you come to my office before you leave?"

Maya's heart dropped. It was no mystery what Mrs. Bridges wanted. "I'll be right down."

After packing her tote bag, Maya headed to the main office, dreading what was ahead. As she passed the secretaries, they looked as if Maya were a student in trouble. Ignoring their stares, Maya strutted by them and knocked on Mrs. Bridges's open door.

"Come in, Ms. Richards," Mrs. Bridges said, without looking up from her computer. "I wanted to quickly touch base about the math program. I hear we're doing well. Close the door behind you."

A bundle of nerves, Maya pulled the door close as she entered the office, then sat in a chair farthest from Mrs. Bridges's desk. This was the first time Maya had been in the principal's office all school year. With the exception of a framed certificate on the wall and a tall potted plant in the corner, not much had changed.

"How good are we?" Mrs. Bridges asked, as she wrapped up a response to an email.

"They have a competition next Thursday. If they win, we'll represent the district in the Harrisburg tournament," Maya said and nervously played with a button on her coat.

"I've been bragging to my colleagues," Mrs. Bridges said proudly and turned to face Maya.

"You're a good teacher," Mrs. Bridges said and paused. "Before you go, Ms. Richards . . . what happened earlier with Mrs. Garrett?"

Maya swallowed hard, and then prepared to own up to her misconduct. "I was wrong and should've waited until after dismissal, but—" Maya looked away, realizing that she had no real defense.

"Mrs. Garrett is a veteran teacher," Mrs. Bridges responded, and folded her hands on her desk. "I know teachers think I'm unfair when it comes to her, but Mrs. Garrett's going to retire in two months. It won't hurt to give her a little breathing room. I'll talk to her about Patrick, but you should probably talk to her."

"I need to apologize," Maya replied as she got up to leave.

"One more thing," Mrs. Bridges said, and Maya's legs started to tremble. "You know I don't like to meddle, but you remind me of my daughter. Forgive me if I sound like a mother, but I feel you need to know that peace of mind is a gift. If anyone tries to rob you of that, cut them loose. You're one of my star teachers, Ms. Richards. I want to see you climb the ladder of success, not fall down."

Feeling like she'd disappointed her boss, Maya wanted to crawl into a corner. Mrs. Bridges had to be referring to Lloyd. "I won't let anything interfere with my job." If she weren't at the school and Ms. Covington wasn't standing outside the door, she would've cried. "And you sounded just like my mother."

"I hope you listen to your mother."

In that moment, Maya saw a tender side to Mrs. Bridges and smiled. "Not as much as I probably should." Mrs. Bridges had always been a pillar of strength and a good role model during the seven years Maya was employed at the school. Until now, Maya realized that she hadn't really expressed her appreciation, so she walked to the door and before opening it turned around. "Thank you, Mrs. Bridges . . . for everything."

When Maya made it home, she changed her clothes and made a cup of green tea. As she sat in the kitchen, sipping on her warm tea, Maya graded a stack of tests to help keep her mind off of Lloyd's deceit and the events of the school day. But her efforts weren't fruitful. After two hours, she'd only marked five vocabulary tests.

Maya was happy when she heard Gwen's ringtone, and quickly answered. She hadn't talked to Gwen since the move, and Maya was eager to talk about the mess she'd gotten into.

"I'm engaged!" Gwen shouted and Maya dropped her cell phone.

Could this day get any worse? Maya thought as she picked up the phone. "Congratulations," she said dryly. "I'm happy for you."

Listening to Gwen share the details on how Justin proposed on a secluded riverbank, Maya tried her best to sound enthused. But as hard as she tried, Maya couldn't muster up the energy to be as excited as a sister should.

Gwen talked nonstop about her vision for the wedding, and hadn't picked up on Maya's sullen mood. It didn't matter that Maya wasn't bubbling with enthusiasm. Gwen had enough excitement for an army of women. Maya leaned back in her chair and sipped on her cooled tea. How could her *younger* sister get married first?

Maya didn't mean to tune out of the conversation, but Gwen talked so fast it was hard for her to keep up. "I need to call you back. I have a meeting in two minutes," Gwen said, and shamefully, Maya was relived.

After hanging up, Maya set the phone down and lowered her head on the table. "What are you trying to do to me, God? Am I not praying enough? Do I need to go to Bible Study more? What am I not doing right?"

It didn't take long for tears to surface, and as Maya lay still, she begged the spirit to soothe her. But after the seconds turned into minutes, and she was still experiencing pain in her heart, Maya tried to usher in the spirit with a song, just like her mother had done on numerous occasions. Normally, it took time for Maya to come up with a song, but today one came to mind without delay.

"Not another second or another minute. Not an hour of another day. Lord, I need you right away." She sang through her tears, and slowly sat up. Maya hadn't heard Smokie Norful's gospel hit since it dominated the airwaves, but the lyrics seemed to effortlessly flow out of her mouth. Though Maya sang slower than the original version, each word had an effect on her spirit. And when she sang the last note, Maya was reminded of a sermon First Lady Williams delivered one Sunday in church.

"Trouble will come in like a flood, but God has a plan for you."

Maya closed her eyes and prayed that she'd seen the end of her flood.

The sound of Claudia's gospel ringtone made Maya jump and she reached for the phone next to her arm. Quickly, she dried her face and took a deep breath before answering the call. "Hey, Claudia."

"You've been avoiding me long enough. And unless you want me to drive to Lansdowne, I suggest you start talking, now."

Maya realized that the longer she kept her feelings bottled up, the more she'd react to the smallest of things out of character. She never wanted to explode on someone the way she had with Mrs. Garrett. So Maya warmed up her tea in the microwave, and told her best friend about Lloyd's wife.

When she was done, Maya could tell by the sighs and moans that Claudia wanted to say, "I told you so." Instead, Claudia sighed and said, "God has something better for you."

Maya had heard that line more times in the past six months, than she had all her life. And while she struggled to believe the words were true, Maya knew better than to test God. But if He truly had a better plan for her life, she desperately needed Him to make that plan clear. And soon.

Chapter 23

It was a beautiful day to be on lunch duty. The trees were green, the flowers in bloom, and the sky a bright blue. Maya strolled across the schoolyard, admiring a group of girls jumping rope as they chanted the words to a double-dutch rhyme. As she reminisced about the days she would jump until the streetlights came on, Maya saw Mrs. Garrett observing a game of touch football at the far end of the yard. Before Maya realized it, she was headed in that direction.

"I guess spring has officially arrived," Mrs. Garrett said as Maya approached her.

"Y-Yes," Maya said meekly and inched closer to the fence where Mrs. Garrett was standing. Gazing toward the football field, Maya swallowed her pride. "I'm sorry for the way I acted yesterday. I was upset at something else and took that frustration out on you."

Mrs. Garrett placed her hands inside her coat. "That wasn't like you. You've always been so pleasant."

"I wish I knew what else to say."

"You're still pining over your ex-boyfriend, sweetheart. Anyone can see that. I don't know why some men are afraid of marriage. Men like that either end up alone for the rest of their lives, or marry when they're too old to really enjoy it. Be glad it's over, Ms. Richards. Your fella was selfish to lead you on for so many years. I understand that pain. But don't be so eager to get involved with someone new. Some pain needs a long time to heal."

It didn't take much for Maya to know that the veteran teacher was talking about Lloyd. In the last week, Maya couldn't find one person to say something positive about her relationship with Lloyd; which to Maya was odd, because before they started dating people thought Lloyd was a great guy.

A basketball rolled by Mrs. Garrett and she stopped it with her foot, before kicking it back to the basketball court. "And you weren't completely wrong, I may be too hard on Patrick. The truth is, he is doing better."

"I appreciate you saying that, but I shouldn't have confronted you in front of the kids."

"I can't disagree with you there, but you opened my eyes. Everyone is capable of change, and you're proof of what tireless dedication can do for one child." Mrs. Garrett cracked a smile.

"I really am s—" Maya began, and then stopped when she noticed a small crowd heading toward her. Amidst the crowd, she saw Patrick holding his forehead. As he got closer to her, Maya thought she saw blood.

Before Maya could react, Mrs. Garrett rushed into the crowd and pulled Patrick away from the other children. "Go back to the playground!" Then, after studying the knick in Patrick's forehead, she determined that he wasn't in any immediate danger. "The bleeding is slow," she told Patrick with care and placed his fingers over his wound. "Keep pressure on your cut, okay?"

Patrick nodded and Mrs. Garrett faced Maya. "The nurse isn't in today, so you'll have to take him inside and clean him up. I'll cover your class."

Maya gently guided Patrick inside the building and worried about the attention he may receive as they walked through the main office. Unfortunately, there was no other way to get to the nurse's office.

"What happened?" Ms. Covington yelled dramatically when she saw the blood on Patrick's forehead.

"The kids were a little rough in the schoolyard," Maya said, hoping to let on that Patrick wasn't badly hurt, but Ms. Covington walked away from her desk and followed them down the narrow hallway. Before reaching the nurse's office, Maya faced Ms. Covington. "Do you mind looking for Mrs. Marshall? Mrs. Garrett is with my class, now, but I'm sure she has an art class, so can you ask Mrs. Marshall to cover for me for about a half-hour?" Maya figured that assigning Ms. Covington a task would make her feel important while keeping her away at the same time.

"Sure. Do you need me to call Mr. Gregorio?"

"I'll give him a call later," Maya said, and stepped into the nurse's office.

Although she would've preferred to stay with Maya, Ms. Covington backed away, and Maya sighed with relief after closing the door. "Now," she said, directing her attention to Patrick, "do you want to talk about what happened out there?"

"I was running with the ball and tripped over my feet. I almost had a touchdown," Patrick explained as he eased onto the patient table.

Maya fumbled through the medical cabinet and grabbed a bottle of peroxide, cotton swabs, medical tape, and a roll of gauze. As she listened to Patrick talk about the game, he seemed more concerned about not scoring than falling hard on the gravel. Maya dipped a few cotton swabs inside the peroxide bottle, and when she set the bottle on the table, Patrick stopped talking. "This won't sting," Maya tried to assure him, but Patrick flinched when the tip of the swab touched his skin. "Trust me, Patrick." Maya tenderly rubbed his forehead with her fingers. And then, feeling more relaxed, Patrick let Maya dab at the cut until it was clean.

"Thank you," Patrick said after Maya bandaged his wound.

"You're most welcome." Maya put the materials back in the cabinet. "Now, sit still for a few more minutes while I call your father."

As Maya dialed, Patrick noticed that Maya hadn't asked him for the number. "You know my dad's number by heart?" he queried, with a trace of a smile.

"You gave me plenty of practice," Maya replied as she waited for Mr. Gregorio to answer. *Please pick up.* If he didn't answer, she'd have to ask Ms. Covington to look up his work number, and Maya really didn't want to do that.

On the fourth ring, Mr. Gregorio picked up with a slight hesitation in his voice. But when he recognized Maya's voice, he perked up. "I thought you were one of the other teachers," Mr. Gregorio confessed, then started talking about his day.

Though Maya wished she had time to talk, she needed to let him know this wasn't a social call. "Solomon," Maya interrupted, and Patrick looked at her with a huge grin. "Mr. Gregorio," she quickly corrected. "I'm in the nurse's office with Patrick. There was a tiny incident while he was playing football today."

Mr. Gregorio listened to Maya as she explained the details of Patrick's injury. When Maya was done, he sighed. "I can't take off today, but I'll tell my sister to take him to see his doctor. I'm glad you were there with him. I don't think another teacher would've cared for him the way you have. Let Patrick know that his aunt will pick him up after school."

"Okay," Maya agreed and smiled softly. "Please call me with an update. I'd like to know that he's okay."

After saying their good-byes, Maya hung up the phone and happily gazed out of the window, temporarily forgetting that Patrick was in the room. When she finally looked in his direction, Patrick's face was lit up. "Your aunt is coming to get you. She's going to take you to the doctor." Maya helped Patrick off the patient table and walked to the door. Patrick was still grinning. "You okay?" Maya wondered why he was so full of smiles.

"I think I'm all better now."

And as they headed out of the office, Maya had a feeling Patrick was referring to more than just the cut on his head.

Maya had called Mr. Gregorio three times since she got home from work and he'd yet to return her call. She was beginning to worry. The cut on Patrick's forehead looked like a minor bruise, but one could never be sure with a head injury. She sat on her couch, watching reruns of *Cold Case* with her cell phone in hand and praying he'd call soon.

The doorbell rang, catching Maya off guard, and she leaped off the sofa. She was so focused on receiving Mr. Gregorio's call that she'd forgotten about the cheesesteak she ordered for dinner.

As she walked to the door, Langston, who'd been resting for the past hour, sprang from under the coffee table and scurried ahead of her. *That's strange.* He didn't normally run to greet strangers. But as she stepped into the vestibule, Maya saw Lloyd's shadow and understood Langston's actions.

Through the glass window, Maya stared into Lloyd eyes, hoping he'd see that she was annoyed by his presence. He should've stopped by yesterday when she was vulnerable and weak. Today, there was nothing he could do or say to make up for the pain he'd caused.

Maya stood at the door, questioning whether or not she should open the door. There were so many reasons not to, but Maya needed closure. With that as the main reason, Maya unlocked the top lock, and as she unlocked the last one, looked at the smirk on Lloyd's face and changed her mind.

On her way back to the living room, Langston darted between Maya's legs and jumped onto the top edge of the chair by the window. Knowing he wasn't allowed on furniture, Langston let out a strong meow when Maya picked him up. Although Maya knew Lloyd was on her porch, she was still startled when he knocked on the window.

"Maya, please let me in. I only need five minutes of your time."

"Go home to Queenie, Lloyd," she told him and closed the blinds.

"I don't want Queenie." He banged on the window again. "I want to be with you."

The porch light next door came on and Maya imagined what her neighbors thought about Lloyd's behavior. They probably weren't used to all the commotion. Afraid that someone would call the police, Maya rushed to the door and unlocked it. "No more than five minutes, Lloyd. I mean it."

Relieved that he was allowed inside, Lloyd started to take off his shoes, but Maya stopped him. "You can keep them on. You won't be staying long."

Not wanting to aggravate her any further, Lloyd took off his coat and followed Maya into the dining room. "Can I at least take a seat?" He pulled out a chair.

"I'm not in the mood for sarcasm, Lloyd. What is it you have to say? I have papers to grade tonight and it's getting late."

Desperate to make Maya see his point of view, Lloyd played by her rules without a fuss. There was no good place to begin his story, so he sat down, placed his coat on his lap, and started where he thought mattered most. "I didn't mean to fall in love with you so fast."

"In love? I doubt you love me, and I assure you I'm not in love with you."

Saddened by Maya's confession, Lloyd didn't want to believe what she said was true. "You may not believe me, but my marriage has been rocky for years. I tried to make it work, but Queenie's attitude toward me changed. Before I knew it, we had two kids and—" Lloyd placed his hands on the table and rubbed them nervously. "Well, I told myself I'd just be in a miserable marriage for the rest of my life. Then I met you. And when you and Kenneth broke up, I thought God had given me a chance to finally be happy. I do love you, Maya, and I think deep inside, you love me too."

"Let's not go there with love again. You need to be concerned about your marriage. If you felt that strongly, you should've worked on getting a divorce *before* approaching me."

"I admit I went through this the wrong way, but my kids—"

"Don't put this on your innocent kids, Lloyd. If you really wanted a divorce, you would've gotten one. No one can keep you from them."

"But you don't know Queenie."

"I think I got a pretty good taste of her. You can still be a good divorced father in your *own* apartment. Why don't you get that?"

Full of regret, Lloyd reached across the table for Maya's hand, but she pulled it away. "It pains me that I hurt you. I want to make this work. I promise that I—"

"I can't believe you. There are no more promises!" Maya stood up. "There's nothing for you to do, but go home to your family."

Lloyd, too, stood up and grabbed Maya's arm. "I can't do that. I refuse to do that. You mean more to me than just a fling, Maya."

"I'm so special that you misled me to believe that you were single."

"I'll never forgive myself for what I've done." Lloyd tried to pull Maya close to him, but she refused. "You have no idea what life at home—"

"First of all, Queenie said you were a happy family until I came along. And second, I wouldn't cheat on my husband if I wanted a way out. I'd pray about it and leave before starting something new."

"Maya, please . . ." Lloyd reached for Maya again, but this time she moved to the other side of the room.

"And I certainly wouldn't lead someone on. I'd let them know right away that I was married. You played with my emotions and lied to me, Lloyd. How can you be that cruel and call yourself a man of God?"

Lloyd's upper lip twitched as he tried to come up with an explanation that would make Maya feel better. "I-I know how this looks, but Queenie and I aren't happy anymore. She knows I want out."

Staring into his eyes, it dawned on Maya that if she didn't end things now, she would be like so many other women who got caught up in loving a married man. Although she did like Lloyd, she wasn't *in love* with him. "I can't be a part of this, Lloyd. It's just not right."

"I'll move out!" Lloyd moved closer to Maya. "I'll live with my brother if that will keep us together."

"Don't make any moves because of me." Maya shook her head. Living with Robert was another thing Lloyd had lied about. "At this point, I'm not even sure I want to be your friend. Any trust between us is gone."

"I can't just walk away." Lloyd refused to give up. "What am I supposed to do with all this love?"

"Invest it into Queenie. She seems to love you more than I do." Every muscle in Lloyd's face seemed to drop, but Maya stared at a painting on the wall. She didn't want to fall for any weakness in his eyes.

"I guess my five minutes is over." Lloyd turned to leave.

Standing as still as a statue, Maya waited for Lloyd to let himself out. She couldn't believe that she would be alone all over again. Maybe that was the way God had intended.

"Can I use your bathroom before I go?" Lloyd asked as he walked out of the room.

Maya huffed loudly. Lloyd was looking for any way to prolong his exit. But it didn't matter what he did this time, Maya wasn't going to change her mind. She wanted him to leave her house, and her life for good. "Hurry up," she replied, and went into the living room. Maya hoped that she'd be able to catch the end of *Monk* on television.

Before she could get comfortable on the sofa, Lloyd ran downstairs with a wild look in his eyes. "Who do these belong to?"

Maya looked at the balled-up sweat socks and football jersey in his hand and sighed. How dare he question her! The clothes belonged to her cousin, Eddie, but she didn't give Lloyd the satisfaction of knowing that. "What were you doing in my guestroom?"

Lloyd threw the clothes on the loveseat. "Are you seeing someone else?"

"I'm not seeing you." How could he have the audacity to ask such a question? "And what I do from this point on is really none of your business."

The doorbell rang and a confused look crossed Lloyd's face. "Are you expecting company?" He headed for the door.

Shocked at his behavior, Maya jumped off the sofa and ran after him. She tugged his arm when she reached him. "What's wrong with you?"

"I won't let you be with someone else," Lloyd charged, still advancing toward the door.

"I'm not the married one here. Did you forget that?" Maya pulled harder on his arm, forcing him to stop walking. "For the record, I ordered dinner from the deli, and when I open the door, you need to leave." Maya pushed her way around Lloyd and took out a twenty-dollar bill from her pocket. After she paid for the sandwich, Maya nodded for Lloyd to leave.

"Look, I panicked. It's just that I don't want to lose you. I guess the socks could belong to anybody. I know you're a good girl."

Lloyd was grasping at straws, but Maya didn't bite. "My cheesesteak is getting cold."

As Lloyd inched toward the door, he frowned. The battle to win Maya's heart was over, and he had lost the fight. When he reached the door, Lloyd attempted to change her mind about him one last time. "Can you at least pray about us before you release me for good?"

"You're unbelievable. You should've prayed about us before you asked me out on a date."

Lloyd refused to give up. As he backed onto the porch, he held the screen door with his hand to keep it open. "We're not done discussing this, Maya."

"We are tonight," Maya exclaimed and slammed the door.

Chapter 24

Half-asleep, Maya answered her cell phone without checking the screen. At 5:15, she figured it was a family emergency, or perhaps Mr. Gregorio calling about Patrick.

"Good morning, Maya," a woman said.

Immediately, Maya recognized the voice. But why was Queenie calling so early? And why was she calling her by her first name? They weren't friends.

"I know he was with you last night," Queenie continued. "Why can't you leave my man alone? Are you *that* desperate?"

Maya looked at the alarm clock next to her bed and yawned. She had at least another thirty minutes to sleep before getting ready for work. "Look, I don't know what kind of games you and Lloyd are playing, but I wish you'd leave me alone."

"You should've thought about that before you slept with my husband. Why did you let him in last night if you don't want to be bothered? Did you have to let him in last night?"

Thinking more clearly, Maya wondered how Queenie knew Lloyd had stopped by her house. Though Maya didn't think Lloyd would tell her, she couldn't be sure. "This has gone too far," Maya mumbled, then thought about how Claudia would handle Queenie and decided to get tough. "Lloyd says that he doesn't want to be married to you. You need to be concerned about that and not about why I let him inside my house. I didn't ask him to come over here in the first place."

Queenie was silenced, but not for long. "I asked you to stay away from him."

"As a woman, why can't you understand that? Are you that hard up for a man?"

"From my point of view, you're the one looking desperate." Maya wanted to tell her about Lloyd's desire to move out, but felt she'd already done enough damage. Besides, if Lloyd was serious about leaving, Queenie would find out then.

Stumped by Maya's gumption, Queenie screamed colorful obscenities into the phone.

"I don't have time for this. I have to get my students ready for a tournament today," Maya yelled, prematurely ending Queenie's tirade. "In the future, I suggest you deal with Lloyd, not me."

"Don't you dare *suggest* anything to me. I *suggest* you—"

Maya disconnected the call. A shouting match was the last thing she wanted to engage in so early in the morning. Maya put her cell phone on the nightstand. There was no point in trying to go back to sleep, so she got out of bed. "Lord, please let today end better than it started."

On her way to the bathroom, Maya's phone rang again. Knowing it was Queenie, Maya let the call go into voice mail. As she prepared for her shower, the phone rang three more times, and each time Maya ignored it. The next time the phone rang Maya stormed into her bedroom and turned off the ringer. "Not today!" Maya shouted and fell onto her bed. "God, please tell me how to make this stop!"

Maya tried to get off the bed, but her legs wouldn't move. Motionless, she recalled something her mother said when Mr. Richards had his stroke. "When you're in need of change, pray without ceasing, and pray until something happens."

If Maya was desperate for anything, she was desperate for change. So she slid down by the side of her bed and began to pray. *Dear God, if you're not angry with me for my part in this mess, please make it go away . . .*

Chapter 25

Despite a fiery morning, Maya's school day ended without an encounter from Lloyd and his wife. As she escorted her afterschool group outside to the bus waiting to drive them to Harrisburg, Maya bypassed the main office for fear that she might bump into Lloyd. At this time in the afternoon, Lloyd usually roamed the halls in search of misbehaving students.

Safely outside, Maya was surprised to see Mr. Gregorio talking to the bus driver. "Hey! Here to wish Patrick good luck?"

Mr. Gregorio stepped off the bus and let the children get on. "I had the day off and wanted to check on him. The doctor told me to monitor him closely for a few days."

Once the children were all on the bus, Maya caught them staring at her through the windows with huge smiles on their faces. She started to say good-bye, but from the corner of her eye saw Ms. Covington running toward her, waving a pink slip in the air.

"Ms. Richards," an anxious Ms. Covington called. "I have a message for you."

Maya couldn't imagine what was so important that it couldn't wait? Her family would've called her cell phone, and Claudia would've come outside. "I'll be right back. Can you keep an eye on the kids?" she asked Mr. Gregorio, and then walked away from the bus. As she approached Ms. Covington, Maya felt an ill feeling in the pit of her stomach, and she knew bad news was looming. "What's up?"

Ms. Covington handed Maya the pink paper. "Here you go." She waited for Maya to read the message.

Maya glanced at the neatly written note and her hand went limp.

You cannot have my man!

Without missing a beat, Ms. Covington caught the paper before it fell on the ground. "I'm not trying to be in your business, but the woman said you'd know who it was from."

Maya's face flushed with embarrassment. "Thank you." She took the note from Ms. Covington's hand. "I think this is a joke."

On her way back to the bus, Mr. Gregorio could tell something was wrong. "You okay?"

Ashamed of the situation, Maya faced him and said, "Nothing God can't handle, right?"

Mr. Gregorio quickly studied Maya's mood. "You know," he began, as Maya stepped onto the bus, "I have the day off, and um, it would be cool to see my son in action. Am I allowed to ride with you?"

"Sure, there was no rule against having a parent chaperone field trips."

Excited, Mr. Gregorio ran to his car, and then boarded the bus. Although there were plenty of seats to choose from, he chose to sit on the same row across the aisle from Maya.

As they journeyed to Harrisburg, Mr. Gregorio did most of the talking. It was hard for Maya to really listen to his stories because her mind was on Queenie and the note. The woman was ruthless, and there was no telling what she would do next.

An hour into their ride, Maya felt her cell phone vibrating through her purse. Afraid that it was Queenie, Maya reached into her bag to turn off the ringer. But when she looked at the caller ID, Lloyd's number appeared on the screen. Maya should've let the call pass, but she wanted to know what had triggered Queenie to act so harshly. "Excuse me, Solomon. I need to get this," she said, and faced the window.

"Hello," Maya whispered, and prayed that it was really Lloyd on the other end.

"Before you go off on me," Lloyd remarked immediately, "I want to apologize. Queenie told me that she called you early this morning."

"Do you know that she called the school and left a message with *Ms. Covington?* And how does she know you came by my house last night?"

"I went to Robert's after I left your house. She assumed I was with you because I didn't answer my phone."

"Why didn't you just tell her the truth? I told you it was over between us."

"Don't say that. I'm going to make things right. Just give me some time. Queenie will calm down eventually."

"This has gotten way out of hand. I can't have Queenie calling my job leaving messages and—" Maya stopped talking when she felt a hand on her arm.

"You should probably handle that later. The kids are staring at you," informed Mr. Gregorio.

"Who's that in the background? I thought you were going to Harrisburg?"

Embarrassed, Maya hadn't realized that her voice was raised. "You can't be serious," Maya mumbled, and then hung up the phone. Unable to look Mr. Gregorio in the eyes, Maya apologized for her behavior.

"No problem," Mr. Gregorio replied in his kind and gentle manner.

For the rest of the drive, Maya and Mr. Gregorio discussed topics that were far more interesting than the phone call. By the time the bus pulled up to the building where the tournament was being held, Maya was in a better mood and ready to help her students compete.

Two hours into the game, they were in the last match, and Ciona and Patrick had qualified for the last round. Only one point away from a win, Maya and other supporters held their breath in hopes that one of them would find the solution first.

Though competing on a tough level, Maya was confident that her students had a chance to win the championship.

Finding the solution took a long time, but after three minutes, Ciona hit the bell first. Cheers from around the auditorium filled the room, but the officials quickly silenced the roaring crowd. Ten seconds later, the head official walked to the microphone, and with a straight face in a monotone, he announced that Ciona had found the correct solution.

"We won!" Mr. Gregorio shouted, and wrapped his strong arms around Maya.

Caught off guard, Maya didn't hug him back. It wasn't that she didn't want to. The embrace felt right. It was mostly because she hadn't expected it to happen.

Mrs. Bridges surfaced from the crowd and individually congratulated each child for their performance. She also thanked Mr. Gregorio for his support, and then hugged Maya. "I knew you'd bring home a trophy," Mrs. Bridges told her. "Have a great spring break, and when we get back, I'll have Ms. Covington organize a celebration and put the trophy in the display case."

In that moment, Maya realized what was most important. Just seeing the sparkle in her students' eyes, and knowing that Mrs. Bridges was proud of her accomplishment warmed Maya's heart and encouraged her to stay focused.

When the bus pulled up to the school, Maya was glad that all of the parents were there. She was ready to get home and relax after enjoying a warm bath. Mr. Gregorio told Patrick to get in his car, while he waited for all of the children to leave with their parents. Once the street was clear, Mr. Gregorio walked Maya to her car parked at the corner. "You know, you're way too nice to be stressed over a man. I wasn't trying to listen to your conversation, but—"

"I know. I haven't been myself lately, but I trust that God will get my mind right soon."

"That a girl!" Mr. Gregorio looked toward his car to check on Patrick. "Any plans for spring break?"

"Not really. My parents and aunts are going to Paris. I'm supposed to have dinner with Claudia's family, but it's—" Maya paused when she noticed a man get out of a car across the street. The streetlights were dim, but Maya immediately recognized Lloyd's smooth stroll. *What is he doing here this time of night?*

Nervous, Maya quickly explained that her ex-boyfriend was heading their way, and asked Mr. Gregorio to leave. She didn't want to get him mixed up in her current drama. But Mr. Gregorio refused to leave her side.

When Lloyd reached them, he invited himself into the conversation, carefully eyeing Mr. Gregorio. Unaffected by his stares, Mr. Gregorio greeted Lloyd with a firm masculine handshake, and then bragged about Maya's math team. Lloyd pretended to be interested, and gloated about Maya's dedication to education. It was almost as if they were keeping score on who knew Maya best.

Maya coughed so they could acknowledge her presence. "Excuse me, but it's late and Patrick is in the car. We should probably get home."

Both men stared at one another, neither wanting to be the first to leave. Given no alternative, Maya took the initiative and got into her car. "I'll see you on Saturday, Solomon." Lloyd's eyes widened.

"This is the last basketball game," Mr. Gregorio replied. "Let's pray Patrick can bring home another win."

"I will," Maya responded, and before she pulled out of the parking space, yelled for Lloyd to go home. It was obvious by the twitch in Lloyd's upper lip that he was angry, but Maya didn't care. At this time of night, he needed to be with his wife and children.

On the drive home, Lloyd had called her cell phone several times. When it was clear that Maya wasn't going to answer his calls, Lloyd sent a few text messages. Though Maya knew she shouldn't read them, every time she reached a red light, she read one of them.

When did u and Patrick's father become so close?

Is Solomon ur new man?
How could u do this 2 me?
I'm on my way to ur house? We need 2 talk!

After viewing the last message, Maya panicked. She looked in her rearview mirror and checked the cars behind her, but it was too dark to see if Lloyd was following her. At the next stoplight, Maya rushed to send him a response.

Ur actn creepy. Do not stop by, or I'll call the cops!

Afraid that Lloyd would create a scene tonight, Maya took a chance and called Mr. Gregorio. There was no one else she could call this time of night. Her parents were asleep, and Claudia would've reacted too harshly.

"I was just about to call you," Mr. Gregorio said when he answered. "You're home already?"

"No, I think Lloyd is following me."

"Well, I can drive over there if that'll make you feel better."

Maya wanted to say yes, but she thought about the hour, and the fact that he was a single parent. There was no need to disrupt Patrick's sleep. "You don't have to do that, but it would be nice if you could stay on the phone with me for a while."

"That's no problem at all." For the next two hours, they remained on the phone until Maya's eyes grew tired and it was clear that Lloyd wasn't going to show.

Chapter 26

"Want anything from the concession stand?" Maya asked Mr. Gregorio and his sister at Patrick's basketball game.

After writing their requests on a sheet of paper from her purse, Maya walked to the concession stand. As she passed the line for the bathrooms, Maya noticed a familiar-looking woman leaning against the wall. Unable to place where she knew the woman from, Maya smiled softly and said hello. Maybe the woman was the mother of a former student. After seven years of teaching, she'd met with too many parents to remember them all.

Maya continued to the back of the room and stood in the line that extended out into the lobby. Because this was the last game of the season, people from all sections of the neighborhood wanted to be in attendance.

As Maya waited her turn in line, she thought about Lloyd. Since he strangely showed up at the school two days ago, she hadn't heard from him. Either he finally accepted that their relationship was over, or he was giving her time to cool off. Whatever the reason, Maya was grateful for the break.

After three minutes of waiting, Maya checked the scoreboard behind her, and spotted the familiar woman gazing at her. The woman was still leaning on the wall while she nibbled on a pretzel, and although the person next to her was talking, the woman's eyes were fixed on Maya. Maybe she was trying to place Maya's face as well.

"Maya?" a female voice called from behind.

Maya turned around and faced First Lady Williams. "Hi," she said, surprised to see her. The first lady hadn't been at any of the other games.

"I'm still waiting to hear from you about joining the curriculum team. I may even have an exciting opportunity for you."

Maya had completely forgotten about the meeting she'd promised to set up. "I'm on spring break next week. Can we meet then?"

"Sure, how about Tuesday at two-thirty?"

Maya confirmed the day and time, and then said good-bye. As the first lady moved down the line, greeting people, Maya saw the mystery woman fast approaching in her direction.

Initially, Maya thought the woman had figured out where she knew Maya from. But as she grew nearer, the smile on her face had disappeared and Maya suddenly felt knots inside her stomach.

The woman was about three feet away, but in a clear and loud voice yelled, "You got a new man already?"

Confused, Maya turned and looked around. The angry woman had to be talking to someone behind her.

"Yeah, I'm talking to you, *Ms. Richards.*"

Immediately, Maya knew that the woman was Lloyd's wife. Once she was standing close to her, she realized that Queenie was the same woman she helped find the bathroom in church some time ago. *How did she find me?*

"Lloyd told me you want him to get a divorce. How does it feel to be a home wrecker?"

Maya looked around again and trembled when she saw First Lady Williams staring at her. What game was Lloyd playing? She hadn't asked him to leave his family at all. Getting a divorce was all his idea. Embarrassed, Maya left the line and ran outside to her car.

"Don't run away from me! I want everyone to know you're a Jezebel," Queenie shouted. "Face me like a real woman!"

Why is Queenie chasing me? Maya rushed to her car. There was no telling what Queenie was capable of doing.

When Maya reached her car, she scrambled through her purse for the keys. She could hear Queenie screaming through the parking lot, and knew it was only a matter of time before she was in her face again. In the nick of time, Maya found the keys and hopped inside of the car.

"I see that you and Lloyd are still talking on the phone." Queenie pulled hard on the car door handle. "I thought I warned you to stay away from him."

Maya hadn't spoken to Lloyd or seen him in two days. What was she talking about? "He's been calling me!" Maya screamed from inside the car.

Queenie yanked harder on the handle. "Come out of the car! If you think I'm gonna let some hot young thang take my husband, you're sadly mistaken."

Mr. Gregorio ran up to the car, carrying Maya's jacket and asked Queenie to leave. But Queenie wasn't moved by his attempt to rescue Maya. She stood back and looked him up and down. "You're a nice looking man. Why do you want to be with a home wrecker? I'm sure you can find someone better than *her*."

"That's for me to decide," Mr. Gregorio replied. "But you're not going to solve anything here in the parking lot with all of these people watching. This is a championship game for kids. Let's act like adults today."

Queenie looked at the small crowd that had gathered in the parking lot, and rolled her eyes. "This isn't over, Ms. Richards. If Lloyd files for a divorce, trust you'll hear from me again."

Maya watched Queenie walk down the parking lot and get into a dark blue Liberty Jeep.

Mr. Gregorio knocked on the window, but Maya was afraid to get out of the car or roll down the window. "It's okay, Maya. She's gone."

Maya took a deep breath and lowered the window. "Solomon, I'm so sorry about this."

"It's cool, Maya. But come back inside? I'm sure Patrick would want you to. Plus, I can keep an eye on you, at least for the next hour."

As humiliated as Maya was, she didn't want to let Patrick down. She looked past Mr. Gregorio and watched the crowd head back inside. It was going to be hard sitting through the rest of the game, but it would be even harder explaining to Patrick why she had to leave. "Okay," she agreed, then rolled up her window and got out of the car.

"What do you think about going to Houlihans after the game? Patrick can stay with Sydni," Mr.

Gregorio said as they walked to the gym. "I think it's time I hear about you and the gym teacher."

Despite the scene Queenie had caused, all seemed forgotten once the game resumed; at least Maya hadn't heard any whispers or comments. Patrick's team didn't win the championship, but he handled it well. Had he lost a month ago, Patrick might've thrown the basketball across the court. Overall, the day ended well, as did the dinner with Mr. Gregorio. As usual, he'd comforted Maya, and reacted to her story without ridicule or callous judgment. Knowing that Maya exercised regularly with Claudia, Mr. Gregorio even proposed that he join the ladies at the gym each morning of the spring break, so he could keep an eye on her. Mr. Gregorio was exactly the friend Maya needed.

When Maya parked her car, she was surprised to see her mother sitting on the porch furniture. Someone at the game must've informed her about Maya's confrontation with Queenie. It was the only reason Maya could explain her mother's unexpected visit.

"Hey, Pumpkin," Mrs. Richards said after Maya climbed the stairs to the porch.

"Hi, Mom. How long have you been here?"

"Maybe twenty minutes. Do you have time to talk to your aging mother?"

"Do I have a choice?" Maya unlocked the front door.

Inside, Maya poured each of them a glass of ice tea, and then sat at the kitchen table. "So," Maya said, "do you want to tell me why you're really here?"

Mrs. Richards looked at her daughter. "Well, I heard about the falling out at the church annex. Want to tell me what happened?"

"Not really." Knowing the truth would disappoint her mother. It was best Maya didn't share any details.

Mrs. Richards was quiet for about a minute before responding to Maya. "I know I drive you and your sister crazy sometimes, but you never declined to talk to me." Mrs. Richards drank the rest of her tea, and then opened a box of cookies on the table. "I called one of my usher friends from White Rock today. She said that Lloyd hadn't been to church in a very long time. Do you really like this guy?"

Hearing about another lie Lloyd had told frustrated Maya. "We're not together anymore, Mom, so you can relax."

Mrs. Richards sighed. "I can't relax, Pumpkin. Some woman accosted you at a basketball game.

I don't think I'm overreacting this time with my concern."

Maya got up from the table and put away the dishes on the drying rack. "The whole thing was a misunderstanding, Mom, that's all." And although there was no guarantee that Queenie wouldn't try to harm her again, Maya told her mother, "I'm sure it won't happen again."

"I know you're not telling me the truth, but I'll let it rest for now. I want you to know that I don't like what I see. Lloyd has come into your life and there's been nothing but trouble. You've distanced yourself from your family. He's not dependable, and certainly isn't an honest man. I mean, he lied about going to church. What decent man does that?"

Hearing the truth wasn't easy. Maya knew she didn't have a good defense for her mother's assessment of Lloyd, and he honestly wasn't worth defending. "I messed up, okay, Mom!" Maya slammed a cabinet door closed. "I made a bad decision. Can we please drop it?"

There weren't many times when Mrs. Richards was silent. But somehow she knew not to push the issue further. Instead of responding, she shoved another cookie inside her mouth and helped Maya put away the remaining dishes. "We're leaving for Europe on Monday. It would be nice if you joined the family for dinner after church tomorrow."

Nonchalantly, Maya lit the scented candles along the windowsill. "Sure, Mom, I'll be there."

Chapter 27

Three weeks had passed since the Queenie episode, and although there was no reason for her to surface, Maya was still on edge. Who knew what could trigger another incident? But with Gwen in town, and staying at her house, Maya tried to mask her frenzied state and had taken the day off work to get fitted for a dress. Gwen had already left the house so that she could meet a few college friends for breakfast, giving Maya time to get dressed without rushing before joining them at the bridal shop.

While Maya tied the strings of her espadrilles, she talked to Mr. Gregorio on speakerphone about attending Patrick's upcoming awards ceremony at church. Langston played with the dangling strings until Maya shooed him away. Thinking it was a game, Langston charged to the front door. Less than a minute later, the doorbell rang. Maya walked to the door and froze when she saw Lloyd. "Lloyd's here," Maya groaned.

What did he want? "I'll call you back in a few minutes, Solomon."

Leery of Lloyd's presence, Mr. Gregorio warned Maya not to let him into her home. "And don't be afraid to call me or the police."

After hanging up, Maya cautiously approached the open door, and as she neared Lloyd, she could smell the evidence of hard liquor through the screen. He must've been drinking half the morning.

"Why aren't you at work?"

"I couldn't take being away from you any longer. I heard from Ms. Covington that you took off today. I've missed you so much."

"What do you not understand, Lloyd? It's over between us, so please stop trying."

But Maya's words fell on deaf ears. "We can get married. I filed for a divorce. Soon I'll be a free man."

Annoyed, Maya realized that no matter what she said, Lloyd wasn't going to listen. "Did you drive?" Judging from the stench seeping through his pores, Lloyd had no business behind the wheel of a car.

"I had to see you," he said with watery eyes. "What am I supposed to do with all this love I have for you?"

"You're supposed to give it your family, because Lord knows Queenie isn't going to let you go. And even if Queenie did sign papers, she'd torment our lives forever. That's not something I'm willing to deal with for the rest of my life."

"Can I come in to talk?" As he grabbed the handle of the screen door, he lost his balance and almost fell backward.

Maya wanted to tell him to go home, but feared that he'd have a car accident and hurt himself, or someone else. "Look, I need to leave. Can I call you a cab? You shouldn't be on the road in your present condition."

"I can stay here until you get back," Lloyd mumbled, barely keeping his eyes open.

Maya sighed. "Wait here." She went to the dining room to get her purse. When she returned, Lloyd was sitting on the steps. Maya rolled her eyes at the sight of him and locked the door. "Let's go, Lloyd." She helped him to his feet. "I'll drop you off at Robert's house."

Too intoxicated to argue, Lloyd stumbled behind Maya and got into her car. Watching Lloyd struggle to fasten his seatbelt, Maya couldn't figure out why she let him into her life.

As Maya drove to West Philly, Lloyd dozed off to sleep, waking up every four minutes to express his love. When she stopped at the stoplight before the Gray's Ferry Bridge, Maya glanced at the SUV dangerously close to her bumper. At the next light, Maya inched forward and the SUV did too. Before the light turned green, Maya caught a glimpse of the "QUEEN" license plate and punched Lloyd's leg. "Get up; Queenie's behind us!" she shouted. How long had she been tailgating?

Lloyd jumped up and looked out the back window. "What does she want, and why are my kids in the car?"

Maya couldn't drive away rapidly in the two-lane street, but she was tired of being followed. As soon as she could, Maya swerved to the side of the road and parked. "Get out!" From the side-view mirror, Maya saw Queenie park the SUV and race toward her, dragging a large garbage bag. "Get out, right now!" she screamed at Lloyd, fearing Queenie was about to damage her car.

"You won, Ms. Richards," Queenie belted. "He's all yours, so take *all* his crap with you."

Without hesitation, Queenie stopped by the side of Maya's car and emptied the contents of the garbage into the street.

At the sight of his clothes flying about, Lloyd sobered up quickly and got out of the car and tried to retrieve them. As he darted in and out of traffic, Queenie ran back to her car and ordered her daughters to help. It didn't take long for Lanecia to follow her mother's actions, but Lauren visibly wanted the chaos to cease. She stood on the sidewalk, crying hysterically and shaking.

Maya couldn't stand the sight anymore. As soon as traffic slowed, she sped off. But Maya wasn't out of the woods yet. She heard Queenie shout, "Stay with your father!"

In a short amount of time, Queenie was on Maya's trail again. Only this time, she kept her hand on the horn. "Jesus, what does she want with me?"

Maya sped down the expressway and into the South Philly neighborhood, but she couldn't shake Queenie. Where were the police when she needed them? Wasn't the horn bothering other drivers?

Scared for her life, Maya turned a corner and parked in a well-lit parking lot across from the bridal shop. Queenie pulled into the lot too, and as she passed Maya's car, shouted, "You ruined my marriage, Jezebel!"

Maya locked her car, and then rushed across the street to safety, or so she thought. As she opened the door to the bridal shop, Maya was pulled to the ground. "I'm never gonna sign the papers!" Queenie squealed. "You'll never have him!"

Laying on the ground, Maya rolled into a ball as Queenie called her names and threatened to ruin her life. Maya felt a kick in her back, and feared what was coming next. Not much of a physical fighter, Maya fought the only way she knew how. *Jesus,* Maya cried repeatedly, and right before Queenie's fist landed on her face, Gwen charged out of the store and pushed her out of the way. Stunned, Queenie challenged Gwen, but held her tongue when she saw eight other women, including Mrs. Richards and her sisters come outside.

"Someone call the police! My daughter's being attacked!" Mrs. Richards screeched, and dropped to the pavement to comfort Maya.

At a loss for words, Queenie considered her odds, and then slowly backed away. "Watch your back, Maya Richards," she yelled, and then ran back to the parking lot.

"I'm so sorry, Gwen," cried Maya, still lying on the ground. "I'm so sorry."

"Was that the same woman from the basketball game?" Mrs. Richards asked in tears.

Gwen knelt by her sister's side once Queenie was gone. "You need to press charges before this really gets out of hand, Maya. If she would go through the trouble of following you here, who knows what else she's capable of doing."

Maya reached for Gwen's hand. "Please," she sobbed, "no police. I'll take care of this tomorrow. I promise." Though Maya didn't have a clue how to stop Queenie, she didn't want the police involved because she'd have to admit, in front of her mother, that she'd unknowingly had an affair with a married man.

"Do you know this woman, Pumpkin? Was that the same woman from the basketball game?" Mrs. Richards queried. But Maya couldn't reply. She was too ashamed to share the truth.

Seated in between Mrs. Richards and Gwen, Maya listened to the first lady deliver a powerful sermon at the Mother's Day brunch. No one had discussed what happened at the bridal shop, but Maya knew they were intrigued. Never in Maya's life had she been surrounded by so much drama.

"I don't often watch sitcoms," First Lady said. "But I was visiting my mother last night, and she wanted to watch *Desperate Housewives*. Now, I know the show is partially classified as witty and light, but as I watched, I took the plot to a deeper level."

The first lady removed the microphone from its base on the podium, and walked off the small stage. "As women, we have to learn how not to appear desperate. Sometimes, when it seems that our prayers aren't answered, we feel God hasn't heard us and tend to take matters into our hands. That's a desperate move. Some of us need to thank God for not answering some prayers." First Lady Williams continued to circle the room. "My sisters, be careful of the prayers made in a desperate state. So you're thirty and still without children of your own. So what? Let's not be like Sarah. She was so desperate to give Abraham a child that she asked another woman to sleep with him."

The first lady walked back to the stage, and continued her message with more fire and zeal than anyone had ever seen. "Some of you turned forty this year and wondered when God was going to send you a husband. It's okay to pray for a husband, but what if God has something far greater than marriage in mind for you? Remember Leah and Jacob? Leah did anything to please her man, yet he never really wanted her in the first place. He wanted Leah's sister, Rachel. As a result, Leah went through extremes to try and please Jacob. That was a desperate move."

As the first lady wrapped up her sermon, Maya's leg shook rapidly. The message had touched Maya's spirit, and if she weren't sitting next to her mother, Maya would've shouted, "Amen," and run around the room.

"God is your all!" the first lady shouted. "No matter what path He's chosen for you, He will sustain you. But you've got to trust Him. Acting out of desperation only leads to trouble. Trust God, my sisters. Trust God."

First Lady Williams put the microphone back in its base, then walked back to her table as shouts of praise filled the room.

As several woman cried out to God verbally, Maya closed her eyes and silently poured out a prayer. *"Please help me, Lord. I want to do better. I don't want to be desperate anymore."*

Chapter 28

In a packed room of family and supporters of the basketball league, Maya sat at the table reserved for Patrick's guests. All ten seats at the table were filled, including the one designated for Patrick's mother, Lena, and his baby brother. Though Lena's presence made Maya slightly uncomfortable because of their first encounter, Maya was glad she was there. It meant a great deal to Patrick.

"And the child to receive the most improved player of the year is . . ." the youth minister said, as he opened a sealed envelope ". . . Patrick Gregorio! Come on up, Patrick!"

Mr. Gregorio and Lena escorted their son to the front of the room, capturing his every move on camera. Feeling like a third parent, Maya started to cry. Patrick had grown a great deal since the beginning of the school year.

Once Patrick was situated on stage, he received his plaque and accepted the invitation to give a short speech. Without a trace of stage fright, Patrick thanked his parents for keeping him in line, and his family for putting up with his behavior. "I'd also like to thank my favorite teacher, Ms. Richards, for never giving up on me."

When Mr. Gregorio returned to the table, he took one look at Maya and laughed. "You have raccoon eyes," he said and sat down.

Maya gently hit his shoulder, and then excused herself from the table. She wanted to go to the bathroom to freshen her makeup. On the way out of the room, Maya saw Lloyd standing by the door and stopped walking. His behavior was now bordering on stalking. Maya spotted an escape route and headed out of the second pair of doors. Not sure of where she was going, Lloyd followed her. "Maya," he tried to whisper. "Maya, I want to talk to you."

Maya picked up speed, but she wasn't fast enough. Lloyd called her name a few times, and then grabbed her arm to force her to talk to him. "I can't live without you, Maya. You add so many beautiful things to my life. I miss you, love."

Refusing to argue, Maya didn't respond and tried to walk away, but Lloyd grabbed her arm and pulled her into his chest. It was then that she smelled alcohol on his breath. Maya tried to release from his grasp, but his grip was too strong. "Lloyd, you show up drunk to church and expect me to take you back?"

"I'm never gonna let you go!"

"Please, Lloyd, leave me alone!" Out of no-where, Mr. Gregorio appeared.

"You okay, Maya?" Mr. Gregorio asked.

"She's fine, and this doesn't concern you," Lloyd snapped, slowly releasing his hold on Maya.

"I'm fine, Solomon," Maya answered, and straightened her clothes. "Just trying to get to the bathroom."

"Hey, man," Lloyd said, "I think you should leave us be."

"I'm not going anywhere," Mr. Gregorio re-plied, standing firm.

Lloyd eyed Mr. Gregorio and pumped his fists repeatedly. "Look, this is none of your business. Why don't you—"

"No, man," Mr. Gregorio said calmly, yet with a strong base in his tone, "why don't you leave? This isn't the time or the place for—"

"Solomon," Maya interrupted and stood beside him. She was afraid the scene would escalate and disturb the awards ceremony. "Let's just go back inside. I'll fix my makeup later, okay? People are staring at us." Maya tugged Mr.

Gregorio's arm lightly and he hesitantly turned around and headed inside the main room.

"How can you do this to me?" Lloyd called after Maya, hoping she'd come back to him. But Maya didn't turn around. She couldn't. She wanted Lloyd to understand that their relationship and friendship had come to an end, and there was nothing he could do to change her mind.

Though Maya wasn't sure how long Lloyd had stayed in the hallway, she was glad he was gone when the ceremony ended, and prayed that she'd seen the last of his embarrassing stunts.

After taking a warm bath, Maya dressed in lounging clothes and went downstairs to wait for Mr. Gregorio. Maya had left a bag of cat food in his car after a trip to Costco, and he wanted to drop it off so Langston wouldn't starve.

The doorbell rang and Maya checked the time. "That was fast," Maya said, and smiled as she headed to the door. She couldn't see who was on the other side of the door, but it had to be Mr. Gregorio. And as she unlocked the door, she remembered that Lloyd had shown up to church drunk. It could be him. "Solomon?" Maya called, and when she didn't hear a response tried to lock the door, but she was too slow. Queenie had wedged her body in between the door, and then forced her way inside.

"Not again," Maya moaned as Queenie aggressively pushed her into the wall.

"Where is he? And don't tell me he isn't here!" Queenie shouted, and advanced beyond the vestibule.

In pain, Maya limped after Queenie, forgetting to close the door. "He's not here. Please believe me."

"Believe a woman who steals a man away from his family? I don't think so," retorted Queenie as she continued to march through the house screaming Lloyd's name.

When Queenie ran upstairs, Maya took an African mask off the wall to use for protection. As Maya tipped up the stairs, Queenie chuckled like a villain. "Is that supposed to scare me? I see it's time for me to teach you a lesson. You can't have any man you want." Queenie ran up to Maya swinging.

In hindsight, Maya knew she should've run out of the house or called the police, rather than try to handle Lloyd's deranged wife alone. But she had panicked and was only concerned about defending herself. So as the insane woman rapidly approached her, Maya closed her eyes and swung hard, but only grazed Queenie's arm.

Scared, Maya's hand trembled ferociously and she dropped the mask onto her feet. Queenie giggled at Maya's pitiful attempt to hurt her, and swung her around. Before Maya could regain her composure, Queenie knocked her into the railing, causing Maya to stumble and lose her footing. "Jesus, help me!" Maya cried as she tumbled down the stairs.

"Maya?" Mr. Gregorio called, and cautiously entered the house. When he saw Maya laying limp at the bottom of the stairs, he rushed to her side and pulled his cell phone from his pocket.

Hearing Mr. Gregorio call an ambulance, Queenie panicked. And without thinking clearly, she rushed by him and fled the scene.

Chapter 29

Awakened by a familiar gospel hymn, Maya almost panicked when she opened her eyes and realized she was in a foreign place. The last thing Maya remembered before she blacked out was Queenie screaming throughout her house. It was crazy to think that Queenie had kidnapped her, but Maya knew better than to underestimate her abilities. Anyone with enough gall to force their way into someone else's home, might not think kidnapping was insane.

Maya tried to sit up, only her body wouldn't cooperate. As she tried to wiggle her body, Maya felt a wave of pain travel through her.

"Relax, Pumpkin," Mrs. Richards said and held her daughter's hand.

"Mom?" Maya attempted to turn her head to the side, but couldn't because her neck was in a brace. And though her vision was a little fuzzy, Maya could see that her leg was in a sling. Confused, Maya moved her eyes so that she could see her mother clearly. "Where am I, Mom?"

Mrs. Richards gently rubbed Maya's hand. "You took a bad fall, Pumpkin. You're in the hospital. Solomon called the church and they called the house. Your father and I rushed to the hospital as soon as we could."

"Solomon?" Maya tried to recall what had happened, and then like a flash of light it all became clear. Not only had Queenie pushed her way into Maya's house, she'd knocked her down a flight of stairs. And before the room grew dark, the last voice Maya heard belonged to Solomon. "Am I gonna be okay?" From the looks of things, Maya prayed the sling and neck brace were the only injuries she suffered.

"The doctors say you're going to be all right, but you hurt yourself pretty bad," Mrs. Richards said and paused briefly. "Everybody at the church is praying for you."

Something in Mrs. Richards's voice troubled Maya. The way she paused between sentences told Maya that her mother was holding back information. Not in the mindset to press for the truth, Maya closed her eyes. "Did Solomon tell you what happened?" she asked, afraid that he had.

"He mentioned that a woman broke into your house. Did you know her?"

Too ashamed to look at her mother, Maya started to cry. "It was Lloyd's wife."

"Oh, Maya!" Mrs. Richards bellowed disappointedly as she wiped her daughter's tears with her hand.

The throbbing pain Maya felt couldn't compare to her mother's reaction.

There was a knock at the door and Maya flinched. "Relax, Pumpkin. You're safe now," Mrs. Richards assured her.

A short and stubby middle-aged doctor walked into the room and set a chart on a nearby rolling table. "Hello, Maya, I'm Dr. Patel." The doctor's smile was friendly as he checked Maya's vitals, and then pulled a stool close to her bed. "You fell down a flight of stairs pretty hard, Maya. I don't know what your mother has told you, but I want to talk to you about your injuries and answer any questions you may have."

Maya started breathing heavier, in anticipation of the bad news Dr. Patel was about to deliver. And in support of her daughter, Mrs. Richards remained at Maya's bedside.

"As a result of the fall, your pelvis is fractured and your hip is bruised. So you're going to be in bandages for a while." He pointed to the cast wrapped around Maya's body. "You'll have to wear that neck brace for a week or two to help relieve the soreness of the sprain. You also bruised your big toe, but it's not broken. Now, you tore a couple ligaments in your right leg," Dr. Patel explained as he pointed to the sling, "so you'll be purple for a while and in a fair amount of pain. I'll prescribe Vicodin to help with the pain, but you'll still feel a little achy. The healing process will be long, and you'll need therapy, but you'll be fine." Dr. Patel scribbled notes onto Maya's chart, and then said, "You're lucky to be alive."

Although the doctor had said a mouthful, Maya was stuck on the fact that her pelvis was fractured. "Will I be able to have children?"

"Not many people would've survived the kind of fall you had," Dr. Patel replied and stood up. "The pelvic bone is strong, but there was substantial damage and . . . you're in your late thirties—"

"Excuse me, Doctor," Mrs. Richards interrupted tearfully, "but we believe in a God who performs miracles. All things are possible to him who believes."

Dr. Patel's cheeks flushed. "I believe that too, but it's my job to give the facts." He grabbed Maya's hand and squeezed it gently. "Keep praying, young lady, and concentrate on getting better."

When Dr. Patel left the room, Mrs. Richards immediately started praying. As Mrs. Richards asked God for healing power, Maya feared God had taken away her ability to have children. How could she let Lloyd ruin her life? Having kids of her own was something Maya lived for, and now her chance may be gone. "How could I be so stupid?" she blurted repeatedly as her mother brought the prayer to a close.

"Don't get yourself too excited, Pumpkin. You made a mistake, but thank God you're alive." Mrs. Richards stroked Maya's hair. "He's given you another chance to live. That in itself is enough to be grateful for."

"Where's Daddy?"

"He took your aunts home almost two hours ago. I had to make Solomon leave too," Mrs. Richards informed Maya, then reclaimed her seat in the reclining chair. "According to hospital rules, I should've gone home too, but the nurse on duty happens to be an old colleague. She understood that I couldn't leave my child. Claudia's going to stop by tomorrow, and Gwen will be here in a couple of days."

Maya turned her head to the left as much as she could without feeling pain, and stared at the machine monitoring her vitals. She wondered if Lloyd was aware of the damage he'd caused. Did he know that he drove one woman to commit a crime, and possibly caused another to be barren?

"Solomon must be your angel, Pumpkin. That woman might've left you for dead," Mrs. Richards stated, then sat back and hummed the tune to "Jesus is Real."

"I didn't get a good look at her face," Maya told a young policeman the next morning.

"That's okay. Sometimes it takes a few days to remember details, but don't hesitate to let me know if you remember anything about the woman who attacked you," the officer replied, and then handed Maya his card. "The more you can remember, the better the chances we have at finding her."

Maya saw Claudia creep in behind the officer, holding a stuffed animal and flowers, and looked down at the card in her hand. "Thank you," she replied weakly. Maya felt bad about lying to the policeman, but she wasn't ready to press charges against Queenie. She was afraid contact from the police would incite Queenie's erratic behavior even more and push her to cause more damage. It was best, at least for now, that Maya remain silent about her attacker's identity.

The policeman nodded and before turning to leave, greeted Claudia with a friendly smile. "I love a man in uniform. I hope you told him *everything*," Claudia whispered, then kissed her friend's forehead. She then set a brown teddy bear in Maya's arms. "My children thought you needed a fuzzy friend to help you heal." Claudia walked over to the large windows and placed the flowers she bought on the windowsill. "You know . . . this isn't the way I wanted to be proven right."

"How did I get myself into so much trouble?"

"This is not the time to sulk. You should be thankful that Lloyd is out of your life. Mrs. Bridges made him take an extended leave of absence."

"He's jobless?"

"Humph! He's lucky Mrs. Bridges didn't fire him. We all eventually have to pay for our actions. The consequence that Lloyd has to suffer for all of this is his cross to bear. Now stop worrying about him, and concentrate on getting better. I'm just glad Patrick's father was there with you. By the way, why was he there again?"

"He was dropping off a bag of cat food from Costco."

Claudia chuckled, and then sat in a chair by the window. "So that fat cat saved your life?"

"Good ole Langston. But I suppose you want to say I told you so. Why don't you get it out now?"

"Don't be silly, Maya. That's not what friends do. I may have been tough on you and Lloyd, but I just had this feeling that something wasn't right."

"I know." Maya started to cry. "Why didn't I heed the signs? Why was I so foolish?"

"Those better be tears of joy," Claudia remarked. "You're not the first woman to use bad judgment over a man. I made myself sick over Debbie's father. You wouldn't believe half the things he put me through. So don't beat yourself up." Claudia stood up and stood by Maya's bed. "Enough about Lloyd, I want to know what's up with you and Mr. Gregorio. I saw him on my way in and he mentioned that he'd be back later. Are you keeping secrets?"

"No, we're just friends."

Maya's reply wasn't convincing. "Whatever you say," Claudia responded, and sat at the bottom of the bed, "but for the record, I like him.

"I'm done with men. I don't want to make another bad choice."

"You know there is such a thing as speaking things into existence. You shouldn't give up on love. You just need to let God send the man to you."

Claudia meant well, but for Maya it was too late to convince her that love would come her way.

Later that afternoon, Maya was exhausted. Her room had been like a revolving door. The minute one visitor left, someone new entered. Though she was glad to see her friends and family, especially Gwen, Maya appreciated the opportunity to rest her eyes for the last hour. If the nurse hadn't come in to administer medication, she could've slept a little longer. When the nurse left, Maya slowly turned her head toward the door. She couldn't believe how the slightest movement caused such great pain. Although on the surface Lloyd was to blame, Maya had to accept partial credit for what happened.

Drifting in and out of sleep, Maya thought she was dreaming when she saw a tall, thin shadow of a man at the door holding a small floral arrangement.

"Hello, beautiful," Kenneth said and walked into the room. "I heard about the accident and wanted to see you for myself."

"Ken?" Maya hadn't seen or heard from Kenneth since New Year's. Not even at church.

Kenneth approached Maya's bed so that Maya could see a clear view of him. "It's me." He set the basket of flowers on the table next to Maya's bed. "I won't stay long," he said, and kissed Maya gently on the forehead, "but I wanted you to know that I have a very good lawyer friend who can help you press charges on the woman who attacked you."

How much did Kenneth know about the incident? Did he know about Lloyd, and that the woman who pushed her down the stairs was his wife? "I need to think about that." Although revenge was warranted, Maya wasn't sure pressing charges was the right action to take. "Can I get back to you?"

"Absolutely," Kenneth told her, then took a business card from his wallet and set it on the table. "I'll leave her contact information with you. She's expecting your call."

She? Maya wondered if *she* were more than a friend. There was something about the way Kenneth said 'very good lawyer friend' that struck a sour chord with her. "Thank you, Ken."

Kenneth leaned down and kissed Maya goodbye. "I wish things were different between us. I hope you know I'll always be here for you."

Kenneth's words brought tears to Maya's eyes. If only he had wanted to get married or she hadn't pressured him, she wouldn't be laid up in a hospital with a fractured pelvis, cracked ribs, or broken toe. "That means a lot," Maya replied.

Kenneth kissed Maya one last time, and then walked out of the room, and when he was gone, another piece of Maya's heart left with him.

An hour before the end of visiting hours, Mrs. Richards and Gwen came back to the hospital with First Lady Williams. During the visit, Maya told them that Kenneth stopped by to discuss pressing charges against Queenie.

"I can't believe I'm saying this, but you should listen to Ken," Gwen said. "This or something worse could happen to the next woman Lloyd chooses to have an affair with."

"Do what you feel is right," Mrs. Richards added.

Maya wiggled as best she could to relieve an itch on her shoulder blade. "I don't know what to do. I've made such a mess of my life. I made a list and prayed for a man just like Lloyd. I got what I prayed for."

"Oh, sweetheart," First Lady Williams said, and moved from the corner of the room to be closer to Maya. "It's okay to be specific about want you want, but God also knows best. You've got to make sure what you're asking for is in line with what God would want. He knows the desires of your heart."

"People keep telling me that. But I don't think people understand what it's like to walk out on someone you love, and then be surrounded by family and friends who all have special loves in their lives. I wanted to be in love too."

Mrs. Richards started to cry along with her daughter. It was hard to watch Maya on the verge of depression, so she left the room.

"You have so much to live for, Maya," the first lady stated, and picked up a handmade card from Patrick. "Your students love you. The kids at church love you. Your family loves you. How do you think they'd feel if you were no longer around? God chose you to educate His children. That's pretty awesome."

A nurse entered the room and announced that visiting hours were over. The first lady grabbed her handbag and put it on her shoulder. "There's more to life than having a man. I hope this situation helps you realize that waiting on God is the only way to go. You should also think about strengthening your relationship with God."

"What more can I do?" Maya thought she was doing all the right things.

"You have to pray about that. God will speak to you if you're open to listen. It could be that you need to read the Bible more, or attend Bible Study more. You may even need to find a ministry that best suits you. You're great in Sunday School, but I have a feeling your mother coerced you into that." The first lady kissed Maya good-bye. "Don't give up on God, Maya. He still has the best in store for you."

After saying good-bye to her mother and Gwen, Maya closed her eyes and prayed. *I'm sorry for not trusting you and wavering in my faith. I was scared and confused. But if it's your will for me to get married, please let my husband have a genuine and honest relationship with you. If he loves you, I know he'll do right by me.*

As soon as Maya finished praying, a faded image of Mr. Gregorio and his son came to mind, and helped her drift off to sleep peacefully.

Chapter 30

Two months later . . .

Slowly, Maya strolled down the aisle in a peach chiffon gown; the mild pain along her right side causing her to limp. It'd been two months since Maya had fallen down the stairs, and every time she took a step, she was reminded of that dreadful day. The pain was not great all the time, but Maya noticed that a certain style of shoe, or the chance of rain intensified the pressure in her pelvic bone even more.

Maya took her rightful place at the front of the bridal party line and shifted her weight. Mindful of her sister's injury, Gwen had chosen studded open-toed flat sandals, instead of skinny heels for the bridesmaids. Even with that adjustment, Maya prayed she'd be able to stand in one place for an entire hour.

As the matron of honor made her way to the front, Maya looked out into the crowded church.

Because Justin was a photographer and Gwen a writer, together, they knew a lot of people, all of whom wanted to share in their special day. There wasn't an empty seat in the main sanctuary.

On the first row, Mrs. Richards and her sisters sat next to one another in similar cream outfits, with swollen eyes from their tears of joy. Behind them, Mr. Gregorio and Patrick sat next to each other in matching suits. Waving rapidly, Patrick caught Maya's attention, and she winked her right eye. After all that she'd been through with Lloyd and Queenie, she still couldn't believe that God had blessed her with Mr. Gregorio's friendship. From the very beginning, he had been by her side, especially through the bouts of depression and physical therapy. And although Maya gave him good reason to walk away at times, Mr. Gregorio was always patient and kept a positive attitude.

Having Mr. Gregorio around so frequently felt natural; like they'd been together all of their lives, and the more Maya got to know him, the more she hoped their relationship would turn into something deeper. This time she didn't create an extensive list or pray that her feelings would be returned. After such a dramatic experience, Maya knew that she had to leave their friendship in God's hands. She no longer trusted herself to make wise decisions when it came to men. Unfortunately, she had to learn the hard way to let God reign in *all* areas of her life.

The pianist stopped playing the instrumental version of "I'm Gonna Be Ready" when Gwen appeared at the back doors, the traditional bridal hymn began, and she floated down the aisle in her pure white gown, with Mr. Richards proudly escorting her to the altar. The guests stood up and cameras flashed from all directions, causing the hand-beaded accents along the break-front skirt bottom to sparkle.

Admiring her sister's gown, Maya hadn't noticed that the pianist had transitioned to a new song. The look on Gwen's face said that she, too, was confused, but she kept walking toward her soon-to-be-husband.

Without warning, Justin grabbed a microphone from Pastor Williams, and with shaking hands cleared his throat. Then, in a deep and loud voice, he serenaded his blushing bride with his version of India Arie's "A Beautiful Surprise."

"You are everything I asked for in my prayers. So I know my angel brought you to my life . . ." Mildly off key, Justin struggled through the words, careful not to shed a tear, and when he finished the last line, "You are a beautiful surprise," there wasn't a dry eye in the room.

For Maya, every word Justin sang struck a chord in her heart, and as she stared into Mr. Gregorio's big brown eyes, she knew that the moment meant something to him too.

Chapter 31

In an overpriced pair of flip-flops, Maya walked around her old classroom, collecting the instructional materials she'd purchased over the last seven years. With the help of Debbie, Claudia's oldest daughter, she packed the things she wanted to keep into four large boxes. The first day of a new school year was due to begin next week and she needed to clear out her belongings so that the teacher taking her place could set up the room to her liking. Maya knew she'd miss her colleagues and many of the children at the school, but she was ready for a new beginning.

With Mr. Gregorio and her family's encouragement, Maya had talked to Kenneth about filing a restraining order against Queenie. That option didn't seem too harsh, and was something she was comfortable with, though Mrs. Richards made Maya promise to press more severe charges if Queenie threatened her again.

Up until a few weeks ago, Maya had intended to return to her teaching position. Lloyd had lost his position as the gym teacher, and she thought she'd be strong enough to endure another year. But because of her fractured pelvis and sore leg, Maya learned that she could only tolerate a couple hours at best on her feet. Though Maya's doctors seemed confident the pain she experienced from day to day would go away, they explained that fractured bones took a long time to heal. For these reasons, Maya decided to accept First Lady Williams's job offer to become the curriculum director for the school, Monumental, that had been built over the summer. In her new position, Maya wouldn't have to stand on her feet all day.

As Maya and Debbie sorted through various items, Debbie shared the details of a summer visit to Atlanta to see her biological father. It was the first time since she was ten that she'd spent more than a week with him.

Midway through her story, Mr. Gregorio walked into the classroom, carrying a bag of mail. "Ms. Covington said these poured in after the news of your accident spread," Mr. Gregorio said as he handed Maya the bag.

Maya peeked inside the bag and was surprised at the number of letters and cards. She could almost bet that Ms. Covington embellished her reason for being in the hospital. During one of her hospital visits, Maya told Ms. Covington, "I slipped down the steps." But by the time the chatty secretary made it back to West Philly, the story had turned into a scene from a best-selling romantic thriller. How the woman received her information, Maya had yet to figure out, but most of it was fairly accurate.

Though Maya insisted she was capable of driving her own car, Mr. Gregorio was weary. He'd taken the day off so that he could be her personal chauffeur. It didn't matter to him that the dosage for her pain medication had significantly decreased, he was worried that she might fall asleep at the wheel and have an accident. Mr. Gregorio had even convinced Mr. Richards to drive Maya to and from her new job until she no longer needed the medicine at all.

"Hey, Mr. Gregorio," Debbie said from the back of the room.

"Hi, Debbie, it's good to see you again. I hear you're going to China in October." Having been around Maya most of the summer, Mr. Gregorio not only bonded with Maya's family, but Claudia's too.

Debbie stacked a few books from a bookshelf inside a box. "Yeah, I'm so looking forward to it."

"Smart move. You'll be surprised at the job offers you'll receive after you graduate. Best of luck to you," he said, then drew his attention back to Maya. Watching her slowly walk to her desk, Mr. Gregorio sensed that she may be in pain. "Are you okay?" Maya shook her head. Though he didn't believe her, Mr. Gregorio didn't argue. Instead, he stood close to her desk and said, "I was going to pick Patrick up from his mother's house, but I can take you home first. You should probably rest."

"Don't worry about me. I'm sure Debbie can take me home. Go get Patrick. You haven't seen him all month."

He gazed into Maya's eyes. "Are you sure?"

Mr. Gregorio had been flexible with his time since Maya was released from the hospital. Her needs never seemed to be a problem for him, but Maya didn't want to take advantage of his kindness. "Absolutely. I know he's anxious to see you. I'm surprised he stayed as long as he did."

"Prayer does change things. I don't want to burden you, Debbie, so please call if you can't take Maya home."

"I'll make sure she gets home safely," Debbie confirmed.

"Okay," Mr. Gregorio said, and kissed Maya on the cheek. "I'm heading out. Are we still on for the BBQ later?"

"My mom called three times this morning already," Maya responded and laughed. "She's expecting you to help my father on the grill."

"In that case, I better be there early," he stated, and before leaving the classroom, waved good-bye to Debbie.

"You two are so cute," Debbie said in admiration when Mr. Gregorio left. "I hope I find someone special too. Good men are such a rarity."

"Don't rush to be in love," Maya said as she tossed unwanted mail in the trashcan by her chair. Debbie didn't know much about Maya's tumultuous relationship with Lloyd. Claudia had told her children that Maya was accosted by a deranged woman. She figured that's all they needed to know. "Do you pray?"

"All the time. College isn't easy."

"Then you know that God will take care of you. You don't want any unnecessary regrets."

Debbie agreed, and then proceeded to tell Maya about a medical student she was attracted to.

Maya opened a plain white envelope without a return address. She unfolded the anonymous two-page letter as Debbie talked. She didn't recognize the handwriting, but after reading the first paragraph Maya immediately knew the letter had come from Queenie. *What could*

Queenie possibly have to say? Not knowing what to expect, Maya prepared for the worst as she continued to read. She had painfully learned that Queenie was an unpredictable woman.

> *I wanted to say I'm sorry for the way things turned out. I never intended for things to go that far. Instead of the restraining order, you could've pressed charges and made my life worse, but you spared me. Thank you.*
>
> *It was difficult explaining to my daughters why their father couldn't go back to work at the school. I'm not proud of the part I played in this situation, but was afraid I was going to lose my husband.*
>
> *Lloyd and I are still together. I know you think I'm crazy, but I love him, and I'll do what I have to to keep my family together. When I recited my wedding vows, I meant them with my whole heart. 'Til death do us part. You'll understand one day, if you ever get married.*
>
> *Lloyd mentioned that you were in the hospital for a while. I don't know how badly you were hurt from the fall, but I really am sorry. Lloyd and I are going to counseling, so I'm hopeful that we'll get*

*past this. I hope you'll find someone to love
too.*

Maya prayed spiritual or physical death
wouldn't come soon for Queenie. If Lloyd was
really unhappy in his marriage, he would cheat
on her again. As much as Maya felt sorry for her,
she especially felt sorrow for their daughters.
The look on Lauren's face when Queenie made
her throw her father's clothes into the street was
a memory Maya couldn't erase. After reading the
letter a second time, Maya stuffed it back inside
the envelope. *Thank you for deliverance, Jesus.*
Maya replayed the short-lived romance with
Lloyd and the drama with his wife.

"I like him, but sometimes I feel like he sends
me mixed signals," Debbie said, not realizing
that Maya had zoned out for a few minutes.

As Maya listened to the end of the story, she
felt compelled to tell Debbie the truth about her
injury. Her eagerness to be in a relationship may
have cost her the ability to have children, and
even worse, could've cost her her life. Had she
paid attention to all the signs God had placed
before her, Maya could've avoided the situation
altogether. There was no way to turn back the
hands of time, but before Maya left the hospital,

she promised God that she would share her story with other women in hopes that they may be spared the pain she experienced.

"Come have a seat by me, Debbie. I want to tell you a story." Maya shifted in her seat.

Debbie stopped packing then took a seat in a chair next to Maya's desk and patiently waited for her to speak. This was the first time Maya had told anyone all of the details concerning her relationship with Lloyd, and she was nervous. There was no way to tell how a person would receive the information, but Maya knew she had to share. Whatever happened once she was done talking would be left up to God. So Maya took a deep breath and asked God to give her the right words to say.

"I don't want you to end up like me, Debbie. I had people all around me, trying to warn me about a certain man, but I didn't listen. So God taught me a tough lesson." For the next hour, she told Debbie about the last eight months of her life.

When Maya was done, both she and Debbie were in tears. "I know what it feels like to want a companion, Debbie, but please be *very* careful about the kind of man you welcome into your life. And especially be careful about the kind of man you pray for."

Readers' Guide Questions

1. Maya and Kenneth were together for thirteen years. How long should a couple be in a relationship before they consider marriage?
2. How do you feel about Kenneth's views on marriage?
3. Did Maya enter into a relationship with Lloyd too soon after breaking up with Kenneth?
4. Was Claudia too tough on Maya? Was Gwen too laid back? How did Claudia and Maya's family affect her life?
5. Do you believe in love at first sight? Do you think Lloyd really loved Maya as he had confessed? Was there something special between Maya and Solomon from the very beginning?
6. Identify specific situations or incidents when Maya should have listened to or consulted God about her relationship with Lloyd.
7. God gives us a spirit of discernment. Mrs. Richards and Claudia both sensed that something was not right with Lloyd. Why do you think Maya ignored the warning signs? When, if at all, did you suspect that something wasn't right with Lloyd?

8. How did Maya's relationship with Lloyd affect her life and her friendship with Claudia?

9. Queenie mentioned that she knew about Maya long before she contacted her for the first time. Considering Queenie's strong personality, why do you think she kept quiet for so long?

10. Discuss the strengths and weaknesses for two of your favorite characters.

11. Do you think God wants us to be specific in our prayers for a mate? What was wrong with the list Maya created? If you had to make a list, what kinds of characteristics and traits would you include?

12. Name at least three questions a woman should ask a potential suitor. How soon into the friendship should a woman ask the questions?

13. Though Queenie's measures were dramatic, was she foolish for wanting to save her marriage? What would have been a better way to handle the situation?

14. Did Maya have a strong relationship with God? How did her relationship with Him change throughout the story?

15. If you could talk to one of the characters, who would it be? What would you tell her or him?

UC HIS GLORY BOOK CLUB!

www.uchisglorybookclub.net

UC His Glory Book Club is the spirit-inspired brainchild of Joylynn Jossel, author and acquisitions editor of Urban Christian, and Kendra Norman-Bellamy, author for Urban Christian. This is an online book club that hosts authors of Urban Christian. We welcome as members all men and women who have a passion for reading Christian-based fiction.

UC His Glory Book Club pledges our commitment to provide support, positive feedback, encouragement, and a forum whereby members can openly discuss and review the literary works of Urban Christian authors.

There is no membership fee associated with UC His Glory Book Club; however, we do ask that you support the authors through purchasing, encouraging, providing book reviews, and of course, your prayers. We also ask that you respect our beliefs and follow the guidelines of the book club. We hope to receive your valuable input, opinions, and reviews that build up, rather than tear down our authors.

What We Believe:

—We believe that Jesus is the Christ, Son of the Living God.

—We believe the Bible is the true, living Word of God.

—We believe all Urban Christian authors should use their God-given writing abilities to honor God and share the message of the written word God has given to each of them uniquely.

—We believe in supporting Urban Christian authors in their literary endeavors by reading, purchasing and sharing their titles with our online community.

—We believe that in everything we do in our literary arena should be done in a manner that will lead to God being glorified and honored.

We look forward to the online fellowship with you.

Please visit us often at:
www.uchisglorybookclub.net

Many Blessing to You!

Shelia E. Lipsey,
President, UC His Glory Book Club